Husk!

Shayna Grissom

Shayna Grissom

Acknowledgements

Acknowledgments

Firstly, I'd like to thank the people who go out on a limb to read and review indie authors. Out of all the many, many things people want you to buy, you chose us, which is amazing. Thank you. I'd also like to thank my Ride & Die editor, Rebecca Partin, who went and got her editing certificate just for me. She's read everything I've written and has yet to throw a project back and make a run for it. To my other editor, Charlie Knights, I hope your indie journey proves successful. You deserve it! My cover artist, Grim Poppy Designs, who has done all my novel-length covers thus far. You do beautiful work and always seem to understand what I'm aiming for. Lastly, I'd like to thank my husband. All of this is possible because of him.

Contents

PART ONE: CHAPTER 1

It wasn't a college, it was an intervention with college credits.

The grounds were surrounded by a cultivated forest with beaten dirt trails, but the mountains were stacked with towering evergreens in every direction. I was in awe of the majestic peaks with their jagged, imperfect ridges. Idyllic scenery where someone would have no choice but to sober up.

Surrounding the house itself was a manicured lawn of inviting grass, yet no one ventured into them. Maybe there were rules about staying off the lawn, but it would've been perfect for a picnic brunch or sitting around a circle to share pain.

Behind the left side of the house, peaks of green tents emerged behind a fence still emanating of fresh cedar. They were probably greenhouses, which threatened a horticulture class. Nothing about this felt like college. Was I at the right place?

The house itself was large enough to be a private college. Three stories of red brick and brown siding decked with black shingles.

White columns braced the white painted porch. Glancing upward was dizzying against a clear blue sky.

I was a fly gazing up at a brick arachnid with dozens of windows for eyes all staring at me with curious focus. There was nowhere to run.

Not a time to be morbid.

This was a fresh start among many. Dad claimed Harvard was too big for anyone to care who I was, so next it was a place so small I'd be safe. A haven where no one knew how I got expelled from Harvard at the very least.

Glancing around the empty campus, I swallowed the hard lump building in my throat. No one knew because there was no one here.

Seriously, where was everyone?

A warm breeze played with my hair. Maybe the driver got the wrong address.

The bronze plaque embedded into the brick squashed those hopes.

Built in 1897 by Robert Lacourt, the Marten Ranch is Clarkson's finest establishment and honored by the Historic Society. May those who enter these halls find the knowledge that lies between these walls.

Too bad no one attending Marten Ranch Academy was seeking knowledge, inside walls or otherwise. Cue the sad trumpet noise.

Let's be real. The students—if there were any—that came to this prep college did so because it was their last stop. Misfits and delinquents that couldn't cut it in the real establishments came here to let their Ivy League dreams die.

Who was I to judge? A girl who was given every advantage and still couldn't cut it. At my age, my dad was working in a firm while attending college on scholarship. My mom had already starred in two major films. I set a record for getting kicked out of the best schools. It wasn't that I didn't care, it was that I cared too much, and about the things I can't change.

You were a mistake...

I couldn't even recall her voice anymore, but the words were as accurate before as they . Shaking off the memory, I took another step. Just one year and I'd be able to go back to Harvard without a derogatory mark on my record per the agreement between my Dad and the pervert dean.

My red-bottomed heels scuffed against the smooth pavement as I eyed the concrete steps and winced. Those would be murder on my feet. A raw ache was preemptively working its way up my spine. Spite would serve me well as I walked up the steps, abandoning my driver as he stacked my luggage neatly on the ground.

The angry rich girl with the sad past was so cliché. So many people suffered things beyond their control while I struggled with mediocrity and self-imposed expectations. Everyone else seemed to know where they were going, what they were doing. For me, it was like the rest of the world was moving at twice the speed while I was on pause.

Maybe it was paranoia brought on by overexposure to the media at such a young age, but I was convinced that an email circulated around enrollment time. This place would be no different. Everyone watched the documentaries about my mom, and there were always theories about what really happened to her.

The throat clearing and jerking reaction when I stepped into a lecture hall followed by the shifting discomfort. Somewhere between hesitant starts to lectures almost relevant to disappearing mothers and nepotism, heads always turned in my direction.

It was funny how strangers held more certainty about what happened to Mom than I ever had. My dad was understanding for a time; but after the last expulsion, even he was beginning to realize that I was the problem all along.

Peering up at this creepy old mansion, I was wishing I had pocketed some of the cash from donating Mom's things.

But no. My overly-confidant ass donated everything to charity. Dad wouldn't have noticed a bag here or there going missing. Her loads of jewelry or anything else I packed away myself before picking the charities. Of all things, Mom's lingerie sold for the most. Anonymous creeps fully funded three new domestic abuse shelters in the greater New York area.

Lilacs and musk with an undertone of something rancid. I hated the way her perfume still lingered...

Marten Ranch Academy was waiting. I couldn't put it off any longer. My feet were screaming at me to relieve the swelling sting, but my brain flashed a red signal. Run. Danger. Calculus. Still, the mood back home was like a toxic vapor of disappointment. The truth was, I had nowhere else to go. I couldn't go back to Dad with nothing to show for myself. Not this time.

Come back victorious or stop wasting his money. He'd never give up on me, but I wouldn't allow him to invest anymore in a lost cause.

"Okay..." I whispered under my breath as I pulled open one of the double doors. Shifting my weight in six inch heals was not easy, and the thing weighed a ton.

Stepping into the Marten Ranch Academy was a lot like stepping into an old school all-boys academy. Like the places that had been converted after everyone realized misogyny didn't pay as well. Wood on wood everywhere. Lemony polish forced its way into my sinuses, and I couldn't help but wrinkle my nose.

That's when a woman in a baby-blue skirt suit with matching vinyl heels came clacking down the hall. "Carlie Whittaker, Hi!"

She was attractive in a way that suggested just the right amount of effort to frame her statuesque demeanor. Her makeup was a solid nine even in the afternoon. I couldn't tell how old she was, but the confident authority in her voice told me all I needed to know.

"You must be the dean," I said, extending my hand.

Dad said you should always shake the boss's hand. It was weird how the little things always stuck when I didn't listen to damn near anything else.

The dean took my hand and shook it firmly, evidently pleased by the gesture. "I'm Dean Feilding."

One thing I noted was that there was no judgment in her eyes. None. She looked like she was genuinely happy to see me. Maybe they were hard up for funding, or she also knew Harvard's dean was trash that preyed on vulnerable girls and dismissed any warning he issued.

"Was the flight all right? I know you came from New York."

"Not the worst, but the time zone always throws me." I wasn't going to be that girl who complained about first class. No one liked rich, privileged bitches, especially me.

"The elevator is reserved for people who need it, so please do not use it unless you must."

My feet screamed in agony as we rounded the wide staircase to the top floor. "No problem."

Not once did she imply that my bullshit wouldn't be tolerated or warn me on the strict curfew. There was no policy boasting or assertion for dominance. Just a brief tour of the school on the most direct route to a bedroom that I wouldn't need to share.

She opened the doors, revealing a spacious, fully furnished room. It was a nice, Edwardian-themed room like a historic hotel. The woodwork continued to be the primary color scheme from the slatted blinds and the four-post bed. There was a circular white shag carpet under the bed. A vanity table with an oval mirror. Thankfully, no doilies were involved.

"You will need to bring your own stuff up here," Feilding advised with a tone of practiced apology. "We keep the staff limited. Dinner is at six, lunch at one, and breakfast is continental from seven to nine."

At least I didn't have to cook.

That usually involved a rotation of washing dishes and scrubbing floors like in the private, all-girls middle school I attended for a hot minute. I hated that because whenever I skipped, I'd get dirty looks from the other girls. Peer pressure was meant to instigate bad habits, not reinforce the good ones.

My eyes fell to my shoes as I weighed the idea of going shoeless just long enough to grab a different pair from the luggage. It's not like anyone would see me bare foot around the place. Fashion was my armor, and I wasn't ready to set down my shield just yet.

"Hey, does this belong to the new student?" A voice wafted into the doorway.

I turned to face a round-faced guy with snazzy glasses. He wasn't overweight, he just had a face that made him look that way. He wore a polo shirt with the school emblem on the breast and gray slacks. It was generic. Two lions and crowns or something like that. A few weird symbols I didn't recognize at an instant. His hair was short and even styled with pomade. I almost mistook him for a professor, but he was far too young.

In his hands were the handles to my rolling luggage. Oh, thank God. I wouldn't have to do it. The image of myself hauling luggage up the rectangular stairs that cased the entryway made me sweaty just thinking about it. Nothing like pitting out in front of people to make a good first impression.

"Oh, this is Jacob," Feilding said with a silent clap of her French manicured hands.

Okay, I was a little confused. This was a private school for the disaster kids, but Jacob was clearly not that. My dad would have cried for joy if I brought him home for dinner.

"Um, thanks, I guess," I said, unsure of the intent behind his gesture. What kind of person just offered to carry up six jumbo suitcases? Was he Mormon? I heard there were a lot of Mormons on the West Coast. They rode around on bikes and did chores to talk to people about American Jesus, something like that. We had the Amish on the East Coast, and they didn't want to convert people. They wanted to be left alone.

"May I come in?" Jacob asked.

He was so formal. "Yes, you may." I couldn't help but scratch at him, but if Jacob noticed, he didn't care. Setting my stuff beside the loveseat, he eyed the signature Burberry pattern on the soft case.

"I like your luggage," he said. "Classics never die. I'll be right back."

A man who respected style.

My mind was already painting a picture as to why Jacob was attending Marten Ranch Academy, and it was nothing I didn't do on spring break after a few shots of Tequila. Some parents were utter bastards. I deserved to be here, but Jacob didn't.

"The day is yours to unpack and rest," Feilding said. "Class starts tomorrow at eight in the library."

Class...as in one?

"Do you mean orientation?"

Feilding's immaculate brows raised. "We have only eight students in attendance after one transferred unexpectedly. The class meets in the library and it's the professors who rotate out when their sessions are done."

Okay, I could appreciate that. With only eight students, Marten Ranch didn't need to adhere to the conventional class schedules. But it only brought me back to the same question.

This was a prep college specifically for troublemakers. Where at best case scenario, we could get our associate degree, unburdened with the task of choosing a major. Why did I get the feeling that my past didn't matter?

"Hey, so..." I started. Not sure where I was going with it, but Feilding sensed my loud awkward pause and filled the gap.

"We don't inquire about academic history," she said. "That creates bias. Besides, it doesn't matter how you came to be here."

It didn't?

Feilding faced me and made that direct, uncomfortable eye contact. Here it comes, the warning. I stiffened and braced myself for the threat. Whatever it was, I'd be sure to defy it.

"I've been the Dean of this school since it opened. Can you guess my expulsion rate?"

Fear crept up my spine. I hated it when my body told me to be afraid of things. Setting my jaw, I shook my head. Whatever her rate was, it was about to increase.

"Zero," Feilding said. She gave a subtle nod and strode out of the room with all the confident swagger of someone who had won an argument.

Touché, lady.

That set the bar pretty high. If I got expelled, it would mean tarnishing a reputation as pristine as Feilding herself. A smirk arched along my face. It was an invitation to do my worst, but I needed to graduate college. It was bare minimum.

Jacob was huffing it up the steps and rolling the suitcases. He appeared in my doorway once more but this time he had all the remaining bags. "May I?" he asked again.

Instead of taunting him, I nodded. "Thanks, those steps were murder."

"There's ice in the kitchen," he said. "You should soak those feet. Most of us walk around bare foot or in slippers. Everett doesn't even change out of his pajamas most of the time."

I noted a hint of disdain and logged it for future reference.

Being a part of the in-crowd wasn't hard, but maintaining that status was. With just eight students, it must have been even harder to establish who was in and out. I always enjoyed watching people battle it out for popularity. It was so trite. They knew it didn't matter once they graduated, right?

Dean Feilding made it clear that she didn't know what happened between me and the last dean. Or if she knew, she refused to care. I inhaled a breath that felt too big for my lungs and the room suddenly felt twice its size.

Maybe this place was what I needed, even if that meant admitting the dean at Harvard he was right.

"Do you have any questions?"

Shit. I forgot Jacob was still here. That wasn't awkward at all.

"Sorry, I'm just out of it."

"Jet lag?"

No, but I nodded anyway.

"Do you want me to bring you some water? We have bottled waters in the fridge."

His niceness wasn't an attempt to flirt. I could tell by the way he was inching toward the door. For whatever reason, Jacob was just kind, I guess.

Like a school nurse that got accustomed to tummy aches and swollen tonsils. He was one step away from carrying around those little bean-shaped bowls that were impossible to vomit in. It was like holding a paper umbrella in the rain. Useless when someone was spewing like in the Exorcist.

"I'm okay," I said. "Thanks, though."

Jacob left, allowing my feet the sweet release from my heels as I fell backward onto the bed. It smelled like expensive detergent, which is to say, it smelled like nothing at all. I stared at the blue-linen canopy for a time, allowing myself to think or feel whatever, but nothing came other than boredom and an increasing need to explore.

Propping myself up on my elbows, I notice a crisp, white letter propped against the vanity mirror. That wasn't there before. Grinning at Jacob's ulterior motive for bringing the luggage, I hurried over, my mind racing with possibilities. An invitation to a secret party? A threat from the in-crowd asserting its dominance?

Practically giddy with the possibilities, I snatched the folded letter from the table. The weight of the paper was thick, good quality, cardstock. Nifty.

I read the note and snarled with disgust.

CHAPTER 2

Dear Carlie,

Hello and salutations! Welcome to the Marten Ranch Academy. We're so excited you're here. If you need anything, all of us will do whatever we can. Seriously. Need a study group or directions? A tampon or a Xanax? We got you. Unless sobriety is what you need, then we will endeavor to maintain that as well.

Whatever you came from or whoever you want to be, be it with us.

Sincerely,

Class of 2026

What a letdown.

They weren't threatened by the new, stylish student, and they weren't inviting me to their parties either. It was a simple, generic welcome letter that probably sat in a stack somewhere. Though on further inspection, it looked handwritten. The scratches of the pen were uneven and made the occasional divot in the thick parchment.

Holding the paper with both hands, I stared at it. Trolls left more personal death threats on my Instagram than this. There was an attempt to be humorous with tampons and Xanax, but it was gutless. There was nothing I hated more than soulless platitudes and generic, idle chit chat.

I mull it over while unpacking. I wanted it to mean more than it did. By the time the dinner bell chimed downstairs, I had decided the reason I didn't like it was because of the unassuming assuming.

No one attending Marten Ranch Academy did so by choice, so the class was attempting to assert what they knew about me based on that fact alone. So much for *Tabula Rasa*...

Not trusting Jacob's advice, I wore shoes to dinner. Michael Kors, to be precise. It wasn't hard to find the dining room. I could hear voices coming behind two pocket doors downstairs. Rolling them open, I prepared for the awkward silence, but instead, seven people clapped and cheered.

Shocked by the weird welcome, I sort of froze. It was Jacob who maneuvered out of his chair and approached me. "Hey, we saved a seat for you." He pointed at the only empty chair in the dining room.

Flushing and sweaty palmed, I was grateful for the directions. I don't know why, clearly a place was set up for me and I could see it from where I stood. I just didn't see it until he said something.

Seating myself between two girls about my own age, they both turned and smiled like they had saved a seat for me at the lunch table. It was so nice...weird.

"Did you get our note?" Jacob asked.

"Yeah, thanks."

"Sorry if it came out weird," the girl to my left said. "We don't get out much."

The self-deprecation had me easing into the seat.

"I'm Heather," left girl said.

"And I'm Felice," girl on the right added.

With quick glances at each, I got the measure of them.

Heather was a granola chick, and Felice wore the latest season's fashion. While Heather's long blonde hair had probably been growing since she was twelve, Felice had an almost-black chin-length bob with razor sharp edges. Felice's face was pale with blushed cheeks and long, dark lashes. Heather wore no makeup, but her face had that soft healthy glow of someone who took vitamins and drank collagen smoothies.

There was no way those two could be friends. Felice screamed New York whereas Felice was clearly California. Yet, their postures were relaxed and casual like they'd known each other for decades. I glanced around the room and everyone was reverberating the same, chill vibe.

"Hi, I'm Carlie...but you guys already knew that."

"Where are you from?" Heather asked.

"Upstate New York."

"Clearly not Amish," Felice purred. I laughed at that, and she grinned. "I didn't think so. Nice shoes."

"You too," I said, noting she had somehow acquired backordered Prada. Who did she kill for those, I wonder.

At the end, there was a Hispanic girl with sleek, shiny black hair. She stared silently with black eyes and a soft pout. Every school had a resident goth chick, and Marten Ranch is evidently no exception. Still, even this goth had a classic kind of look that never went out of style.

"This is Estella," Jacob said with a polite gesture.

I nodded, and like a typical goth, she only stared. No offense was taken. I actually liked the blank apathy. It meant she didn't care what I did and that she wouldn't waste words. I could light the ranch on fire, and she might very well smile.

Got to admire a person who finds their niche. In every lit class, there were at least two goths. They delved into every Gothic with fevered, nail-biting anticipation all the way to the end. I liked watching the flames dance in their eyes when the lit professor coaxed the deeper meaning of the book's ending.

The cathartic ending to a traumatic event. An understanding that wealth and privilege means nothing in the face of true hardship. The unwavering heroine's will to fight for what's hers. Only by burning away the old and decayed can a woman reject the status quo. If they're lucky, the insane servant will gladly stay behind.

Spoilers: the house always burns down in the end.

"I'm Travis." A guy with a knitted beanie said.

"Tiffany, the token Asian girl," Tiffany said without irony.

"I'm Everett," he said. I figured that much. He was wearing blue flannel pajama pants. He was looking at his dark hands when he asked, "Are we stating the obvious, or can we just skip it?"

There was an undercurrent of discomfort, but Jacob smoothed it over with a laugh. "Well, that's all of us. Sometimes the professors eat with us, but they didn't want to overwhelm you on your first day."

Dismissing whatever that was, I found it kind of alarming that the professors and students ate together. Wasn't that a conflict somehow? I'd need to be careful of what I said in a pond so small. It was one thing to piss off a teacher I wouldn't see after a semester, but I'd be stuck staring at the professor's pruned face if I tried that here.

"Is that weird?" I asked. "Eating with the teachers?"

"It's weird when Feilding joins us," Everett said. "I think she knows it too, so she doesn't come often."

That was a relief. The last thing I wanted was the looming sense of dread of eating with the wrong fork. The dean gave me the impression that she was strict on etiquette. Dad was self-made, which meant he didn't give a shit about formalities. Left to his own devices, he'd still be shopping at Kroger. His assistant made sure he didn't feel the need.

"It's a small group," Heather said. "When the teachers join us, they kind of just want to be regular people."

"What happens at lunch, stays at lunch," agreed Travis.

Before I could ask anything else, a squeaky cart made its way into the room. Lunch was various deviations of a Cobb salad. There were bread rolls and butter. On the lower rung of the cart was sodas and sparkling waters shoved into stainless steel ice buckets.

While Heather's Cobb salad didn't have hard-boiled eggs or ham, it did have more tomatoes, nuts, and fruit. The plate set before me was the standard arrangement, but Felice had more eggs and a pre-sliced grilled chicken breast.

Felice grabbed a fancy French water, and I did the same.

"We didn't know if you had any dietary restrictions," Heather explained as the pink of her cheeks began to grow. "I hope you don't have any allergies."

At that, nearly everyone's eyes went wide, and their forks froze. "Oh, no, do you?" Jacob asked the question that seemed to be on the hive mind.

"No," I said and marveled as they all exhaled. I felt like I needed to say something for the sake of follow-through, so I blurted out, "I don't like sushi, though."

Why were they so concerned? It was so off-putting. Like I was added among them by default. What if I was some racist asshole or liked to kick puppies on my day off? It was like there was no vetting among the group, just acceptance. Whether I liked it or not. Did I like this? It was hard to explain. Like a bizarre spa treatment. A pool of warmed honey that was easy to sink into. Safe and promising health benefits even if they were minimal at best. Tugging at every hair and fiber, refusing to let go and yet, so warm and gooey.

"I'm vegan," Heather said. "There's so much processing in meats, and there's a ton of mercury in tuna. I want my system to be clean before having children someday."

Was honey vegan? I'd have to ask one day. Scanning the room, I checked the expressions of everyone else, but no one laughed at her. "You plan on doing that soon?" I asked.

"Oh no," Heather said. "Not until I'm twenty-eight."

"I'll eat all the stuff you don't want," Felice said with a grin, but not in a mean way. She was being supportive of a pregnancy planned six or seven years in advance. Very granola.

We ate our varying Cobb salads in a lukewarm silence after that.

There was a casualness about it, as if I had been there all semester. As if everyone wanted to be here and wasn't a colossal fuck up.

I wanted to scream, "Don't you know how lame junior college is?!"

"Your essay paralleling Cavendish to Hemmingway was legit," Everett said to Jacob.

"Aw, thanks!" Jacob said with a soft smile. "Not as expansive as yours, but I tried."

"No one is going to beat a historical consciousness essay," Tiffany said.

Felice was watching the exchange brightly while she ate every bit of meat off her plate. She avoided the lettuce like it'd give her hives. Why even bother ordering a salad then? I supposed she wanted to fit in even if it tasted like solidified water.

Cavendish and Hemmingway were similar since both were severely impacted by war. Trauma has a way of leaking into writing whether the author is aware or not.

"Tolkien could be added to that parallel," I said. "He wouldn't want to be, but he's admitted as much."

Jacob beamed at me while he chewed. "Hm, I didn't know that."

"You like fantasy?" Travis asked. He was leaning back in his chair as slack as possible.

Anxiety simmered in my stomach when I realized everyone was waiting for me to respond. I didn't want to sound so sincere, but...

"Yeah. I like that fantasy can explore politics and justice in a way that isn't boring."

"Wicked," Travis said with a lulling nod.

I felt the heat rise in my face. If I held off the question any longer, I might scream. "So, I got to ask," I said, instantly regretting it. "This is a school for..." I struggled to find the words.

"Assholes?" Travis offered.

"Delinquents?" Everett suggested.

"The disturbed," Estella spoke for the first time.

I nodded and didn't stop nodding. "All those things, but all of you seem so smart."

"Oh, don't get it twisted," Felice said. "We all have a past. Well, maybe not Jacob, but we all did things we're not proud of."

I looked to Jacob for an explanation. "My dad is a narcissist. Unrelated, I'm majoring in psych!" he said with a cheery sarcasm.

"So, this place changed you?"

"We changed ourselves," Heather said. "We stopped blaming our parents, except Jacob, but they deserve it—"

"That they do!" Jacob said, emphasizing his point by making his hand into a pretend gun taking aim.

"And we decided to put aside our trauma to become the people we want to be," Heather finished.

Okay, I get it. It's like The Breakfast Club where teens from different walks of life are forced together and they come to an understanding of one another as well as the world at large. An overwhelming emotion expanded in my chest. Like a bubble that I didn't want to burst.

Was it hope? It might have been hope. Either that or indigestion.

This clique didn't give a fuck about their past and neither did I, but no one ever believed me. Up until this point, people had two ways to regard my highly publicized trauma. The former was to spin a cocoon around me, isolating me from anything that might remind me of something that happened when I was six.

The latter reaction was to use it against me like a blunt, annoying weapon. If I got into an argument, my mom somehow got thrown in. It was the most involvement she'd ever had in my life, but it wasn't like I ever had something equally personal to throw back, so I'd usually respond with a throat punch or inspired car decoration.

But these guys had dealt with the same things and decided to just walk away from it. Something about that was a little odd, though. We were just talking about literary genius and how trauma plays a part in that. Who are we if not walking bags of trauma? Life lessons that were hoisted on us before we knew how to handle the situation. Even if Tolkien understood that war was horrible, it wasn't the same as watching the flesh peel from his comrade's feet in the trenches or seeing someone's head get blown off right beside him.

Those memories weren't something a person could wave away like an offensive appetizer or an uninvited bug. They stayed with you and cropped up when you least expected it. Flashbulb memories taking you back to those horribly visceral times at the pop of a car backfiring.

Yet, this clique claimed they simply walked away from it. Set their knee-jerk reactions to triggers aside like last season's coats. Not possible, but for whatever reason they believed it possible.

So, it begged the question.... Where did the trauma go?

CHAPTER 3

The library was cool.

I don't dedicate my life to books, and I'm not a Belle who would swoon at the sight of one, but I can appreciate a two-story library with a winding staircase. I got there early and perused. It was like any other college classroom, just more books. Desks with laptops crowded the middle of the room facing a projector and a professor's desk.

The books included everything from *The Divine Comedy* to mangas, which was unexpected. Unpretentious and a reminder of all the possibilities books can be for a person. I liked it. The library promised to soothe any kind of negative emotion given half the chance. And the fact that the classes were all held here? Even better.

Five minutes to eight, the students came in together. All seven of them. Sort of clustered.

"You know who else put friends into circles?" Jacob was winding up for a punchline.

"Who, man?" Travis asked.

"Dante," Tiffany deadpanned.

"Yes! You do read the group text," Jacob said, absolutely elated.

All seven of them, all the time. They were the clique.

Felice and Jacob sat together at one desk, Heather and Everett sat together at another. Travis and Tiffany sat behind team Heatherett leaving Estella behind Felica and Jacob. She wasn't isolated, though. Felice and Jacob made it a point to twist in their chairs to keep the residential goth in the loop.

They made their intentions clear the night before. I was one of them whether I liked it or not. There was a vacant space in my heart then. Pulling out my phone, I clicked on the only message in my inbox.

This school isn't the worst. I've made friends. Love you.

An ellipsis faded in and out and my anticipation rose and fell with it. I waited a few minutes—breath straining for release—but the dots stopped. Dad saw my text and didn't answer. Fair. He had every right to be mad at me. Maybe I finally bit the big one. But a pissy, indignant rage rose where remorse probably should have been.

Yeah, offering the dean a blow job in exchange for not expelling me was wrong, but there was something misogynistic about *that* being the thing that shattered our relationship. Not the time I was caught keying the car of his associate's daughter. Nor the time I spray painted a massive dick on that Columbus mural. A consensual sex act between two adults was a no-go, but property damage was fine.

"What are you grinning about?" Everett called.

I wondered what the clique would make of that. They claimed they each had a past, but apart from Jacob, they didn't exactly talk about it. Maybe that was part of their "put the trauma aside," or whatever they said.

"Oh, just thinking about one of the times I got expelled," I said as I walked down the steps.

The air got a bit cooler at the bottom, but maybe it was the discomfort in the clique's smiles. Estella shifted in her seat slightly and said, "Was it worth it?"

"Totally," I said, taking the seat beside her. "I was sent to one of those private Christian colleges, and the art students wanted to paint a mural of Columbus on the side of their building."

This garnered expressions anywhere from surprise to disgust from everyone except Felice, who glanced around the room as if she were wondering what everyone else knew that she didn't.

"There were petitions and even a protest," I said. "But the dean okayed it anyway."

"Gross," Jacob said.

Estella stared at me with utter enthrallment. The flames were lit in her eyes. "What did you do?"

"I snuck out the night before the unveiling and spray-painted a big black dick in his mouth."

Travis threw his head back and laughed. "Tell me you got a picture."

I took out my phone, and all seven of them hovered over it to gander at Columbus performing fellatio.

"That is the best act of vigilantism I've ever seen," Estella said.

Even Felice was laughing. Only, in the corner of her eyes there was a blankness. No true fire like the kind in Estella's. History might not have been a strength for her. Google would fill her in after class.

"Isn't that sort of offensive?" Jacob asked.

"Duh," Felice said.

"No, I mean, to the LGBTQ community," he clarified. "Sure, Columbus deserves to be insulted, but to do that using a gay act is degrading them too."

There it was. Someone was bound to find it offensive for more reasons than one. I honestly agreed with Jacob, but the communal wine went down like sangria, and my choices were limited. With one color and limited artistic options, I went with the worst.

They thought they could be friends with anyone, but what about someone so unabashedly offensive? Someone who didn't care who they hurt along the way just so long as their point was made. The clique thought they could take me under their wing and nurse me into a person worthy of their support. They were wrong.

I never should have had you...

Always on the outside, easily forgotten and never quite trusted. Didn't they get the email? I was only here to get my record back on track so I could graduate and gain access to my trust fund. The sooner they learned that about me, the better. Might as well yank off the wax strip before counting to three. Sorry to crash your altruistic intentions.

"You really had to make that a Black dick?" Everett was still laughing, but he was uncomfortable. I'd nearly succeeded in offending everyone in the room. Delicious.

"Mike would have loved this," Jacob said.

"Please don't mention him," Felice said.

Jacob's face went tense as though he'd said something wrong. What was that all about? An ex-boyfriend, perhaps?

There was a squeak of sneakers on the polished floor as the library doors came bursting open. "Sorry I'm late guys," a man in his forties with a salt-and-pepper beard said. "Rough night."

"It's okay. We were just discussing the evil bastard that is Columbus," Jacob said.

"He only raped, tortured, murdered, and colonized an entire continent," Felice said. "He deserved the dick."

Something about her reiteration set the gears in my brain the wrong way for a moment. She knew he was awful yet waited for everyone else to say so before listing his crimes in order from evil to hellscape. Like she was ticking off boxes on a to-do list.

Before I could dwell on it more, the professor issued me a happily surprised smile like I'd brought him flowers or something.

"Hi there. I'm Dr. Sykes. I teach history and classic lit."

"I'm Carlie Whittaker," I said. "I'm an artist."

At this, Everett choked on his laughter. All the while, I was keenly aware that Estella was glancing at me every chance she could. It was kind of weird, but also cute? She was trying to play it cool, but I'd clearly won her admiration.

Sykes quirked his brow and strolled over, hands in his pockets in that cool, confident way that made my stomach flutter. Tilting his head, he observed my phone. Brows raised, he nodded in approval. "A for Whittaker. But we're still discussing the royal bastards. Namely, Peter the Great."

Peter the Great wasn't that bad. Sure, he terrorized the *Dvoriane*, but I rather enjoyed his eat the rich mentality. Peter was over six feet tall when the average man was barely five foot seven. It was hilarious to imagine a giant ginger with a perpetual eye twitch marching up to a random noble, grabbing him by the beard and sawing it off with whatever he had on hand.

If Sykes wanted to discuss royal bastards in Russia, Ivan the Terrible would have set a new level of precedence. The guy used to throw cats out the tower windows just for laughs.

Trying to push a country into a world of science and enlightenment didn't make Peter a bastard in my opinion. It was more like a parent forcing their kid to eat veggies. Maybe not the best or efficient tactic, but the intent was a good one.

There was a half hour break between professors. Sykes chatted up Jacob about westernizing Russia while everyone else inexplicably sat around waiting for the next class to start. No one was trying to escape what came next.

Had I known it was math, I would have hidden in the bathroom.

After an hour, I came to two conclusions. One, statistics made no sense. I'd say zero sense, but zero could mean anything and any number could be considered zero. And two, I decided that Ms. T was a masochist. Unlike Sykes, who was personable, down-to-earth, and explained historical events in ways that made sense, Ms. T was flying high on improbable numbers.

Her wiry hair floated around her massive glasses, and her broken fingernails pointed at charts and graphs with excitement as if she was making profound points. At least I wasn't the only one lost on the subject. Everyone except Tiffany and Everett was frantically taking notes.

After what was the most brutalizing hour of math I'd ever encountered, it was time for lunch.

Hurrying out of the library before Ms. T could finish her sentence, I caught a dark figure in the corner of my eye. It was Estella, and she was trying to walk beside me.

"Hey, did you catch anything she was saying?" I asked.

Estella gave me a dead-eyed expression. "No, but I programed my calculator for all the equations we're expected to use this semester."

Beautiful Estella. Saint Estella. "I'd really appreciate it if you could show me how."

"Might just be easier if I do it for you," she offered.

"I won't survive otherwise."

I didn't need to understand statistics; I just needed a decent grade to avoid academic probation—if that was even a thing here.

I could smell lunch waiting for us in the dining hall. A dry crackle of smoke lingered on the back of my tongue. "Smoked salmon?"

Who put smoked salmon on a Cobb salad?

"We're in Washington State, after all," Estella said.

Cobb salad was topped with salmon for everyone but Heather. I didn't want to be rude by not sitting between Felice and Heather, but I wanted to sit by Estella. As if the clique somehow understood this request, they sat in a totally different arrangement.

Travis and Tiffany sat across from Felice and Jacob, and Everett and Heather sat across from me and Estella. I couldn't stop my eyes from shifting across the new seating arrangement while Felice suppressed a smile.

"We like to change up where we sit," she explained. "That way everyone feels included."

"It's too small of a group to silo one person off, and that's easy to do when couples are involved," Jacob added.

They were so keenly aware of the social dynamics within the clique that they pushed against conventional norms. Something about that sparked within me. They were actively opposing their own nature to instill equality. It was...righteously cool.

Still, I didn't need friends. I didn't need anyone.

"Heads up: Mrs. Richter is going to want you to write a personal essay about why you're here," Everett warned me.

At this, there was eyerolling from some of the clique, and Felice stabbed at a hunk of salmon with her fork. The cooked flesh flaked against the not so gentle twist. Creative writing was something I'm good at, but the disapproval from the clique made the air feel heavy. At least I wasn't alone in this.

"Well, I can write it, but I don't think she's going to find the essay school appropriate."

Given they were all aware of my inclinations toward graffiti, Jacob had to break it down for me. "Not the action that brought you here. She wants to know the root cause."

"Oh, like Mommy and Daddy didn't love me enough?"

"Pretty much," Tiffany said, chasing a tomato across her plate. "Feilding's attitude is pretty cut and dry, but Richter thinks she's the one in charge here."

"Wannabe shrink," Felice grumbled.

The looming essay wasn't approved by the clique, and I didn't approve of it either. I didn't want to relive the day my life became a series of lifetime documentaries. Family members slowly turned on us, accusing my dad of terrible things for a paycheck and fifteen minutes. Year after year, the family in the Christmas photo got smaller and smaller until it was just Dad and me. Too sad and pathetic to hang on the walls, that only left pictures of me and *her*.

He needed new pictures. Photos to reflect the people we are today and not the state she left us in.

"Hey, would it be cool if I took a photo of you guys? My dad worries."

At this, the clique brightened. "That's really sweet," Tiffany said.

Jacob got on his feet, organizing everyone. When I tried to take the picture, he stopped me. "You got to be in it too! Set the camera to a ten second delay."

I did. Followed by a giggling, mad dash around the long table before I collided with Travis, knocking Heather off balance. Everyone was laughing at me but in a fun way, and...it felt good. A warm hug after trudging through rain without a coat.

"Say cheese!" Jacob sang as he roped an arm around my shoulders.

"You are the cheese," Felice responded.

When we checked, the photo was postcard worthy. Like, it could have been the next brochure photo for Marten Ranch Academy. They were all genuinely happy. Even Estella. She didn't exactly smile, but she made a silly blank expression while Heather kissed her cheek. Felice posed like an attorney in an ad, but Everett was gesturing to her like a hype man, and a smile was threatening to burst from her face.

"This is perfect, you guys," I said, oddly choked up. I bit my lip until it bled to stop that from happening. My tongue couldn't help but search for that bitter, metallic tang.

"Feilding will want that photo," Jacob said.

"I want that photo," Felice said.

"Add her to the group chat," Everett said, pulling out his own phone.

My breath seized in my chest. It was happening. I was being added to a group chat. And not for a group project where it was academically necessary either. Moments later, my inbox was blowing up.

Maybe this wasn't the worst.

Sure, it was fun to be the loner. The anarchist whose name floated down halls and circulated through staff emails, but acceptance felt nice and cozy. It was like how Christmas used to feel when it was a party full of happy, drunk adults. Besides, the only way I could pass these classes was with their help.

With lunch almost over, I texted my dad the photo of us but didn't write a caption. It didn't need one.

Estella hung back with me while the others left. I overheard Travis saying he needed to grab a book from his room and other totally normal things, but my ears pricked at a new word.

"You think she will join?" Tiffany asked.

"It's not up to us," Felice said.

Cryptic.

"What's that all about?" I asked Estella.

Her lips moved around like they were rubber cemented shut before managing, "We have a secret club of sorts. This house has history. It was built by a famous occultist, so we like pay homage to that."

"You guys have a secret society or..." I asked, trying to contain my smirk.

That sounded like the last thing the clique would be into. Estella? Sure, she would be all in, but the others were so pragmatic. I pictured Jacob in his ironed polo and styled hair, trying to strike up a conversation with a ghost.

"So, you linger here often?" Jacob would say.

The ghosts in my imagination took the shape of Marley and Marley from *The Muppet Christmas Carol. Woahhhhhh*!

"Hey kid, nice shirt." Marley would say.

"That's not a kid; it's an old man in disguise!" the other Marley would chime in.

"No, nothing like that," Estella said, banishing the ghost Muppets. "Hey, I got to grab my creative writing books. I'll meet you in the library. Okay?"

"Sure."

And there it was—the reason I preferred to go it alone. There was always a final step I couldn't quite make. The clique was standing on the train while I remained on the platform. Something sharp twisted in my heart, but I had to play it cool. It was better to be alone than left out.

I rolled my eyes. Even I annoyed myself. They had known me for less than two days. I couldn't expect them to reveal their whole asses to me in that time. Whatever homage they paid the occultist was probably embarrassing. Cause let's face it; the clique was cringy. Even the in-crowds feared judgment from the outside.

What would I do if they all started dancing The Time Warp in their underwear? Yeah, I'd laugh. Would I participate? Not a chance in hell.

I didn't have a creative writing textbook, and I was pretty sure no one else did either, so I headed straight toward the library. I had just crossed the threshold of the pocket doors when they shuddered followed by a knocking sound. Like something fighting its way through the walls.

Hesitating, I scanned the doorframe. Crown molding and all the fixings appeared sturdy. Maybe it was all the movement upstairs that sent them reverberating, but the silence that followed was too eerie.

This house has history...

Nope. There were some things I didn't need to know. And with that, I booked it to the library, banishing any inkling of the disturbance from my thoughts.

CHAPTER 4

The first day of classes had come to an end.

After so much extroversion, I craved solitude but found myself unable to remain in my room. Instead, I explored the school grounds on what would be the last sunny days in fall. If change had a scent, it would be autumn air. Dehydrated leaves and wilting greenery muted the sounds around me.

The forest was a cultivated one. Strategically planted, the trees buffered the worn trails as if discouraging people from veering away from carefully laid plans.

I knew if I stayed on course, I'd find something beautiful. A creek with shiny pebbles or a comfortable bench. A reward for staying on the path and trusting its maker's intentions.

Squeezing through a pair of Japanese maples, I wandered left. Not because of some analogy about forging my own path or sense of discovery— the only thing I was liable to find was a dead possum. I did it because that's what I always did. Even as a kid, it was impossible to keep me on the path.

There were several years of my childhood that were not photographed.

Baby pictures filled several albums. My first smash cake, first crawl, a plastic baggie containing my first tooth was taped inside one. Bath time and gummy smiles filled the pages until I turned three.

There was no secret as to why.

"We had to keep you on a leash," Dad griped. "We hated it, but we had a hell of a time trying to keep you safe. Every time we turned around, you were running toward something dangerous. You refused to hold anyone's hand."

Dad had banished all leash photos. There were virtually no mementos from the family vacation to Mexico because of this. I was glad of that. The last thing I wanted was to see myself leashed even if it accompanied a stylish panda bear backpack.

As I waded through the trees, crunching leaves underfoot, I found myself back where I started. Marten Ranch Academy.

When did I get turned around?

CHAPTER 5

*C*an you help Mommy?

    Yes, the blue pills. Good girl! Bring them here.

"Let's count them out together," I read out loud. "There were fifty-one in all. I counted as she swallowed before sinking into the bath."

When I go down, count the bubbles, okay, sweetie?

"I think she wanted me to watch her die so she wouldn't be alone. I didn't want to, so I just waited until her eyes glossed over and ran to Daddy for help. She went away that night and never came back."

The library was silent, like the moments after someone's aunt had too much to drink and announced her husband was having an affair. Wrong.

But I was comfortable in my wrongness. I locked eyes with the teacher and resumed a relaxed posture. She wanted to know the core of why I was at Marten Ranch Academy, so I delivered. Hopefully, it was uncomfortable enough that she'd think twice before giving this assignment to the next student.

Richter was a middle-aged woman with full highlights and a soft, plumpness to her. The way everyone's favorite grandma was personified. Only she wasn't pleased.

"Ms. Whittaker, I think you misunderstood the assignment," she said.

I tensed slightly at that. Everett was holding his head in his hands and staring at the desk. Even Jacob was at a loss for words. I looked to Estella, who merely shrugged.

"You said to make an essay about the underlying reason for attending Marten Ranch..."

"I have no doubt this moment impacted you greatly," Richter said. "But what I wanted was your reasons for coming. Your reason for wanting to be here, not anecdotes from your childhood."

I shook my head. No, that wasn't what she said. It wasn't even phrased in the same way. Flipping through the pages of my binder, I reread the quote I had taken from the other day. "Write a five-hundred-word essay about a personal event that indirectly led you to Marten Ranch Academy." I quoted.

"I meant personal as in why you decided to enroll in this school."

That's not what she fucking said! I had it quoted. Everything in me felt like it was fusing together into one nasty bomb, ready to go off. I didn't *want* to be here. None of us wanted to be here, it was the last recourse.

Before I could continue arguing the point, Richter said, "Class, what's wrong with this essay?"

"There's no agency in your story," Tiffany tried to explain.

"This is real life," I argued. "Like it or not, there are times in our lives when we are not the hero calling the shots."

"Agency isn't always about calling the shots," Travis said. "It's about reaction as well as action. How the character feels and what they want to do even if they don't do it."

I was six. My agency consisted of picking my nose and watching *Cocomelon*. Clearly, I was right, but my insides were tangling in knots. I shared something so personal and was salted like a Wagyu steak.

"I think there was agency," Estella interrupted. "She ran to get her dad instead of doing what she was told."

"Yeah, it's not the character actions that's the problem; it's the lack of feeling and internal thoughts," Jacob explained.

Richter was nodding her head like it was connected to a metronome. "How did this event make you feel? What did you want? That is the basis of all good characterization."

It was a very unpersonal way of attacking my personality, but they didn't understand that. How could I explain that I didn't feel anything? I was six. I didn't know what was happening.

They wanted me to set aside the trauma. Fuck them.

"I was too young to understand what was happening," I said. "I was just happy to receive praise and proud of my counting skills."

At this, Richter's eyes lit up, and she outstretched her hand, "May I?"

I'd rather shove it down her throat, but sure, let's all have a learning experience from my childhood trauma. Awkwardly, I got out of my chair and gave her the essay. She spun around in her chair and wrote out a sentence.

"Let's count them out together," Richter scrawled on the whiteboard. *"There were fifty-one in all. I counted as she swallowed before sinking into the bath."*

"You mentioned that you were proud of your counting skills, so let's add that."

This carried on for the next twenty minutes, during which my embarrassment intensified to staggering heights. My face burned like the time I got drunk and passed out on a beach in Greece. I hated every moment. The only thing that kept me in my seat was the fact that I'd look like a crybaby if I fled.

The clique took turns dissecting the most traumatic moment of my life with surgical precision. Adding flourishes and removing commas. Oh, so careful in avoiding the major arteries that could bleed out at any moment. By the time it was over, I couldn't process the words on the whiteboard.

Was I going to puke? I hoped so.

"Thank you so much for sharing that," Richter said kindly. "It's never easy putting your writing out there."

And as if I was taken off the burner, the heat was gone. Everyone was clapping and issuing words of praise and encouragement. "That was so brave," Estella whispered.

"She's a beast!" Everett howled.

I nodded and tried to smile, but masking hyperventilation is harder than it looks.

Class ended, and I emerged from the room drenched in sweat. Seriously, there were pit stains on my crepe blouse. It was ivory, so everyone could probably see it, but that was the least of my mortification.

The worst part was that the clique carried on like it never happened. I was no stranger to getting feedback, but never from an entire group I was trying so hard to get along with. Fucking Richter. It was like she was intentionally trying to humiliate me. If I had known a group critique was involved, I would have written something else.

A soft hand was on my arm. "Hey, are you okay?" Estella asked.

I didn't slow as I marched up the steps to my room. "I didn't know it was going to be like that."

"Normally, it's not," Estella said with a tone that suggested she found it perplexing too. "I don't know why she felt the need to do that. We usually do those exercises with posthumous works."

There was a click in my brain, like the pieces snapped together. "What's Richter's first name?"

"Barbra, I think," Estella said.

I stopped at the top of the staircase and googled her. Being one of the top teachers at the top schools meant she was also atop the search results. As I read what I already knew, I couldn't stay the tremble in my hands. I tilted the phone so Estella could read it.

"Serves on the Ivy-league trust committee as well as..." Estella read it out loud as if she were asking a question.

"She's on the board of trustees, which means she already knew my reputation."

Estella's black shimmery lips formed an O. "That's fucked."

Richter knew my expulsion records, my history—hell, she probably signed off on my expulsion letter. The clique did exactly what Richter wanted, and they had no idea that she was so complicit. Even at Marten Ranch Academy, my history followed.

I needed to be alone after that.

"There's a thing I need to do," I muttered before pulling away.

"If you need to talk about it," Estella started, but I was already waving her off and speeding to my room. I could hear her calling for me to wait, but there was no way in hell I was going to let anyone see me like this.

I needed a shower. And by shower, I mean curl into a ball on the shower floor sobbing. It wasn't just because of the horrific Richter incident. If I cried every time a professor didn't like me, I'd die of dehydration.

It was the injustice of it. Richter manipulated my peers to create distance between us. Yeah, I'm a shit, I get it, but a true professional would have kept that information to themselves and let the clique find that out on their own.

I was assured by Feilding that my past didn't matter, and yet it was dredged up like some cursed mummy tomb that Estella would cream herself over. Richter tried to gaslight me into thinking I had misunderstood the assignment. Ugh, I was so bottled up and angry all I could do was sob louder as the water ran cold.

To top it off, my dad still wasn't responding to my texts. He'd finally lost all faith in me. Was that it, then? If one offer of a blowjob was all it took, I must not have been all that loveable to begin with.

With aching ribs and numb legs, I made it out of the shower and crawled into bed, still dripping wet. Exhausted and empty. I don't recall falling asleep, or when I started dreaming...

I'm in the clawfoot bathtub back home. The one my mother tried to die in. Bathing in warm honey, it tugs against my submerged limbs, urging me to stay. I hold up my hands and it slides down and between my fingers.

The honey cools more and more until its gelatinous texture makes it impossible to sit up. Hard to breathe. I'm pulling and fighting, but the only thing that has any sense of urgency is the heart pounding in my chest. *I can't breathe...*

In a moment of semi-consciousness, I'm reminded that it's just a dream. The character lacks agency... She should have stopped her mother. Why did she give her the pills in the first place? How did it make her feel to know that her mother was shelving all her failures on her? The character is so weak and stupid, her only thought was gaining her mother's love and approval.

I'm sliding deeper into the tub. My upper lip is submerged.

Take this for agency.

I use my toes to pull up on the drain. The plumbing groans under the slow drain but it's working. The honey sinks to my chin. I'll be just fine; I just have to hang on a little longer...

That's when something crunched. Was it bone? Glancing down I see my foot is going down the drain along with the honey. Bone crushing, skin pulling... I'm being sucked down the drain. I'll be liquidated alive.

Opening my mouth to scream, I find that I can't. The honey has glued my mouth shut. The drain pulls me further. My calf...then my knee. It doesn't hurt because this is a dream, but I can't seem to wake up.

My other leg is forced backwards as the drain gurgles in its attempt to devour my hip. Pulling against it with my arms, I gain some ground. Half of my thigh is pulled from the drain, and it's been sucked dry like a sausage casing without the meat.

There was nothing left of me inside.

So, I let go.

Suction forces me back down faster than before. Shattering and shredding muscle and bone, my left knee was smashed against my forehead as my intestines were sucked down the drain in a slow, spooling motion...

I bolted upright and screamed.

Heaving and gasping, I flailed my arms and legs to make sure they were still intact. They were. I wasn't in a tub. Dad had that bathroom renovated. No more clawfoot. It was just an awful, disgusting dream brought on by stress.

Grabbing my phone, I check the time. My windows say its nighttime, but my heart says early morning. It's only eleven thirty. I took a long nap, and there'd be no sleeping after that.

I hated naps.

Something about sleeping any time other than at night made my stomach queasy as I grappled with the concept of time. The bed was soggy, and my hair was mostly dry, thanks to those Egyptian cotton sheets. Slinking out of bed, I put on a pair of joggers and an oversized black sweater.

When I get in this mood, there's no plan of action. I might have been treading downstairs for a snack just as easily as I would make a Molotov. I don't choose violence. There's simply me and an opportunity, no inhibitions.

The kitchen had all sorts of things. Swiping a bottle of wine, I grabbed a meat cleaver from the magnetic knife holder and gave a hard thwack at the neck of the bottle, just before the lip. Glass cracked, and evidently, I'd grabbed the carbonated wine because a spirited foam shot across the stainless-steel appliances.

I drank deeply, not caring who saw before continuing my rampage. Next door was maintenance. It was nice how they left the doors unlocked. Kicking open the door, I stumbled in and found paint.

***

Daylight was burning through my retinas.

I rolled over before resorting to covering my head with the blanket. My head throbbed, and my joints ached. Also, I needed to puke.

Making it as far as the edge of the bed, I spewed pink bile all over the white shag carpet and groaned. Still hanging my head over the edge, I found myself counting bottles. I recalled the first one. Part of a second bottle, a red that made my tongue feel all dry, too. But there was no way I drank three. I don't even like white wine.

My phone said it was lunchtime, but I found the dining room empty. Not a single Cobb salad or artisan water to be found. But I could hear a faint discussion from outside.

Bleary-eyed and cold, I walked out of the ranch barefoot and found the clique staring up at the side of the house.

Estella's eyes met mine, and she was shaking her head, mouthing words of warning, but it was too late. Richter spotted me. "Real mature, Carlie."

All right. What did I do this time?

Raising my head to the house, I found words painted white across the wall.

Babz Richter is a CUNT

Pressing my lips together was the only way to stop the laughter. Drunk me did not lie.

"I warned you about this one," Richter squawked to Feilding, who noted the graffiti with a passive sort of interest.

"You did warn me," Feilding said. "Several times. Tell me, since when do we critique private essays without consent?"

"I did ask her consent," Richter said. "I asked for her to hand it over."

"Yeah, but you didn't explain what it was for," Jacob was quick to point out.

"Naw, you told her to write that essay. We even told her what to expect, but then you acted like it wasn't what you wanted," Everett said.

"I am all for critiquing," Tiffany said, folding her arms, "but you never critiqued ours in front of the whole class like that."

I might've been drunk still, but I couldn't process what was happening. The clique was defending me? Estella kept trying to get me to do something with her eyes and mouthing words, but it just wasn't translating.

"Is this the part where I pack my shit?"

It was Dean Feilding who spoke next, but her eyes were hungrily fixed on Richter. "No, Ms. Whittaker. I already told you. I haven't lost a student yet, and I don't plan to. Mrs. Richter, in my office please."

For a minute, I started after them. My stomach was too curdled to feel nervous; it was just a habit to proceed when the words 'in my office' were used in that tone. I stopped after the spinning in my head slowed down, and Estella took my hand.

She glanced up at me with those big brown eyes and said, "I told Feilding what happened."

"Can we just take away the whys and ask...how?" Jacob said. Hands on his hips, he was staring at the white paint. "How did you get up there?"

I shrugged. "Beats me."

"Hold up," Heather said. "You were blackout drunk, on a ladder, and didn't die?"

"It's amazing, really," Felice said.

Drunk me did all sorts of things, but none were amazing. Drunk guilt usually got the best of me around five in the morning. This feeling was something else. I had disappointed them, and I think I regretted it. Unlike most people in my life, they weren't trying to shame me. I was voluntarily experiencing that on my own.

Tiffany glowered at me. "You know how hard it's going to be to get that paint off the house? It's a historic landmark. Next time you have a problem, say so. Don't act like a fucking child."

I swallowed the hard lump in my throat. "Agreed."

"It's not going to be that hard," Travis said. "She used water-based paint. Most of it will wash off."

"How can you tell it's water-based from up there?" Estella asked.

Travis shrugged. "All the paint in the maintenance room is water-based. I learned that after trying to skateboard in my room."

I'd figured he was a skateboarder, but that just confirmed it.

"All right," Everett said. "Let's get this cleaned up."

Wait, were they trying to help clean up my mess? "I can do it—"

"Jacob, help me and Travis with the ladder," Everett said. Heather just batted her eyes at him like he was a knight in shining armor.

"We'll get the hoses set up," Felice said.

And just like that, classes were suspended as the group of eight spent the rest of the afternoon washing *Babz is a CUNT* off the side of the building. I was a little sheepish at first. It was all my fault, and I should have been cleaning it myself, but then we got to work, and it didn't feel like a punishment. We were all just cleaning the side of a house and it didn't matter why or who'd done the defacing.

We put liquid dish soap on some shop brushes, and the words fell away like whitewash. Heather grabbed the hose and took a quick shot at Everett while he was on the ladder. He turned around and yelled, "These are my favorite PJs!"

Heather giggled. "Your ass looks good like that."

Everett did indeed have well-defined ass cheeks due to the way his pants clung from being soaked. "All right," he took the compliment.

I resumed scrubbing with the broom, assuming that was the end of it. But when Everett switched places with Travis, he took the bucket of soapy water and dumped it over Heather's head. Her eyes were scrunched shut, but she howled. "There's soap in my eyes!"

Some of the downpour hit Felice. I held my breath as she gave Everett the death stare. Gripping a soaked sponge, she stalked toward Everett.

"Felice..." Jacob tried to stop it, but she launched a massive, soapy sponge at Everett. Missed, and pelted Tiffany alongside the head. Pandemonium broke out. There was soap and water flying everywhere. Before I could duck and cover, I was blasted with icy water from the hose. Armed with a long-handled broom, I shook it overhead and a cold, soapy rain fell over Travis and Felice.

Someone cleared their throat.

Everyone froze to find Feilding standing precariously on the turf. "The house is clean. Whittaker, with me."

Confident that I wasn't going to be expelled, I treaded through the house soaked and soapy behind Feilding, but she stopped me short of the entryway. "You're not going into my office like that, and you're not entirely off the hook."

I nodded, grateful for being heard and not expelled. "Understood."

"Community service all next week."

"Yeah, that's totally fair."

Feilding nodded in agreement that she was indeed totally fair. Or maybe she was pleased that I agreed. It was hard to read her face, and her tone always suggested annoyance, but I'd happily pick up trash or whatever, just so long as I got to stay.

She wrinkled her nose slightly and scanned me up and down. "And no problem will be solved by a vat of wine."

I shuddered at the thought as my stomach threatened to revolt. "No more wine. Ever."

"Good. Off you go."

Returning outside, the clique was standing on the porch waiting for the decision. "Community service," I said.

"Oh, are you picking up litter?" Heather asked. "I'll join and collect things to upcycle."

"I'm not sure, but that might be the job."

"You'd be better off painting fences," joked Everett.

"Hey," Jacob said, clapping his hands together. "Let's do a street team and help the elderly with lawn work!"

I glanced at Estella. *Are they for real?*

Sadly, yes.

"I want to check out the humane society," Everett said.

"Awww!" Heather cooed.

"Old people love being read to," Tiffany said. "I'll entertain them while you guys do all the gross work."

"Well, it's settled then," Felice said. "It's community outreach week! I'll put together a plan so that each day we can focus on different aspects of volunteer work."

"I'll apply sunscreen and remain in the shade," Estella said.

Like a sitcom, they all laughed on cue. Big blank fake laughter followed by hugging each other. So jarring. Like they were puppets.

"Oh," Jacob said, glancing at his watch. "We better get changed and ready for class. We're doing historic reads today, so don't forget your gloves."

Gloves? Estella couldn't mind-transfer that one, but she deliberately hung back with me to explain. "Once a week, Dr. Nelson brings old, rare books. We wear gloves when we read them."

Oh, that wasn't as weird as I initially expected. "Some libraries have that policy."

Estella nodded. "I have extras if Dr. Nelson doesn't."

All in all, it was a weird day. Slept through two classes, got in trouble, and was massively hung over, but the clique seemed oblivious to pessimism. Estella radiated negative energy, but if I learned anything from statistics, negative wasn't good or bad; it was simply another value.

And that seemed to be how the clique perceived it.

Tiffany wasn't happy about the graffiti, but she didn't hold it against me once it came sloughing off the wall. Any animosity for my actions fell away when we sat together in the library, pulling on black latex gloves.

Dr. Nelson was somewhere in his sixties. Balding and in a brown suit, he reminded me of someone who sold insurance instead of a PhD in history and archeology. He handed out various books to everyone. I got a book called *Decisive Moment*, a book about the exact moment to take a photo.

But when it came time to give one to Estella, Dr. Nelson extended a book and didn't let go until her eyes met his. "It was quite hard to find this. I suggest you get photos."

Her eyes instantly watered, and there was a silent exchange between them. What was that all about? I hoped he wasn't a perv; otherwise, I'd be testing Feilding's patience once more.

Estella's book didn't have a title, and the cover wasn't... Well, it wasn't starched linen. It was leather of some kind. The hair on the back of my neck raised as it occurred to me that it wasn't cowhide.

"What is that?" I whispered.

"I'll explain after class."

What the hell was Estella into? I stole glances at her book at every chance I got, but I couldn't read any of it. Was it in Latin? My book was cool, but it wasn't in Latin and didn't have a bunch of creepy symbols all over it.

Dr. Nelson's eyes drifted in my direction as if he were noting a group of pigeons cooing on a ledge. He didn't speak on it. His nose was also stuck in the first edition of *The Wizard of Oz*.

The class droned on at a lurching pace. I wanted to know about her book. What was she reading? Was that human skin? I assumed Estella would be into dead things, but this was a whole other level. It was like the rest of the world no longer existed. She snapped photo after photo with an attachment for her iPhone camera to get more professional photos.

Click, flash

Click, flash

If anyone else in the clique noticed, they ignored it except for Felice, who turned and smiled at Estella with a devious sort of smile. I got the feeling that whatever Estella was up to, everyone was in on it but me.

CHAPTER 6

I practically herded Estella up the stairs and into my room over a book.

My fifth grade teacher would be so proud. She always said that anyone can find what they need most within books. That was after I did a book report on *The Cat in the Hat* because the assignment was about *any* book. Evidently, she didn't find the parallels between the cat's shenanigans and unwanted help enlightening.

My bedroom door clicked shut. "Spill it."

Estella climbed onto my bed and folded her legs like a kindergartener. I sat down and did the same to face her.

"It's not like there's a major for the occult. Ancient history and archeology are as close as I can get. Nelson gets me."

I was able to figure out that much on my own. "So, you believe in ghosts and witchcraft and stuff."

"There are things in this world we don't understand," Estella said. It wasn't creepy the way she said it. More like she was trying to soothe an anxious child. "I want to learn about them. The book Nelson gave me was a Bruja's grimoire. Shortly after Spain invaded South America, witchcraft became a popular way to frighten military away."

It certainly had that effect on me. "That wasn't a cowhide cover, was it?"

The way Estella's eyes lit, and the slight smile threatened to form was familiar. I knew rebellion when I saw it. This was her way of lighting fires. "Human skin doesn't burn as easily. It's thicker, and Spain provided a lot of it."

My stomach flipped, and I swallowed the bile spurting up my throat.

"So what language was it in?" I asked.

"Nahuatl," she said. "Or at least a version of it. I was so busy taking pictures I haven't done any transcribing yet."

"That's fucking wicked," I said breathlessly. Estella knew an ancient language? I knew how to ask for alcohol in just about every language where I've vacationed, but that didn't exactly impress anyone.

"I focus on South American occult, but my favorite thing is to find correlations between different Pagan and Demon worship."

"Do you ever...try it out?"

I don't know why I was asking, but it seemed like the next logical question. Estella's eyes became distant, like she was remembering something she'd rather not. That only spurred my heart to beat quicker. She must have tried at some point, but maybe it didn't go the way she wanted.

"Only once."

Before I could ascertain more juicy details, Estella blinked back into reality and said, "Oh hey, while I'm here. Let me see your calculator."

It was abrupt enough that I got the hint. She didn't want to talk about it anymore. I got off the bed and grabbed my calculator from my Gucci bag. I stopped and frowned at the clean slice through the fabric. When did that happen?

"That's weird," I said, holding up the bag for Estella to see. "There's a cut."

"I guess you'll just have to get a new one."

"It's not ruined forever," I said. "I'll just send it to my tailor. If she can get wine stains out of white satin, this will be no problem."

Estella stared at me for a moment. "You don't just buy another?"

I looked at it again and shrugged. I suppose I could, but it seemed a waste of a perfectly good bag. "This was the last year Gucci used this particular canvas for their bags. It's a classic."

"Felice just buys things to wear them once."

A pretty common occurrence among fashion lovers. It wasn't that I couldn't relate, no one likes an overflowing closet, but I could never bring myself to do that. The bag had a clean cut. It wasn't damaged beyond saving.

Ignoring the itch to grab my phone, I said, "There's history in fashion. One day, items like this will be preserved and kept on display. Their value doesn't end after a season. I like classic pieces that never go out of style. One day, someone might put my wardrobe behind a glass case."

Estella nodded. "Very cool."

While she worked on my calculator, copying formulas from hers to mine, I couldn't help but ask more questions. Mostly, it was to move past the silence. Estella might have been perfectly comfortable in the stillness, but I wasn't. The last thing I needed was to check my phone for a text from my dad...again.

"What about ghosts," I asked. "Are those real?"

"Maybe. I have a theory that spirits are beyond most human comprehension. Even if we do experience them, we rationalize and change our own memories until it was just a gust of wind or something."

"What about people who go looking for them?" I asked, thinking of all those TV shows where people actively search for them.

"Even them," Estella didn't lift her eyes from the calculator. "They go to places with creepy reputations to find proof, but in all likelihood, they've been ignoring the ghost in their own home without realizing it."

"So, houses with history aren't any more haunted than a new suburban housing complex?"

"I didn't say that. It's just that we tend to ignore what we can't explain."

"Is this place haunted?" I asked.

She stopped punching the keys and raised her eyes to mine. "This house is haunted by power, not spirits."

I squirmed a little at that. It felt like I was back at summer camp, and we were all telling ghost stories by the fire. I was all tense and ready for someone to jump scare us. At any moment, Estelle was going to hold a flashlight under her face and tell us the bad guy had been in the house all along.

Haunted by power... Her words were profound and poetic.

Power did have a way of haunting people. Like when the lottery winners always ended up worse off than before they won. Or like celebrities who'd fallen out of popularity and began doing bizarre things to try and bolster their careers.

A house like Marten Ranch was once a modern marvel and probably the pride of the constantly damp state of Washington. But once the owner presumably died, everyone struggled with what to do with it. Make it a tourist attraction? That didn't work. If the school was shuttered, these halls would be empty once more, searching for purpose.

"If we can't remember seeing ghosts, what's the point of them?"

Right away, I felt stupid. Lots of things existed without human purpose. What I meant to ask was; If ghosts don't chase power, why do they linger?

As if understanding my true question, Estella said, "There are dozens of theories about ghosts. From alternate dimensions to souls that can't move on. I don't know where they come from or why they're here; I just know that they have no point."

I nodded, tangling my fingers in my lap to keep from checking my phone. "We want them to have a purpose."

At that, Estella hit enter for a final time and said, "There. No more battling with statistics."

"Thanks," I said. "Seriously, I'd be screwed if you didn't help me."

Dinner that evening consisted of two large charcuterie boards, seasoned and roasted potatoes, and a pasta with lemon basil. Heather blanched as she eyed the cheese. Her hand reached out, trembling. In a moment that appeared almost a lapse in willpower, she wiped the peppers and olives that were isolated in tin cups.

"Not going to lie," she said. "I miss cheese."

"I just love your determination," Felice said while pointedly nibbling on a white cheddar six inches away from Heather's face. "You have so many convictions."

Tiffany was sitting by Felice today, and I was sitting between Travis and Everett. Jacob was between Heather and Estella. I wanted to sit by Estella, but the clique was adamant about diversity.

"Not convictions," Heather said. "Just goals. When I'm pregnant, I'll phase dairy back into my diet. Meat, too, after I stop breastfeeding." There was probably a manuscript of plans somewhere in Heather's room. "And my children will decide their dietary needs on their own. Just so long as it's organic, non-GMO, and without all the extra crap the machine puts in our food."

By 'machine,' I assumed she meant the food industry. It was a vendetta of a different sort. I could appreciate that. "They're all owned by the same three companies," I added.

Her eyes went wide. "They are! Just a massive conglomerate to make us sick and addicted. I'll hire the best chefs to make our food, so it's not like my future children will be missing out on anything."

"Reputable farmers need all the help they can get," Everett said. "Knowing my meat comes from a free-range farm where they love their animals means a lot to me."

Heather stared up at him adoringly.

"How long have the two of you been dating?" I asked.

There was some laughter from Felice and the couple, and my heart dropped. I said something wrong, didn't I?

Felice leaned in and whispered, "Supposedly, they're not a couple."

"We just don't want to put a label on it," Everett said.

At that, I eased a little. So, they were dating but not actually dating. Got it.

"We're young and should have young experiences," Heather said. "So, while we really like each other, we're open to all things."

"Yeah, they are," Felice said, and giggles erupted from the clique. Even Estella was laughing. I did too, but it was awkward. Was their initiation ritual some kind of class-orgy? This place was getting interesting.

Did they wear black latex gloves and organic condoms? I imagined Heather had some reservations about swallowing. Jacob probably showered once before and twice afterward. I couldn't imagine Estella participating, but perhaps that was why she stood apart from the rest of the clique.

"Where's that Gucci bag you usually carry around?" Felice asked. "The one from nineteen seasons ago."

It wasn't weird that Felice noticed. She was the only other female in the house with a passion for fashion, but my mind couldn't help but jump to *that* conclusion. "There was a cut along the side. I'm sending it to my tailor for repairs."

"Shame," she said, swirling her red wine. "It was borderline vintage. You might as well toss it. They lose value when repaired."

"Not true," Tiffany cut in. "Art is restored all the time, and it's just as priceless."

Felice faced her, and it was like the spotlight had been taken off me. "I'm not talking about your obsessions; I'm talking about *ours*."

It was the first time I had seen a move toward exclusion among the clique. So, there were rifts and ranks. They tried their best to hide it, but all in-crowds had them, and Tiffany, the art lover, was somewhere on the bottom rung. In one brief conversation, Felice had elevated my rank in the social hierarchy.

"Art is in the eye of the beholder," Jacob said, steadfast on neutral ground. "Whether it's a painting, a bag, a sculpture. All provoke thoughts, meanings, and feelings."

At this, Felice hedged a little. "Of course, but you have to admit, the art Tiffany is referring to is untouchable. Purses are just purses. Artfully crafted or not, they don't hold up to Michelangelo."

And just like that, the spotlight was turned off. It seemed to me that Felice had some mean girl tendencies, and it was Jacob's job to keep them in line.

"Well, you know how I feel about a nice pair of shoes," he joked. "The right pair can make the heavens sing."

"I've experienced that many times," I said.

The errant tension in the room eased, and the conversation lilted to the week's agenda.

"All right," Felice said. "I broke us up into two teams, alternating by the day, of course. Tomorrow, Heather, Everett, Jacob, and Carlie will help the animal shelter. Travis, Tiffany, Estella, and I will be volunteering at the senior home."

"Sounds good to me," Jacob said.

Everyone else was nodding in approval. Estella didn't look thrilled, but that was probably her neutral face. "Maybe we can get out of class early," Travis suggested. "Beat the traffic."

"I don't think Nelson will care," Estella said. "It's for a good cause, after all."

My experience with animals was...lacking.

A dog bit my face when I was four, so that was out, and my parents didn't want cats scratching the furniture. Hopefully, they wouldn't pick up on my fear. Everyone said animals could tell if someone was a bad person. What if the shelter pets deemed me unworthy, and the clique picked up on it?

Focusing on the anxiety of community service was busy work for my brain. It kept me from the real concerns that another round of classes came before growling dogs and snapping teeth. I'd have to face another writing session with Richter after my stunt. Maybe she'd trip down the grand staircase before then.

Cause let's be honest. She was going to find another way to punish me. What if she made a few calls and got ahold of my dad?

I checked my phone again. Rather than a message from him, I got one from Estella.

You notice something is off, don't you?

With Felice? I replied.

You need to be more careful.

I eyed her from across the table, but she wasn't looking at me. A spiral of dread made me forget all about dinner or who I was with. *Did I upset her?*

No. You excited her.

CHAPTER 7

The edge of the seat pressed hard into the back of my thighs. I had chewed a layer of my bottom lip clean off, and it stung in the open air. What fresh hell would Richter bring for the remainder of my academic studies—however long it may be.

I flinched as the door opened, and a pair of sensible heels clacked squarely against the hardwood.

In the place of a plump, tweed-suit-wearing woman was a slim frame with a blonde French twist. Dean Feilding.

My brain took a hard shift. Had Richter been fired? My eyes darted around, looking for a reaction from the others. The clique wore similar expressions of confusion but waited for Feilding to explain.

It didn't take long. In a smooth, confident voice, Feilding said, "Mrs. Richter's conflicts of interest became all too apparent after the graffiti incident. Marten Ranch Academy is dedicated to our students, not the board. Starting tomorrow, Mr. Lindt will be leading this course."

Reading between the lines of that announcement, I got the feeling that Richter wanted more board oversight and say in who attended. Feilding didn't strike me as the sort of woman who relinquished power easily.

Felice tilted her head, unsure of how to respond, but that was the only reaction the clique issued. The dean sat down at the professor's desk and said, "I want a short essay about what you think attending college is about. We will be sharing these, so bear that in mind."

The next half hour was a gnawing silence. I stared at the page, asking myself the question multiple times. What did I think attending college was about? It was such a stupid, generic question, given by Feilding since she probably didn't know we were studying great female writers. I'd much rather draw comparisons between Shelly and Woolf.

Maybe I'd write something horribly sarcastic. Nothing brought out my worst inclinations like generic questions and expected attitudes. Feilding wanted five-hundred words about learning and finding myself, so I'd give it to her.

But my pen stopped short.

Feilding went to bat for me. The clique helped me clean and were going to volunteer so I wouldn't be alone. Or maybe just because they loved community service, I don't know. The point was everyone in this room deserved a genuine response from me. It was the least I could do.

"All right, class, finish up," Feilding said.

I exhaled. Eyes fixed on my paper. A nervous tingle came over me. It was probably the most vulnerable thing I'd ever written.

"We'll start with Felice and work our way across."

Felice's essay read like a valedictorian speech. It was all about creating our own narratives and changing the world. The words themselves were nothing I hadn't heard before, but I had to blink back the tears for some inexplicable reason. It was like she was speaking at youth's funeral.

Feilding closed her eyes while listening, her head bobbing slightly as though she were keeping rhythm. I had to stop myself from nodding too.

"It's a fascinating use of mnemonics," Feilding said. "Did everyone notice it?"

The dean stood up and wrote out a series of lines and carrots. "What Felice did there was use the rise and fall of her speech to emphasize certain words, making them more memorable. If done correctly, one can instate powerful emotions in the listeners."

"Where did you learn that?" Jacob asked, turning to face her fully.

"Oh, I learned by watching former President Barack Obama. My personal hero."

I blinked. Unsure of what to make of that.

"It was so sweet," Heather said, drying her eyes. "And so, so true."

Everett nodded. "The delivery was amazing, but I feel like you leaned too hard on it."

The spell of Felice's words was slowly unwrapping, and I realized the same. There was no way in hell I was going to say Felice Lakewood's essay was empty...but it was platitudes and clichés wrapped in a Bath and Body Works gift basket. All the same cheap products, just a different smell.

Tiffany opened her mouth and said, "I think you could have dug deeper..." She hesitated when Felice turned around and fixed her a stony expression. "But with five hundred words, it's hard to do that."

Estella flipped through three pages and said, "I went way over the word limit."

It was my turn to comment, and Felice was staring at me. "I really enjoyed the delivery. Maybe one day you can show me how you do it?"

She smiled, but there was something in her eyes that said, *not in your wildest dreams.*

As the rest of the class read their papers, I couldn't deny the increasing tension. I had been gripping my pen so hard that it stung and left indents on my fingers. Every time I tried to chew on my lip, it bit back as if reminding me it had nothing left to give.

One by one, each of the clique shared a near-identical version of Felice's essay. None were presented as well, and some had more personal anecdotes involving an auntie or the cleverness of whales. Otherwise, it was like all the essays were written by the same person.

If they noticed, they said nothing of it. They praised one another on the unoriginality of their thoughts and how inspirational Tiffany was as the only student to receive a scholarship to attend the academy.

I hadn't chewed my fingernails since high school. That stopped when I started getting acrylics. It just wasn't as satisfying; however, my fingers found a corner of lifted cuticle, and I peeled nearly up to the knuckle.

Why were they like this? Like they were empty of any genuine thoughts. Maybe they were just nervous because Feilding was leading the session? Something about it was deeply unsettling. Like I was sitting in a room all alone with robots.

When it was Estella's turn, most of that discomfort slipped away. My bottom lip was swollen, and the flesh of my pinky finger was bleeding under the thumb I applied pressure with. But the moment she opened her mouth and spoke, it was like the room bloomed into full color once more.

I was in a library with friends and the dean. The room smelled of old books and dust, and it was starting to rain outside. Inhaling a deep breath, I went lax in my seat.

Unlike the others, Estella's essay was about all the things she wanted to do and how college was the steppingstone to get there. It wasn't a great essay, and she mumbled half of it, but she was real.

"You have more goals listed on that essay than I've had in my entire life," I told her. "It's freaking amazing."

The others commended her on her dedication as well but critiqued that her presentation could be better. Fair.

By the time it got to me, I was too exhausted to even care what they thought. Nothing could be worse than Richter's class-led pummel. Here we go...

"The truth is, I don't know who I am. I've spent most of my life defining myself with rebelliousness and anger, but maybe I can be something more. For the first time in my life, I want to be more."

The clique and even Feilding clapped when I finished.

"What an inspiration," the dean said. "Going to college is all about learning who we are and what we want to be."

"Oh my God," Heather said. "You totally nailed it!"

"We get to decide who we are now," Jacob said.

I nodded, understanding for the first time what the clique meant when they said to set aside the trauma. My past had defined the way people treated me and, in turn, how I reacted. It never occurred to me that I could just dismiss it and pursue what really mattered to me.

"But what is it that *you* want?" Estella asked.

My face flushed. I had hoped no one would pick up on it. I didn't know what I wanted to do with my life; I had only just figured out that it was my own.

"Still working on that part," I said, ignoring how hot my face was.

"Nothing's wrong with that," Heather said. "Some of us still hang on to dreams, no matter how infeasible they are. You'll find it when it's time."

I mouthed a thanks, but then Everett came into focus. He was glaring at Heather. She wasn't talking about me at all.

"Excellent work today, class," Feilding said. "Continue your readings, and Lindt will resume the curriculum tomorrow."

As we left, Estella got in front of me. "I didn't mean to embarrass you," she said. "I was just curious."

"No, it's okay. Our essays were polar opposites. You know what you want, and I wish I did."

Estella clutched her books to her upside-down cross necklace and said, "I know what I want, but the world doesn't make room for studies like mine."

I grinned. "You just have to make more noise." That was something I did know about.

We were heading out when I overheard Travis say, "Tell me she isn't ready."

"It's not up to me!" Felice replied with an exacerbated tone. "I don't even know if the sanctuary is ready."

What was the sanctuary? The hype of positivity gave way to the reminder that the clique was still shutting me out. Though, based on this new information, it sounded as though there were some extenuating circumstances. Did an orgy get out of control leaving their sanctuary in a state of disrepair? I had to restrain a giggle.

"We can check in and see," Jacob offered.

Before I could hustle toward them to hear more, they split off in several directions like a herd escaping a predator. "What were they talking about?" I said, but as I turned, Estella was gone too.

CHAPTER 8

A dog with bulging eyes stared at me. Despite his mouth being closed, his tongue was hanging out and threatening to lick the carpet. Short hair and stout, his face was a pile of wrinkles on his squished face. His graying black and white coat was coarse and there were a few bald patches around the incessantly wagging tail.

"He's one of our favorites," the volunteer said. She was probably nineteen, wearing a white T-shirt with the humane society's logo printed in silk-screened black. Her blonde hair was in a ponytail, like she came ready for a workout.

"He's..." Horrific? Grotesque? I didn't know much about dogs, but usually, there was more dog than tongue.

"Quasimodo has a macroglossia. It means his tongue is abnormally long."

It was waiting for something, but I didn't know what. Panting and wagging, it finally worked itself into a state where it began honking at me. Should I touch it, or...

"You don't have much experience with animals, do you?"

"Nope."

I turned my head for a moment, and Everett was gone. Then, on the other side of a glass room, I spotted him. Just one athletic Black man and a sea of fur. It was like the cats knew he was their friend and fought for every inch of space on his lap. Like some kind of cat whisperer, it came so easily to him. He smiled at me and made a petting motion which a cat happily inserted himself as an example.

Returning to Quasimodo, the unrelenting little dog waited patiently for me to figure it out. I really didn't want him to lick me, but that was probably unavoidable, given his condition. I patted his head, and the stub of his tail began to waggle frantically.

"Aw, he likes you."

I exhaled and relaxed. Petting the dog was nice.

The dogs in the other room were barking. Heather and Jacob were assigned to walk the dogs. Having no experience with animals, I opted to do front desk work. It was something I did for my dad on summer breaks or between schools.

So, there I was, wearing a white T-shirt, helping the others do intake. Quasimodo sat at my feet while I printed out brochures, receipts, and forms. Most people were coming to look at the animals. A mom with a couple of kids adopted a kitten, and someone rang the bell.

It was distracting me from the work of setting up the three additional printers the humane society had yet to connect to their computers, but it was cute to see how happy the animals were when someone took them home. Like they knew they were being adopted.

"So, what's Quasi's story?" I asked, observing the little paws on my leg.

"His owners were breeders," the blonde said. "They couldn't sell him, so they brought him here."

Scooping the dog up from under the arms, I plopped him in my lap. "But they made him. The least they could do is take care of him."

"They didn't put him in a bag and toss him into the river. They brought him to us," she said. "He couldn't nurse, so we had to bottle feed him. He has special needs that require more work than most owners are willing to deal with. So, we decided he's the mascot."

I was petting him so hard that his wrinkly skin was pulled back with each stroke. His eyes would temporarily bulge harder, but he seemed to like it.

Speaking of the vet, a woman in a white coat was being shadowed by Everett. Listening to bits of their conversation was funny. I couldn't understand it, but they were so animated. Like he finally met someone who spoke the same language.

"He wants to be a vet, but his girlfriend is against it," the volunteer said.

"Why?" I asked. She glimpsed Quasi on my lap and smiled before turning back around at the desk.

"I don't know. He looks happy here."

It was a strange thing to admit, but I was happy here too. Not that I wanted to become a veterinarian or anything like that, but it felt like a good place to be. I couldn't describe it, but there was a tranquility here that wasn't present at Marten Ranch. The walls felt sturdier, more secure somehow.

Probably because they didn't occasionally rumble without cause. I was on the top story. The only space above my room was an attic. I doubted rats could make my light fixture shake. Either way, it was unsettling. I needed to get out more.

Quasi curled up in my lap and fell into a hard sleep when a man came in with a dog. It was a brown, furry mutt with wide-crying eyes, and my heart just dropped.

"I need you guys to take her," he said.

The volunteer was on her feet and trying to soothe the poor dog. She explained there was a surrender fee, to which the man threw three hundred dollars on the ground before storming out. For a minute, I thought he was going to yell at her or hit her, but he left, and the dog frantically tried to follow before letting out a wail.

"Oh my God," I uttered, clutching Quasi to my chest.

"Come here," the volunteer soothed. "Good girl."

She picked up the money and led the frantic dog into another room while I just stood there like an idiot. That guy really did just dump his dog and leave. I mean, duh, people did that all the time, obviously. But I'd never seen it firsthand. The dog didn't understand what was happening. It was beyond cruel.

The volunteer came back out. "We have her in a quiet room to decompress. Once the vet looks her over, we will finish intake."

"That was...traumatic," I said.

Quasi was panting in my arms. I was probably holding him too tight because he was starting to cough again.

"Yeah, people suck. That's why I prefer animals."

I could see why.

***

Hushed conversations and scant whispers came from every direction in the night. Just when I thought I was following one, they went silent, forcing me to find another trail. They had to be going in the same direction. The sanctuary wasn't some ominous presence; it was a place the clique convened in secret at night.

Then again, if it was an orgy, maybe they took turns hosting. I really didn't think it was a sex thing.

This house has history...

A soft light sent a black and white stripe rippling across the wall. Someone was using a candle or a small flashlight.

Hurrying down the stairs, careful not to trip, I rounded the banister and chased the fleeting footsteps, only for the light to vanish. Leaning with my back against the wall of the library, I steadied my breath. Jesus Christ, it wasn't some life-or-death pursuit, but I was panting.

The pitch-black had set me on edge, that's all. It was all-consuming as I chased the clique to a private rendezvous to which I wasn't invited. I just wanted to know what it was. That way when they did decide to invite me, I'd be ready.

Knowing my luck, it was probably some kind of Girl Scouts but for adults. Future Leaders of America or some crap that wasn't worth stumbling around at two in the morning, in the dark.

Whatever it was, they were in the library.

My fingers found the knob, and I pressed my ear against the seam. Silence.

The moon reflected in the large windows, slats of light illuminated an empty room. The books remained stationed on their shelves, but there was something on Estella's desk. I moved closer and felt it. Book-shaped, but it didn't feel like a book. I flinched with recognition.

Dr. Nelson gave Estella a rare book. A Bruja's grimoire, its cover made from a Spanish soldier's skin.

What the hell was that doing here?

CHAPTER 9

*C*runch...

    Crunch, crunch...

There was something so relaxing about picking up litter. With my makeshift harpoon, I stabbed cans and paper alike and shoved it in the black garbage bag slung over my shoulder. Not every day of volunteer work could be fun. Nor could it be as tumultuous.

I had a dream last night that I went looking for the clique and only found Quasi sitting on my desk. His giant tongue rested on a stack of books as he whined, waiting for me to come to him. Only, when I did, the room shook and shuddered.

Waking up before things got too scary was the norm for me.

If only reality wasn't so creepy. I was awake when I found the flesh-covered book in the library. The next morning, I attended class like nothing had happened, and the book wasn't discussed.

"They had to choose a sunny day for this," Estella said, appearing beside me. She wore a wide-brimmed black hat and sunglasses, and she radiated the smell of sunblock. Greasy and thick yet somehow tinged with coconut and zinc.

"Better than a rainy day," I said.

Her eyes shifted toward me. "Rain would be better. I like this state for that reason."

Crunch...crunch...

"It doesn't rain as much as everyone says," I noted. "I thought it would be torrential every day."

"Maybe it has rainy seasons."

Crunch...

"What part of Mexico are you from?" I asked.

"Just outside Polanco. Mexico City."

At that, I beamed. A distant memory of shopping with my dad in a place that felt like Beverly Hills's richer cousin. "Hey, I've been there!"

CRUNCH...

Estella stabbed at the errant beer. Easy, Norman Bates. "You don't like it there?"

"I like Día de Muertos, but I'm not allowed to attend unless my brothers come too. I want to see the ruins of our ancestors, but I can't unless I have security. I can't even take a shit without someone asking why."

I cringed. That would be annoying. "Are you the baby sister?"

She nodded.

Sometimes being the only child was a good thing. I could only imagine her brothers didn't understand Estella's interests. They probably complained about being tasked to look after her. Security wouldn't complain, but they probably made it hard for her to get away with crossing those taped-off areas or red ropes.

The only way Estella could explore the world was through books. No wonder her world was painted in black and white.

I wasn't about to bring up the book from last night. The last thing I needed was for the clique to think I was stalking their nightly activities. Even Estella – who I'm pretty sure wouldn't say anything – was a risk to my covert operation.

"Hey, I got to try out the calculator in statistics," I said. "It was a total lifesaver."

"It's the only way to survive that class. Next semester is calculus or something more grounded in reality."

Might as well be a foreign language. Only instead of French, it was German, and I still had no idea what anyone was saying. "Please tell me you have formulas for that too."

Estella only grinned. That probably meant yes.

In the distance, Travis was sitting with a homeless person under the shade of an oak tree. They were sharing one of those massive malt beers found in any convenience store. "What's his story?" I asked.

I couldn't imagine him doing anything that would result in a suspension. I couldn't imagine him doing anything at all.

"You mean why is he at our school?"

"I thought it was for troublemakers."

"Sadness is trouble for parents," she said.

My heart ached at that. I couldn't imagine Travis being depressed. He was quiet and laid back but soulful and sort of dreamy. He seemed perfectly content under the oak tree. his homemade beanie on his head despite the heat.

"Taking a break?" Estella asked when we approached.

"Just doing some outreach," he said, smiling at his new friend. Despite his ragged clothes, his face and hair were clean, and so was the large backpack sitting next to him. "Paul here was bored waiting for his work shift to begin."

"You have a job?" I asked, only to blush, realizing how rude it sounded.

Paul nodded. "Same job for twenty years."

He had a job but was homeless. I didn't understand. My frown enunciated my confusion, and Travis said, "Loads of homeless people have jobs. Rent is expensive."

"I was living out of my car," Paul said. "But it got stolen, so...here I am."

If someone had a job, they should be able to afford a shitty studio apartment at least. It wasn't fair. "It just doesn't seem right," I said, casting my eyes to the pair of shoes that cost more than Paul probably needed to make rent.

"Are you kids hungry?" Paul asked, reaching for a plastic bag. "You've been out here for a while."

The four of us sat under the oak tree and shared a bag of Doritos. The crunching noise was now between my teeth. We didn't say much. Just watched cars merge onto the freeway. Sometimes we'd laugh when a car nearly caused an accident or watch someone veer across lanes.

"Get off your phone!" Paul complained.

Even I didn't use my phone when driving. That was what Bluetooth was for, jeez. "I'm a destructive ass, but at least I don't try and kill people in the process."

"You're not destructive," Travis said without taking his eyes off the freeway. "You're an activist."

I could only stare at him, trying to figure out what he meant. Graffiti, arson, and the occasional riot were not things activists did. "I've never held a sign or asked someone to sign a petition in my life. I don't even vote."

"Carlie," Estella said. "Think back to every time you've gotten in trouble. Why did you do it?"

"Because I was drunk and pissed off?" Seriously, it was like they didn't know me in the slightest.

"Yeah, but why were you pissed?" Travis pushed. "Columbus getting undeserved accolades..."

"Or because the school forced your professor to change the curriculum?" Estella added.

"That dean you tried to lure into a sex act...I attended Harvard before I tried to kill myself. He was a known perv. You were trying to expose him, weren't you?"

There was too much to unpack in Travis's words. My brain jarred and twisted back again. I didn't know what to say or how to say it.

Travis wasn't ashamed of his past. He shouldn't be, but there was sort of a black garbage bag beside him. Not the one full of litter, a different one. Like, he'd have to carry that with him for the rest of his life. He'd always need to disclose it with doctors, and everyone would think about it when they talked to him.

"He has an account with my dad," I said. "The worst part is that my dad pretty much stopped talking to me after that. He chose an account over me."

"That's bullshit," Paul said. "I wish I could tell my daughter I'd never choose anyone over her."

"You don't see her?" Estella asked.

Paul shook his head. "I see her every day. She just pretends she doesn't know me."

Crunch...

***

Laying in my bed, my eyes and ears followed the sounds between the walls. The skitter scatter was followed by what sounded like someone dragging their knees across wood. Sort of bumpy, like their knees bounced off the floor. My imagination was getting wild, and so was my heart rate. I didn't dare move. Not even to breathe.

The sound stopped, only to resume in the far corner of my room before leaving altogether.

I tried to rationalize it with thoughts, but images of horror film monsters kept flooding my mind. Crawling things with misshapen bodies and melty skin. Clutching my blanket, I pulled it up to my face and hyperventilated as quietly as I could.

Just a rat. Just a bunch of rats. They sound louder than they are. Probably dragging food or nesting materials. Or a fucking corpse.

A giggle from outside my door, followed by a "shush," eliminated the panic. I sat up. Maybe they heard the noise too and came to investigate. Slipping out of bed, my bare feet felt the shag carpet between my toes.

"Hello?" I whispered, stepping out of my room.

I was pretty sure it was Everett that shushed the laughter, but no one answered. They headed left even though there was nothing but a closet followed by a dead end. I opened the closet door and flipped on the light.

For a horrific moment, I imagined a monster appearing in the corner. Braced for the worst, a scream was ready in my throat, but nothing was there. Just a vacuum and cleaning supplies on a metal shelf. A mop and roll-away bucket.

Once again, the clique eluded me in their nighttime mischief. Where the hell could they have gone?

I checked the library. Not because I was holding out hope that I'd catch someone sneaking around. Mostly, I just was just too restless and afraid that the noises from the attic would be waiting for me when I returned.

The night air was growing colder. Shivering, I wrapped my arms around my chest and ignored the icy touch of the floors against my feet.

I was missing something major about the house. Something the clique had discovered. Perhaps that was why I wasn't invited to the sanctuary. Felice kept saying it wasn't up to her. If it wasn't up to the queen bee, then it must have been up to me to find it on my own.

Then again, I could have been misreading the situation. I had a tendency to do that. For all I knew, Feilding had to sign off when I was good and committed or something.

"Ms. Whittaker?"

I gasped and jerked away. Soul leaving my body. Arms slapping in the direction of the disturbance. Dr. Sykes jumped back. "Woah, sorry. I didn't mean to scare you."

Every nerve hummed and tingled as I laughed and swatted at the professor again for good measure. "You scared the shit out of me."

He was also breathless. Hands on his knees and laughing. "Same."

"What are you doing here?" I asked.

"I heard a weird noise in the walls," he said. "I followed it to the library."

I shook my head. That couldn't be right. I heard the noise in the attic and then Everett in the closet. But I had been in the library for only a few minutes and didn't hear anything. "I heard it in the attic but not around the library."

At least it wasn't just me. That was both reassuring and alarming at the same time. At least if a professor mentioned it to someone, they would take him seriously.

"I'm pretty sure it's rats," he said.

"No way. It's way too loud."

"I'm from Brooklyn, Whittaker. I've seen rats that could make off with a small child."

Inhale. Exhale.

"That doesn't make me feel any better."

"I'll talk to the dean tomorrow. Get an exterminator to take care of it. This is a big old house. I wouldn't be surprised if raccoons were nesting between the walls."

"Come on, I'll walk you back to your room."

He turned on the flashlight from his phone when we got to the stairs. I expected an awkward silence, but Sykes had a charming way about him that made me feel at ease. "Okay, I'm not sure which room is yours. So, lead the way."

I hung a left down the corridor and stopped short of my room. "This is me."

"Do you want me to check your room before you go in?"

Yes. I wasn't going back in there if I heard anything else.

"No, I'll be okay."

"Okay. I'm on the right wing of the first floor. Second door on the left. If you need anything. Otherwise, don't be afraid to call one of the other students."

I nodded as my stomach bottomed out. Suddenly aware that his hand was on the small of my back. He wasn't trying to be weird, just reassuring, I think. Swallowing the lump in my throat, I went back into my room. Something inside me screamed at me to lock the door.

The monsters are not in between the walls. They're the smiling, familiar faces.

CHAPTER 10

Volunteer work had been completed, and I was officially off the hook. Feilding approved with a nod Friday night and said, "Did you learn anything in the wild?"

I blurted it all out at once. Like a confession. The heat engulfed my face and chest, but I didn't care. My dad wasn't there for approval, so I had to get it from somewhere. I told her all about Paul and Quasimodo. How seniors were left to fend for themselves alone in their homes, and the devastating amount of litter for such a small town.

"Everyone is alone," I said. "They're alone, and no one cares."

Feilding stared at me so hard I thought I'd pop like a bubble. "But you care, don't you, Carlie?"

Blinking back the tears, I nodded. "It's stupid, I know—"

"It's not stupid," Feilding said. "It's not bad to care for the welfare of others. Even if you're privilege expects otherwise."

Easy for her to say. After meeting Paul, I researched the cost of rent. The clothes I wore to pick up litter cost more than rent for a year. Even if I did sell all my belongings and donate everything I had, it would be the equivalent of a piece of space trash flying into a black hole.

I was useless, and it fucking sucked.

"I guess I've always been sheltered from it," admitting the greatest sin of all. "Private schools, manicured campuses. It's not like I was unaware that things were hard..."

"Beneath that vain exterior, you have a kind heart," Feilding said. "And I suspect you'll find ways to make an impact. Even small ones."

I left the dean's office feeling so light but dizzy with questions. Mainly, when did authority approval start meaning something to me? There was a difference between Dean "hand on the thigh" and Dean Feilding, though. I respected her in the way I used to respect my dad.

That wasn't fair.

My dad had no idea what I was trying to prove. Even I didn't. Not until Travis pointed it out to me the other day. There was no point in explaining it to Dad, though. He wouldn't believe me any more than the board would believe countless girls. How could he when the dean smelled danger and expelled me?

I fell into my bed and decided I would sleep no matter what. The raccoons or whatever in the attic could fall through the floor and go feral on my face, and I wouldn't so much as flinch. Ambien would make sure of that.

People using Ambien have reported experiencing the following symptoms: daytime drowsiness, headache, stomach upset, diarrhea, constipation, loss of memory, worsening depression or anxiety, loss of memory, abnormal thoughts, macroglossia, agitation, weird fucking dreams...

Someone was panting in my ear.

"Not now, Quasi..." I said with a weak swat.

Their breath was hot, and something wet pooled along the collar of my school polo.

But the panting persisted. Rapid breathing marched to its own rhythm. It ceased the moment I opened my eyes.

That was beyond disturbing.

Reaching for my phone, I unplugged it from the charger and checked the time. It was six in the morning. On a Saturday. Unbelievable.

The croissant thudded on my plate and was only stopped by a cluster of grapes. I didn't actually want to eat it; I just got it to make my plate less bare. Armed with a mug of coffee and a pile of single-serve creamers, I sat down across from Estella. She was reading a book and didn't look up until fifteen minutes later.

"Woah," she said at the sight of me. "Rough night?"

I nodded as I drank the last bit of coffee.

"You ever fall asleep but feel like you were awake the entire time?"

"Alcohol has that effect." She said it as a fact, but it felt like she was implying that I was drunk. Between volunteer work, class, and homework, I didn't have time to drink. It didn't help that the clique was the "high on life" type, and there was no one to drink with. Not like that ever stopped me before, but if I drank alone, it meant something illegal would follow.

"I didn't drink last night. I even took an Ambien, but it felt like I was laying there awake all night while having this creepy dream…"

I could hear the panting against my ear.

"Sounds like something is bothering you," Estella said.

Life bothered me. I supposed that should have been her line and not mine. Estella was wearing a fresh coat of black polish, and her hair was slicked back into a high ponytail, making her face more pointed and goth than usual.

"There are weird noises coming out of the attic above my room," I said. "Sykes thinks they're rats or coons. He heard them too." I added the last bit just in case she didn't believe me.

Estella frowned. "He was in your room?"

I shook my head. I just said the house might have an infestation, and that's where she went with it? "No, he heard it along the library walls."

"Anyways," I said, forcefully steering the conversation. "He said he was going to ask Feilding to get an exterminator."

The conversation died, and I desperately needed another cup of coffee.

While I was grabbing another handful of creamer pods, I saw Estella was texting somewhat furiously on her phone. She glanced my way and put her phone back in her pocket, then went back to her book.

Something weird was going on. It didn't take a psychic to know she was texting the clique's group chat that didn't include me. I knew there was a group chat without me because they'd formed a new one when we all swapped phone numbers. They didn't just decide to form a group chat right then and there.

It was another door closed to me, like the one to the sanctuary. The more aware I was of the partition, the more it itched and scratched against my already raw nerves. What did I have to do? Watch *The Sound of Music* until my eyes and ears were bleeding? Get a Disney character tattooed on my ass? Sing the praises of Noam Chomsky?

Everyone was entitled to their space and all that. The clique didn't owe me anything, but after spending my entire life as an outsider, I finally wanted in. Not just want— I craved it. A bestie, a crew of people I could lean into, knowing they felt safe enough to do the same.

I thought the clique's acceptance was too good to be true, and it was things like this that put doubt in my mind.

Sitting back down, I stared at Estella. She knew something was up because she squirmed under my gaze. *What is it you're not telling me? What do I need to do?*

Relenting, Estella closed her book and said, "There have been some rumors about Sykes. Just keep a distance from him, and if he does anything weird, let me know. Okay?"

"Like what?"

Her black lips formed a pout. "I'm not supposed to talk about it. Nothing proven, just vibes."

In my experience, vibes were usually enough. "I got those vibes from him too."

Estella nodded, but she either didn't understand what I wanted or she was avoiding it.

"What's with the sanctuary?"

"It's not ready yet," she said. "But when it is, you will probably be invited."

I squirmed in my seat a little. Finally! "Anything I should know beforehand?"

"You're welcome to attend, but you don't have to participate," Estella said. "I still haven't."

Curiosity was gnawing at me. "Is it a sex thing?"

She giggled and said no. Most definitely not a sex thing. "So, why haven't you participated?"

Estella shifted in her seat. "I don't need to."

But the others did. My mind went to Travis and his mental health history and Jacob having asshole parents. Whatever these guys were doing, it was helping them move past their trauma. "Is it...like a keta-mine treatment?"

Her smile widened. "Yeah, but foolproof and without drugs. It takes time to get everything arranged, and we don't know if it will even take to you yet."

"Hm," I said.

New tactic. If their little initiation ritual wasn't ready—or I wasn't ready—and I suspected the latter, the best thing to do was to play it cool. "Just an FYI, drugs aren't my scene."

It wasn't that I hadn't experimented or had some agenda against them. On the contrary, I had tried them all and found them not worth it. The aftermath of coke was like getting a rug burn on the inside. Heroin was too risky. Molly involved a lot of maintenance and self-awareness. I didn't exactly enjoy being overwhelmed by feelings, even if they were the good kind. Hallucinating was not great, and no psychedelic uncle that hung out with the teenagers could convince me otherwise.

Pot was okay, but there was this clingy stink of pot culture I just couldn't handle. Moral of the story: drugs are boring.

Estella raised her laminated brows. "You just said you took Ambien."

"That's a prescription; it doesn't count."

There was a note of amusement on her face. Before I could stop myself, I plucked one of the grapes off the stem and threw it at her face. There was an instant where Estella went cross-eyed as the grape came hurtling toward her.

In a snap, she opened her mouth and caught the grape. Locking eyes with me, she ate it. "I have three brothers," she said. "You're going to have to try harder than that."

And that is when I decided I had found my person.

CHAPTER 11

"So, should we call it?" Tiffany asked the silent room.

It was eight thirty, and Dr. Sykes was a no-show. Which was annoying because he gave us this massive assignment over the weekend that involved creating a timeline of a specific period in Europe. He winked at me as I drew the paper out of Travis's beanie.

"The Enlightenment."

Sykes gave a low whistle, and I knew the project was going to end me.

If I had a week, I could squeeze the Magna Carta and scientific reasoning between the Napoleonic Wars and the Bill of Rights, but the Enlightenment fanned all of Europe into a frenzy that lasted over a hundred years, and that was a lot to wedge into the length of a sheet of paper.

And now the professor wasn't even here to collect it.

"It would have been nice to have an extra day," I muttered under my breath.

Estella silently laughed while chewing on the end of her pen. "Still mad you got the Enlightenment?"

Furious.

"If I made the effort and showed up, the least he could do is the same."

"I'm sure there's a good reason," Jacob said.

"Maybe he had an emergency with one of his kids," Heather suggested.

I frowned and straightened. "I didn't know he had kids."

If he was married and had kids, why did he sleep in his room so much? On the night we ran into one another, it was the middle of the night. He implied that he'd be in his room if I needed anything. Looking back on that moment with new information made me feel gross all over. Like I was complicit in whatever kept him away from his family.

I looked at Estella. *Remember what I said about rumors and vibes? Yeah...*

September was long gone. Before I could even register it, Halloween was approaching. While I had still made no progress in discovering the sanctuary, there was a lot to brag about when it came to my grades. Thanks to Estella, I was passing statistics, and Feilding said I was doing well.

Communication with Dad was still strained. He texted me to tell me that I was going to start getting my allowance again, but it was so unlike my dad I suspected his secretary had sent it.

Your weekly allowance will resume bi-weekly starting the fifteenth.

I might just have to call him and get it over with. Phone calls were consuming and nerve-wracking, but old people preferred them. Maybe he needed to hear my voice to remember that I was still a person and not some bad nightmare.

Whatever I did, it had to be soon because Christmas break was fast approaching. Nothing was worse than being an uninvited guest. Especially in what should have been my home.

"I'm here!" Sykes shouted as he pushed open the doors to the library.

He slid across the waxed floors. Disheveled, wearing no tie, I'm pretty sure he was wearing the same clothes from Friday. Estella and I exchanged brow wiggles.

What the hell is that about?

I don't know...

"Right," he said between gasps. "Sorry I'm late. The missus and I have been struggling lately."

I leaned back in my chair. Oh, no. Whatever he was about to do, I wanted no part of it. Lingering notes of rum exuded all the way from the front of the room where the professor sat on his desk.

"You see, sometimes couples grow apart. And there's nothing you can do about it. It's not your fault, and it's not their fault."

I got the feeling this was the speech he gave his kids as well, only we weren't his kids, and none of this was relevant to European history. I didn't want to know about the professor's story, mostly because I got the sense it was dripping with bullshit.

"Sykes," Everett said. "It's cool, man. How about you just take a nap in your office. We'll start fresh tomorrow."

"That's a good idea," Jacob said. "I could use an extra day to work on this project."

"Me too," I added.

The tears were coming on, and we were all too reluctant to move. "But there's never, ever a good reason to turn on your spouse. That is the ultimate betrayal. To abandon them in their time of need. To take away their children like you're some kind of monster..."

I fully turned to Estella. Eyes wide. *You believe this shit?*

We've been on to him since the beginning of the school year. He's going to do the work for us.

Jacob stood and gave Dr. Sykes a pat on the back. "You're okay…"

Felice was leaning in, practically salivating at the display. The others were glancing at the door like they wanted to make a break for it. Heather looked as though she would burst into tears at any moment.

The clique was immobilized by conflict. On one hand, they seemed to suspect him of something and wanted him to admit it, but there was that wholesome need to be supportive of a man who appeared to be in pain.

"If I asked you guys to testify on my behalf," Sykes said between rubbing at his teary face. "Do you think you could do that for me?"

The sirens were going off in my mind. Red and flashing. Something was not right. Jacob was still trying to calm him, but I knew what this was. Predatory behavior. Sykes was rallying those around him with charisma and sympathy, no questions asked.

Spoilers: If someone asks you to go to bat for them on the basis of "they're lying; it's not true," it means you're being used.

"Of course we will," Felice said, standing from her seat.

I moved to stand, but Estella grabbed my shoulder, pushed me back down, and shook her head. Was she serious? There was no way I'd let the Care Bears get involved with whatever legal trouble Dr. Sykes had gotten himself into.

"I knew I could count on you guys," he said. "You're good kids."

"Why don't you come and tell me all about it?" Felice said, taking him by the hand. "My father has some excellent lawyers…"

"I'm a professor. I can't afford that."

"It's on the house," she promised as they left the library.

I waited as long as I could, but I was certain Felice and Sykes were still within earshot. "What the fuck was that?"

Everett let out a tense sigh as he comforted Heather, who was full-on ugly crying. Travis leaned back and nodded at Jacob. "You good, man?"

"Yeah," he said with a sigh. "That was a lot."

"Why would you let Felice help him?" I asked. "We don't know what he did, but it must have been pretty bad."

"Don't worry about Felice," Tiffany said. "She saw this coming a mile away."

Shaking off the tremble in my hands, I realized they were right. Felice's dad did have an army of lawyers, and she intended on joining their ranks one day. Just because the clique was bookish and wholesome didn't mean they were suckers.

We were barely halfway through the semester and down one professor, probably about to lose another. I'm sure bigger schools lost teachers all the time, but it was more apparent when there was only one class.

"Let's go out for a walk," Tiffany said, coming to a stand. "Heather, you want to walk outside?"

She nodded and let Tiffany help her to her feet. "Let's go get some coats on."

"Excellent idea," Jacob said.

Not the first conclusion I came to, but the last thing I wanted to do was stick around in the library. It smelled like desperation and patriarchal tears in here.

***

A walk really was what I needed.

Our breaths made clouds, and our shoes crunched on dead leaves. Everett didn't bother putting pants on, but that seemed to just be his thing. Travis was wearing a new beanie as if the old one was tainted by Sykes. It was the same blue and grey yarn but in wider stripes than the last. Tiffany wore a faux fur-trimmed snow coat with an expression of steely determination.

I walked with Estella behind Tiffany and Heather.

"She was really upset by that," I said.

"Heather struggles with confrontation."

"So much for putting the trauma aside."

"That's the downside of our motto," Estella admitted. "It doesn't account for new trauma or varying levels of it. What we saw as uncomfortable will probably give Heather nightmares for weeks."

I arched my brow. *Weeks?*

"When our cat died, I didn't cry," Estella elaborated, taking a high step over a fallen branch. "I was sad, but he was old. Death was a release for him."

"Sure."

"My brother, Diego, sobbed like a baby. He never really connected to a pet before Rum Tum."

I got what she was putting down. "Heather doesn't have a lot of experience with people being people."

"Absentee parents and homeschooled by a constant rotation of nannies. At one point, a nanny quit, and she was left alone for like three months before anyone noticed."

"Shit."

And I thought I was the loner. There was a canyon-wide difference between choosing to be alone and being isolated without recourse. I couldn't even imagine. Dad hired a nanny when I was young, but when he was off work, she was off duty. Her name was Sigrid, and she always insisted on hanging up the laundry rather than using the dryer. She was the one that cultivated my love for fashion.

"Like me, Marten Ranch is her first real experience being in the world as an adult, but she lived in some remote area because her parents are guru brainwashed. So, no exposure whatsoever."

We were losing the others. Everett was a blip in the distance while Jacob struggled to keep up. Travis had slowed down to be with Heather and Tiffany, but they were far enough ahead that I couldn't make out their faces.

Without a word, we picked up our pace. Trudging up a rocky hillside, I started to gain on the others, but Estella and her short legs had a harder time. What was a few steps for me was a climb for the girl barely making the five-foot mark.

"That's just it. We don't know what will happen," Travis said. "But we do know the rate of conviction— if he even serves time."

"I just don't know," Heather said. "We consented. It's different."

"His daughter didn't consent," Tiffany said. "He won't hurt anyone ever again."

Heather was sobbing again.

I stopped short. The ramifications of their words were a gravitational pull on my insides. Estella went on that whole wise wizard lecture about how situations could impact people differently, but that's not at all why Heather was upset.

The clique knew more about Sykes than I realized, and they were up to something. I was more impressed than anything. I didn't think they had it in them and based on what they just said about Sykes and his daughter, he deserved whatever came his way.

What were they planning? The final image of Felice leading Sykes away warped from her being led by a conniver to her leading a man to the slaughter. My internal urge for justice tugged at me; I wanted to know what they had in store for him.

No, I couldn't ask. I was playing it cool, and it was a strategy that had been paying off. The clique was getting sloppy, letting things slip within my proximity.

"Hey," I said, approaching. "I'm sorry you had to see that, Heather. It was a lot."

Tiffany nodded and continued rubbing her back. "It's for the best."

"He deserves the worst," I said.

Travis's eyes met mine. He hesitated for a moment as if he were unsure if he was allowed to lift the rope to let me in, but he nodded. "She's right. Our justice system is a failure. This is the only way."

"If his daughter stands trial, it will be devastating," Tiffany said. "Worse than what happened to her."

I didn't even think about it. The idea of a child standing up there, getting interrogated by lawyers. Trying to confuse her into tripping up on the stand. Making her think that she was wrong just so they could win a case when everyone knew he was guilty. If he walked, she'd have to live with the fact that it was due to whatever she hadn't said.

Heather wiped the snot from her nose, and I found myself biting my cheek to keep from crying myself.

Estella approached, panting and huffing, breaking the spell that I was in on whatever happened next. Tiffany laughed and said, "You okay there, Delgado?"

"I am an indoor girl."

Up ahead, Everett and Jacob were waving at us. They were no longer specks. I could make out their faces. While Everett was totally unphased, Jacob had his hands on his knees, blowing white-hot clouds like some kind of red-faced ice monster. It wasn't all that far ahead, but it was an upward trajectory that had Estella shaking her head.

"I'm not going up there."

***

That night, I sat on my bed and stared at my door. Whatever the clique had in store for Sykes, it would happen tonight, and I was going to find out. They couldn't deny me if I caught them in the act. I had already signaled that I was down for vigilante justice, and once I was a witness, there was nothing left to do but make me a partner in crime.

Somewhere in Marten Ranch, there was a dungeon or something, and they were going to lock Sykes away for good. What happened when we graduated, though? Who would deal with him? Everett was graduating this year. I heard him talking to Heather about applying to Davis for the vet program.

I'm pretty sure even Feilding could hear that conversation all the way from her room. It went against Heather's ten-year plan.

"We can't sustain the lifestyle we want for our children on a veterinarian salary," she said. "Besides, if you're still in school, there's no way I can get pregnant at twenty-seven."

"Hey," he soothed. "My parents can't wait to be grandparents. They got you."

"No nannies," Heather said. "I'll stay home, and you need to put in the effort as a father while being a student."

"Just as long as I can go," he said. "California would be great for kids. Lots of sunshine and like-minded peers."

This seemed to soothe Heather's worries, and she resumed her planning based around the California campus. Whatever floated her boat.

But if some of the clique were graduating, that meant that they'd need to pass the torch. Like me, for example. Whoever came the following year would need to be trained and aware of the pervert locked in whatever secret room they had him in.

There was still no noise coming from the hallway. I glanced at the clock. It was only eleven. Still too early, I guess.

Another thought occurred to me then. What if they didn't intend on keeping Sykes captive?

A shudder racked through my spine. There was no way. The clique was not capable of murder. They were barely capable of mismatched socks. More likely, they had pooled their resources to make sure Sykes was put away for good. They were probably researching in their sanctuary about the best ways to ensure a maximum sentence with Felice's army of attorneys on speaker.

Soft footsteps sounded around the stairway landing. Barely audible, that I wouldn't have noticed had I not been waiting.

My departure was silent. I left my door slightly ajar for a reason. I kept my lights off so that when it was time, my eyes would have fully adjusted to the night. As I crept out of my room barefoot in the dark, I caught a glimpse of a shadow moving to the opposite wing.

Slipping along the walls, ducking in the shadows, I trailed after two figures. One is practically half the size of the other. One of the guys, either Travis or Everett and the small one had to be Estella.

This time, I saw which room they entered. I hesitated, steadying my breath, waiting for sounds. There was a hitching noise, followed by something sliding across the carpet...then nothing. Opening the door, I found the room empty. It was Tiffany's room.

The décor mirrored my own, but she had silver-framed photos on the nightstand. A young Tiffany standing in front of what was probably her grandparents beside a photo of an Asian man smiling at the camera. Probably her dad? She barely talked about her home life. Most of us didn't.

I walked a wide circle in the room that looked like mine but wasn't. Her carpet wasn't under the bed; it was beside the wardrobe. I stopped short and stared at it. All the strands were swept in one direction. Flat and smooth, the synthetic material shimmered in the moonlight.

Grabbing the wardrobe from the back, I pulled it in the opposite direction of the carpet's brush pattern. I overestimated, and the wardrobe swung out so hard I stumbled to catch it. It moved as freely as a door, revealing a pitch-black doorway to somewhere unknown.

Oh, I did not know if I wanted to walk through a secret corridor in an old house in the middle of the night. That was a good way to end up a heroine in a horror story.

This house has history...

But did I want to know how they snuck around, or didn't I? All of a sudden, I wasn't so sure. The sanctuary sounded really cool, and I wanted to know the secret. What bound the clique together despite such differences— I mean, other than trauma?

Then again, they were my friends already and Estella said she didn't participate. I didn't need what was on the other end of this creepy passageway. She was enough for me.

I grabbed the wardrobe and started to pull it back into place when a man screamed. His cry was a distant echo, but in the silence, it might as well be an alarm clock next to my head.

Hot, tingly panic washed over me. What if someone was hurt in their stupid little rituals?

Stomping like a kid who didn't want to go to school, I fumbled with my phone and turned on the flashlight. Fine...I'll go.

The secret hallway was just a wall cavity. Sheetrock was cut away, exposing support beams, and the floor continued unpolished. Still, it was a really wide gap between rooms. Holding my phone up, I inspected all around the entrance. Maybe it led to an unfinished attic space or something.

Urged by the silence that followed a creepy scream, I stepped over the threshold and inhaled. "Okay, this might be how I die."

Dramatic? Probably, but it was sketchy.

The wall cavity was just wide enough for a single person to walk through easily. It was a straight shot for several feet before taking a hard right. Despite the occasional cobweb, the floor was swept clean. No dust, no trail.

When the path split into two ways, I was stuck at an impasse. *Okay, screamer, if you want to be saved, do your thing...any time now.*

Anxiety to pick the right path was eclipsed by the need to hurry, so I went right again. By this point, I had lost all sense of direction. I could have been anywhere on the top floor. And based on the sounds that came from the attic, I knew that I didn't want to go up.

Only, there was no ladder or way to go down when I took yet another right, so I doubled back to what I thought was the original split and took a left, but that only resulted in a dead end.

The hairs on the back of my neck were standing at attention. I was burning up with nerves, and my sweaty skin was developing a dusty film. Ugh, my stomach was so queasy. Couldn't we just get this over with already?

Releasing a big breath, I ignored the uncertain shakiness in my feet. It's okay. I can do this. It's not as cramped as I think. The walls are not closing in on me. I'm not lost.

Taking the next few rights, the floor before me took a steep decline. It was new territory and, more importantly, heading away from the attic. I was going down and around in what was probably a spiral around the main stairs.

Seeing electrical wires stapled along the walls and pipes bracketed against the studs was massively comforting. I was still in the house, just in places where only electricians, plumbers, and the clique frequented.

A low, achy groan sounded from nowhere.

The phone slipped from my hands and fell light first on the ground. Everything went black except for the small halo of light on the floor. Debris shifted around me as dust floated around the light. Panic swelled in my throat, and I was gasping for fresh air.

Swiping the phone off the ground, I hauled ass, searching for the nearest exit. Running was something I did in high school, but it had been years since I sprinted. Too freaked out to remember proper breathing techniques, I heaved and gulped dry swallows. Pounding my fists errantly, searching for any way out.

The walls narrowed, and my helpless gasps only echoed in my mind. The thing in the attic would find me. It was coming for me. And whatever it was, it was large enough to shake the whole damn house.

With all sense of direction gone and no way out in sight, I rounded a corner only to find myself at a dead end. That was enough to break me. A sob snuck from my throat. I shook my head in denial. I needed to get out right now.

That was when it registered.

The studs in the wall created a ladder upward. There was a square cutout in the ceiling. Not caring where it went, just so long as I was out of the wall cavity, I climbed. Raw wood splintered in my hands and feet, but I pushed at the cutout. It gave, but something was on top of it, holding it into place.

I had to get out. I needed to get out right now.

The square section slid, exposing the underside of a carpet. I laughed and clawed at it with my fingernails until they snagged. The carpet was moved to the side, revealing the underside of a bed. I squeezed through the limited space and wriggled out from underneath. Inhaling the familiar scent of Coco Chanel, I laid on my back and cried with relief.

It was only when I came to my senses that I realized I was lying on the floor of my own bedroom.

CHAPTER 12

I woke the next morning on top of the covers, wrapped in the throw blanket drug from the end of the bed. I vaguely recalled not wanting to soil the sheets with whatever I brought back from the wall cavity. Sitting up, I leaned over the bed and felt for the nightstand I shoved under the bed to block the secret hole.

It was still safely wedged under my bed and undisturbed. After taking a shower, I dressed in a striped AllSaints sweater and jeans. I pulled on some knee-high boots and attended class just as I always did.

Secret pathways throughout the house or no, I had a growing GPA to manage. Last night was more like a fading nightmare in the light of day. After scaring myself stupid and having a panic attack in a claustrophobic setting, I was ready for some reality.

Estella gave me a closed-mouth smile when I sat beside her. "Sykes is late again."

We both knew he wasn't going to show, but I was willing to play along. "You think he's making a run for it?" I asked loudly enough for the clique to turn their heads in my direction.

"My father's office advised him to turn himself in, no contest," Felice said. "Maybe he took their advice."

"We can only hope," Jacob said. "I'd like to think that deep down, he wanted to atone for his crimes."

Everett only glanced at them before looking ahead like he didn't hear it. Heather was staring vacantly forward like she was barely hanging on. Tiffany stopped reading her book to elbow Travis, who was head down on the desk. A glimmer of drool pooled where his mouth was.

There was no denying it. Everyone was off today.

Frustration crept up my muscles then. We were all alone. There was no reason to keep up the charade. It was like the time we spent the week with my aunt and uncle in Paris right before they got a divorce. The tense silence at the dinner table where they pretended everything was normal when we all knew it wasn't.

They had done something to Sykes, and he probably deserved it.

But...maybe I didn't want to know. If the clique got caught, I had nothing to do with it. For once, I would be the innocent party. What would I do if I learned they chopped him up to bits and buried him in their compost pile in the garden? Heather was an expert on recycling. That girl could repurpose anything, even child molesters.

I skipped breakfast, and now I was so queasy I was starting to regret it.

"I need to eat something," I said. "Maybe the breakfast is still in the dining room?"

"Probably," Estella said. "I'll come with you."

She slipped her books back into her satchel, and we got some coffee and pastries.

"I know things are sort of weird right now," she said while I ate my raspberry Danish. "But it will be back to normal in a few days."

"Did you guys kill him?" I asked point blank.

Estella was shaking her head before she could sputter out the words. "No, of course not. We didn't do anything to him. Felice tried to help him, but he didn't want to be a better person. He only wanted to get away with it."

I stopped nibbling on my Danish. I believed her. It would be like the clique to try and get a bad person to do the right thing. The screaming I heard last night might have been the disgraced professor's sounds of anguish being confronted with the truth.

"So, he ran."

"He ran," Estella said with a sigh.

Of course he did. Sykes was probably on the next flight to Mexico, never to be seen again. Whatever they dug up was intended to force him to surrender, but it had the opposite effect. I suppressed the urge to laugh at the naivete of their plan. No wonder they were acting so defeated.

My heart tugged as I thought about the nightstand under my bed.

It was still beyond creepy that there was a crawlspace large enough for a person under my bed. The labyrinth of hallways meant that anyone could go anywhere unseen. It wasn't like the clique made the house, but they clearly used them. Even dusted too.

"We plan on turning everything in to the investigators," she said. "It's the least we can do."

"What about a fundraiser for his family?" I suggested.

The newly single mom would need all the resources she could get. For herself and her kids.

Estella's eyes grew wet, and she gasped. "That's an amazing idea. If all our families pitched in, she'd be set for years."

That would also mean I'd have to call my dad. Something I had been putting off for months. He was good for it, though. I knew he'd cut a check. If he didn't, I'd donate the allowance that had been piling up.

"Let's go tell the others," I suggested.

Estella was already on her feet.

***

Instead of studying European history, we were all calling our parents for donations. Felice was on the phone with her daddy's attorneys setting up the GoFundMe in Mrs. Sykes' name, but her dad was in meetings for the next several hours.

"This is such a good idea," Heather said while she was on hold, waiting to get ahold of her own parents. "I feel so much better about all of this now."

The only one who wasn't calling her parents was Tiffany. She instead made the brave decision to call the FBI to hand over the stockpile of information someone—probably Felice—had found by using a private detective.

I could only stare at the manilla folder with a half-inch stack of paper inside and wonder if there was anything like that on my mom. There had to be. Her disappearance was only Lifetime's favorite original series.

Maybe I'd do some snooping of my own when I returned home for winter break. My phone was heavy in my hand. If I wanted to help the fundraiser I started, I needed to dial his number. To get anywhere near the files on my mom, I'd need to be welcome home. Neither would happen unless I grew a pair and called my dad.

Why was it so hard to push the icon? It would dial, and I would say, "Hey." I would tell him about how great school was going. About my friends and how we were trying to help the professor's family. It would be easy and not awkward at all.

What if it went to voicemail? He was probably busy at work.

"You can do this," Estella whispered in English before sounding off on someone in Spanish. She was annoyed with whoever answered. Estella rolled her eyes and said something that probably wasn't a kind greeting.

Brother?

She nodded. *The eldest brother.*

Ah, daddy junior wanted to screen the call. She was on hold for less than a minute before another male voice answered, and her voice raised with agitation. I cringed and wondered which unfortunate brother picked up by accident.

If Estella was willing to go through all her brothers to get to her dad, the least I could do was leave a voicemail to mine.

"Yeah, Mom, you can just transfer the money to my account, and I'll take it from there," Jacob said slowly. "Mounts, Mom—we have the same last name, remember? It's ten in the morning. How many pills have you taken? Should I call Fernando?"

Across the aisle, Travis seemed to be having an easier time of it. "He bailed on her and the kids. We just want to make sure they won't be homeless...Yeah, I feel fine. Great, actually. Happier than I've ever been."

"Yes sir," Everett's expression was uncharacteristically stern. "Just trying to take care of our own, you know? All the proceeds will go directly to the family, sir."

Heather wasn't even talking to her parents unless her dad was a Guru named Aman Das. Whoever he was, he had full access to her family's money.

I groaned as I dialed my dad's cell phone.

The first ring drilled on with anticipation. If he never answered until the third ring, and by the sixth, it went to voicemail. The second ring was cut short, and I straightened with surprise.

"Hello?"

"Dad," I sputtered. "Hi."

"Hi, Carlie. How is everything?"

I couldn't help but smile as the corners of my eyes stung with tears. "It's great," I said with a laugh.

"Yeah?" He was happy. I could hear his smile and smell the fine tobacco on his suit jacket.

"Did you get the picture I sent you?"

"Um, I did, but it didn't load on my phone, so I had my secretary print it... Ah, here it is." He was shuffling through what was probably a mountain of paperwork on his desk. "Oh, honey, this is sweet. Are these your friends?"

"Yeah! You'd love them. Seriously, they are like the best people ever."

"Ms. Feilding says you're doing excellent. You have no idea how happy that makes me. Shouldn't you be in class, though?"

"I am," I said. "But there's been a situation."

At that, the tone of his voice dropped. "What happened?"

He was probably expecting the worst. I couldn't blame him. "I'm fine. It really has nothing to do with me, but the class is organizing a fundraiser for a professor's wife and kids."

"Oh." Was he surprised? Relieved? I wasn't sure. No one ever liked a fundraiser phone call from a family member, but I had to press the advance.

"Dr. Sykes... He was a bad guy. We're trying to raise money to help his daughters..."

How much did I want to tell him? Even I didn't know the extent of it. Too afraid to look in the manilla folder, I had enough information about it for a lifetime.

"Say no more," Dad said. "Who do I send the money to?"

I reached my hand toward Felice with grabbing fingers. She handed me the paper, and I gave Dad the site information. He then relayed it to his secretary while I was still on the phone. "Okay, it's being taken care of. This is a really nice thing you're doing," he said. "I'm really proud of you."

My heart sort of lurched in my chest. I didn't know what to say. The clique was a good influence? Up until this morning, I thought they'd murdered someone. They had a secret society. Oh, and there might be something living between the walls of Marten Ranch. So naturally, I'm thriving, Dad! "How have you been doing?"

"Oh, you know. Same old. Are you coming home for Christmas?"

"Of course."

"Keep up the good work, honey," he said. "And don't be a stranger. I hate those texts. Call your old man."

I giggled and wiped an errant tear from my cheek. "I will. Thanks, Dad. Love you."

"Love you too, honey."

I dropped the phone on the desk and sagged into my chair. How did one phone call zap all the strength from my body yet lift my spirits at the same time?

"Dad came through," Felice said, staring at her phone. "And wow, did he come through!"

That didn't surprise me. There was nothing that Dad loved more than a good charity. He'd auction his underwear if he thought they would sell—he held no illusions that they would. Ironically, Mom's lingerie did sell. For nearly a million. Supposedly, there was some weird subculture that grew in the wake of her disappearance that coveted her intimate possessions.

I hated the internet sometimes.

By the time Ms. T came in to teach math, the class had raised a quarter of a million dollars. It became the most popular fundraiser of the day, so random donations were beginning to trickle in. By the end of the month, Ms. Sykes wouldn't need to worry about money for a very long time.

Oblivious to the energy in the room, the math professor began lecturing eight emotionally spent people while Felice took notes on the fundraiser and was blatantly texting someone an email during her lecture.

Ms. T didn't seem to notice or even care. All that mattered to her were the numbers. In a way, it was a relief. I had no idea what she was talking about, but the timbre of her voice and feverish excitement about trajectories drowned out the noise in my head.

"And once again, we find ourselves in the same predicament," Ms. T said. "Say it with me, class!"

No one said anything.

But her hands continued to wave like she was orchestrating a symphony. "Correlation does not equal causation! Just because two events appear related on the graph, it does not mean they are even remotely related."

"While these two events have similar patterns of occurrences, it does not mean they are interrelated. Only long-term data or independent study of each phenomenon can determine if they are in fact joined in some way."

I tilted my head and nodded.

Ms. T was finally making sense.

The house was creepy. Noises came from the walls. These two things might have nothing to do with each other. After exploring the night before, I learned that the clique was using the wall cavities to travel in secret, and that had everything to do with the noises I'd been hearing.

Did that mean the clique was up to something insidious?

I glanced around the room. Travis had fallen back asleep. He was leaning back in his chair with his mouth wide open. Heather was braiding a section of her hair.

Jacob was buffing his nails. Where did he get a nail buffer? Did he just keep one in his pocket at all times?

The clique didn't have an evil bone in their bodies. They were one step away from being honorary Girl Scouts. Still, I hesitated. They were rather effective when it came to digging up information on Sykes. They fumbled when it came time for delivery, but well-meaning.

***

The dining room smelled like hard-boiled eggs and triumph.

Everyone had their own version of the Cobb as tradition, but mine was still just the traditional, unadulterated classic. The clique devoured their lunch like a group who'd just come back from a run. Food lifted the mood, and soon, they were back to their usual selves.

"Ms. T was really on point today," Jacob said, dabbing his face with a napkin.

"It was a good lecture," Tiffany agreed. "I just wish I had more energy to participate."

Heather was eyeing the grilled chicken on Travis's plate beside her. She closed her eyes and inhaled as if the smell alone might be enough to satiate her.

Across from her, Everett's fork went still as he watched her.

No one was forcing Heather to be vegan except for herself. We supported her, but no one would hold it against her if she swiped a bite of chicken from Travis. I doubted he would care. Felice noticed too. "Have you done any bloodwork recently?" she asked.

It was almost enough to tear Heather's gaze from the chicken. "I don't really like doctors."

Felice sort of nodded back and forth, like she was trying to form the right words. "It might be worth looking into. If your iron is low, it can make you feel tired, give you cravings."

"Just get the low dose," Jacob said. "Otherwise, you'll be a bit constipated."

"Maybe I should look into supplements," Heather said with a dreamy tone.

Estella raised a brow at me from the far end of the table. *See? Back to normal.*

She was right.

I took a swig of my artisan French water when something clunked around in the ceiling. Everyone froze, and our eyes drifted upward. We sat in silence, observing the light fixture shake as the lights flickered.

No one said anything. My eyes found Estella's. *Is it now?*

CHAPTER 13

The noises only increased in the weeks after Sykes left.

While Dr. Lindt picked up where Richter left off, Dr. Nelson took over history. He made no outright announcements or anything like that, but on his first day, he said, "The professor with an actual history degree is making some changes to the curriculum."

We all got a new syllabus that swapped around a few things, but no major changes. It was like having an opinion on whether someone should watch The Hobbit before or after Lord of the Rings, but whatever.

Something knocked around behind the bookshelves, and Nelson stood there with his brows furrowed as his eyes followed the noise. He said nothing of it, but the next day there was a van with a dead cartoon rat on the side, and people were crawling inside and out of Marten Ranch.

With all the drama, Halloween was overlooked by all except Estella, who lit white candles around her room and made a line of salt at the threshold of her door.

"The veil is said to be thinnest on this night," she explained while I sat on her bed, helping her bundle white sage with twine.

"Did you ever get around to transcribing that skin book?" I asked.

Her face remained unmovable when she took out a spiral notebook and joined me at the bed. "Ancient healing remedies, for the most part. How to deliver babies breach and slow bleeding after birth."

I suspected that wasn't what she'd hoped to find. "Well, keeping mothers and babies alive was important."

"Turns out Brujas didn't exactly believe in their ancient Gods any more than people believe in God now."

That was comforting to know for some reason. Like, there were always holy rollers, but there were also skeptics. It was cool to see that even in ancient times, people had varied opinions. They weren't masses of unthinking idolizers. Only the most extreme made history, I surmised.

"But that wasn't what you were hoping for," I said.

She shrugged, fiddling with a bundle of sage. "I can't make correlations between gods if they don't write about them."

"Like how some people think Allah and Jesus might have been the same person."

"It's possible, but Egypt is very good at record keeping. Tutankhamun's father met a monotheist around that time. After that, he decided there was one God and changed the country's entire religion. Even changed his name."

See? It's always the extreme ones that go down in history. "Did he worship Jesus or something?"

"This was before Christ," Estella said. "But some theologists think that this was an early form of Christianity, before Jesus."

The only experience I had with religion was church on Easter and weddings. Dad just didn't have time for it, or maybe he stopped believing when Mom went missing. My grandparents were very Christian, but only in public.

"And like how all pagan beliefs have weirdly similar stories," I said.

Estella's eyes brightened. "There's always an end of days, a hero among men, even similar types of demons."

She leaned over and opened the drawer to her nightstand, producing a book. Linen covered but still old. Not as old as the skin book, maybe. This was a printed edition.

"Unlike everyone else here, this school was my first choice. Robert Lacourt was a demonologist. He built this house in a specific location, and the design was entirely his own. It's said he made the house with secret paths to trap the demons he summoned."

Well, that was unsettling. "Is that why everyone just ignores the weird noises in the walls?"

At that, Estella erupted into giggles. "I seriously doubt that."

I opened the book and flipped through the illustrations, landing on one page that had been dog-eared. I made a tisk tisk noise. "The clique would come undone if they saw this."

"It's my fatal flaw," she said with a flare of drama. "I can't resist dog-earring pages. Don't tell them. Jacob might cry."

"Your secret is safe with me."

Moving past the abysmal sin, I observed a hairy (or was it scaly?) monster with horns and a massive mouth. It was taking a chomp out of someone's torso. "Devouring demon?"

"That is one that pops up in nearly every culture," she said. "Different names, different appearances, but always the same ability. It feeds on souls, flesh, whatever. What made Robert so fascinating is that he believed he could alter a demon's nature. Make them work for him."

"Did it work?"

"Well, he disappeared suddenly, so I don't think so."

As much as I loved talking about gruesome things with Estella, there was a commotion outside the door. We both jerked our heads at the shouts. Stepping over her salt line, we hung over the balcony to see what was going on.

"You got a whole colony between these walls," a man in a full-body white suit said.

"Rats," Feilding said with a hand on her heart.

"Raccoons," the man clarified. "One of them dug under your crawlspace cover."

I had the overwhelming urge to take a shower. A few weeks ago, I was roaming around in the wall cavities looking for the clique with bare feet. How much raccoon shit had I stepped in? I shivered all over. "Gross."

"That explains a lot," Estella deadpanned.

Several workers came in with cages. They stacked them one on top of another with a rattling clang. The cages filled the entryway, which was larger than the average studio apartment in New York. How many raccoons were there?

"Want to go back to talking about demons?" I asked. At this rate, the conversation was preferable.

Jacob slinked out of the library and promptly shoved his hands in his pockets like he was afraid to touch the cages. Back against the wall, he tried to move around them before another worker came in with cages in each hand. Having brushed Jacob with one, we watched as Jacob rushed to the elevator, punching the up button until the metal gates closed.

I couldn't help but snicker at that. "Someone should tell him that raccoons carry rabies."

"No one is more aware of that than Jacob."

A snicker escaped my mouth. From the level below us, Tiffany leaned over the railing. "So, uh, is class canceled today?"

Feilding in her wine-colored skirt suit with matching heels did her best to remain calm and collected. That was hard to do surrounded by cages. We were harboring half the county's raccoon population between the walls. What would the board think? Oh, the scandal!

"That's probably for the best, Ms. Nguyen."

The upset in the day was a relief, to be honest. Not because class was canceled—I was impartial to that. It was easy to enjoy class when I wasn't failing. More because the creepy noises were indeed animals and not something sinister or even the clique's doing.

Correlation did not mean causation. Scooby Do unmasked the villain, and it was a trash panda.

Estella turned to face me with a grin. "Want to do something rebellious?"

I choked back my disdain. Like she would even need to ask. "Would the clique hate it?"

She nodded, hands twisting behind her back like she was holding a surprise gift. "We can invite them and watch them flee the room screaming."

No one could pique my interest quite like Estella. "I'm down."

***

The mass text summoned the clique. With nothing better to do and nowhere to be, they came to Estella's room. She had lit her black candles for "dramatic effect" while everyone sat in a circle on the floor.

"All Hallows Eve is said to be the night when the veil is thinnest," Estella said, setting the stage.

Of all people, Jacob was sitting up straight, fully amused. I suspected he appreciated a good show. Tiffany was texting with one hand while the other was being clutched by Heather—who looked like she might pass out.

Everett's eyes followed Estella, but it was anyone's guess if he was buying it. Felice was observing the clique as she often did. One look at Travis and I knew just what he was doing on a day with no classes. His eyes were glassy, and his mouth drooped slightly.

"Are we summoning spirits?" Jacob asked.

Felice rolled her eyes. "In the afternoon?"

"The Bruja's grimoire only had a few spells, but there was one that might solve our little infestation."

"They already caught one, and trust me," Everett said. "They're not little."

Tiffany snickered at that.

I went from feeling like a co-conspirator to a bystander. The urge to be one of them clawed its way up my back. I should have asked her what we were doing before the rest of the clique came in. This was Estella, I reminded myself. We were actually friends. We texted outside the group chat and developed a silent language. I didn't need to know what she knew; I needed to trust her.

Gnawing on my bottom lip, I waited to see what she did next.

"This," she said, unveiling a tall mason jar of various dead plants, "is a remedy from the Bruja herself. It's supposed to ward off scavenging animals and insects."

It looked like those things people sold at craft fairs when they spelled it *faire*. I half expected a resin-crafted fairy with butterfly wings to be sitting inside. There was a skull poking up from the moss. A mouse skull, maybe?

"Is this what you do in your room when you're not hanging out with us?" Tiffany asked, eyes on the jar.

It totally was. I recognized a bundle of white sage inside. So that's why we were making those. My inclusion needs were fulfilled.

We were each given a smaller jar, sealed with a lid. Inside was a bunch of dried, spikey flowers with dead petals hanging limp under the thorns. They might have been red once, but now they were brown. Estella's eyes flickered to me and at my jar. The meaning was clear. *Don't open that.*

Estella sat beside me in the circle. She chanted in what I assumed was Aztecan or whatever ancient language she called it. Nahuatl? It was effective. She could have been reciting a grocery list for all I knew, but the goosebumps ripped along my arms, and the hair at the nape of my neck prickled.

She took out a grill lighter and lit the contents of the big jar. It smoked and sizzled, blackening the glass as an earthy, sour smoke fizzled from the mouth of the jar. "What do you see in the smoke?" Estella asked.

"Are we supposed to answer?" Jacob asked.

Everyone scowled at him for annihilating the vibe. "Yes, Jacob," Felice said. "She means us."

"Okay, just checking."

At this point, the smoke was taking over my vision, but it didn't hurt when I inhaled it. No one was coughing or waving their hands. I turned to look at Estella, but that's when I saw something weird. The smoke stopped short of us. Our circle contained the smoke. Like a pane of glass, the black cloud worked its way upward only to spiral back into the circle like a tide unable to breech the cliffs.

Spooky.

Returning my gaze to the depths of smoke, I searched for shapes, but it was just black smoke.

"I see a fox," Everett said. "With a big bushy tail."

"I see flowers blooming," said Heather.

"A sunset," Travis said.

But all I saw was smoke. I tried to see their faces to see if they were for real, but the smoke was too thick. On my hand was Estella's, and I squeezed it, not sure what was going on.

"Oh, my God," Tiffany said. "I see a boat paddling on water!"

Jacob was next. "I see fish? It's like I'm inside an aquarium."

That was when I saw it. Coming straight at me was the demon in the book from earlier. It gnashed at me with its sharp teeth. It wasn't completely clear, more like a smoky cartoon which somehow made it less shit-inducing, but I fell back as tendrils of smoke grabbed it and yanked it away. "Monster," I uttered.

Estella was staring at me then. The smoke obscured her expression, but it was like she was worried.

Lastly, Felice let out a noise of annoyance. "I don't see anything. Just blackness."

"You mean the smoke?" Heather asked.

"No, just vast, dark, empty."

"Everyone open your jars," Estella said. "You too, Carlie."

My hands were so sweaty I had a hard time, but the lid came loose. About that time, everyone was yelping and crying out. Being the last to open my jar, I was the last to get hit with the scent. Pungent, tear-inducing muskiness rammed straight up my nostrils.

The smoke was gone, and the fire in the jar was nothing but a wispy smolder.

I gagged, coughing on bile. I wasn't the only one. Jacob heaved into his own jar. Everyone's faces were curdled and annoyed.

"What gives?" Tiffany asked through her coughs.

"Imperial Crown," Estella explained. "Wards off critters, smells like skunky cat piss."

Travis was still smelling his. He glanced up at the disgusted faces and said, "You think I can smoke this?"

CHAPTER 14

C
lasses were canceled for several days after the raccoon fiasco, and then there was the weekend. Good old Feilding wasn't about to let us get off so easily. Instead of library sessions, we all got an email of required reading.

Not just one book, but three subject-dense materials full of eye-drying content. One was War and Peace, which was the easiest of the three. The second was a statistical analysis case study, and the third was all about Catherine the Great's art collection.

I had to Google a summary of the last two, and even then, I collected notes from everyone else. The clique was always happy to help like that. Tiffany even offered to explain the statistic book in a way that actually made sense.

"You're really good at this," I said.

"A lot of good it does me in the art world," she replied.

"Isn't there a lot of math involved in art?" I recalled something about a golden ratio and how Da Vinci sketched a perfect circle.

Her frown softened at that. "You're a lot smarter than you let on."

"You want my notes on War and Peace?"

She snatched those notes from my hand before I could blink. I read it a few years ago, but I missed so much the first time. The depth of despair and the character's desperation was far more intense to me now than it was before. Maybe I had just grown up a little in the last few years.

I came downstairs for breakfast, still mentally preparing myself for Monday, only to find the clique wasn't in the dining hall. Where was everyone? I checked my phone just to be sure, but it was seven a.m. on November fourth; it was Monday.

Were classes canceled again, and I just didn't see it? There was nothing in my email. I texted Estella. *Hey, where is everyone?*

Library. Don't come.

I went to the library.

Estella turned to look at me and shook her head. Her skin was paler than usual. She was either wearing a lighter foundation or...no, there was a greenish tint to her cheeks.

Everett was puking into a flowerpot that housed a plastic tree in the corner of the room. Everyone else was huddled around the teacher's desk. Some had their backs turned, like Heather and Travis. The rest were facing something.

I approached, and the sickly-sweet smell hit me first. I caught a glimpse at a black and white tail before moving in front of Estella to behold the dead raccoon splayed out on the professor's desk.

Well, half a raccoon. That's when I vomited.

Never in my life had I instantly puked like that. There was always some kind of precursor. The way back of my mouth would pool with saliva or the spins. Bare minimum, I'd feel it coming up, but this was immediate. Like a sucker punch to the chest.

"Don't worry about it, Carlie," Jacob said. "Most of us had the same reaction."

Hands on my knees, I steadied my gaze on the floor. Blood was dripping off the desk in a constant *tap, tap, tap,* like the leaky faucet in the bathroom. Sometimes it helped me sleep after I quit taking Ambien. I'd have to get maintenance to fix it over break.

There was a man screaming in the other room, followed by a familiar hurling. This wasn't a single occurrence. A high-pitched scream came from somewhere else in the house. I was willing to bet it was Feilding.

"I need to get away," Heather said, charging out of the room.

So many questions were in my head, but all my brain could do was make a buzzing noise. Someone took my hand and led me out of the library. I figured it was Estella, but when I sucked in the fresh air outside, I looked up, and it was Felice.

Her face was mostly blank, but there was a slight frown. "Stay here. I'm getting everyone else."

The clique spent the next ten minutes outside shivering before Everett gently slapped Travis's chest with the back of his hand. "Come on, man, let's get some blankets or something."

"Feilding said we can hang out in her private library," Felice said, emerging from the house. "Nothing dead is in there."

The dean's private library was a room that connected to her office. It had a massive fireplace and floor-to-ceiling bookshelves on either side. There was a coffee table surrounded by floral print sofas. It was probably a tearoom or something once upon a time.

"Open the window," Heather told Everett. "I can't get that smell out of my nose."

"Or the image," Tiffany said.

There was a stack of logs and kindling, so we did what every teenager did when there was flammable stuff— we made a fire.

After sitting for a long time in silence, I finally sorted out what I wanted to say and how I intended to say it.

"What the fuck was that?"

"Maybe a wild animal—" Jacob started.

"No," I cut him off. "No. That's not what this is. Enough bullshit."

"Carlie..." Estella soothed, taking my hand with both of hers. "We don't know."

"I think we do," Heather said, glaring at Estella. "I think that spell you cast a few days ago caused this."

"It wasn't even a spell," she said. "I just put some stuff in a jar with some peyote. The dried flowers in the jar were in the Bruja's book. They were the thing to ward off animals."

Heather's eyes went wide. "You gave us drugs without our consent?"

"Not enough to intoxicate you," Estella said. "More like a contact high."

I mean, normally, I would have been mad, but given the circumstances, it was like being angry at an ice cream cone melting in the middle of a volcano explosion. "For the record, I don't do hallucinogens," I said.

"I'm really sorry, guys," Estella said. "I wasn't trying to scare anyone. Things have just been so tense."

Of course they were tense. Two teachers down, one of them vanished mysteriously, the house was infested with raccoons who were now being ripped apart, and their carcasses were strewn about the house.

"What we saw in the library," Everett said, pointing his finger toward the door. "That was a warning. A blatant threat."

That was my sentiments exactly. "Whoever did that wanted us to get the message, but what's the message?"

"Maybe it's not for us," Tiffany said.

"It was in the library where they knew we would be," Travis said. "Fuck this. I'm smoking a joint. Anyone want some?"

Heather was the first to reach for the lit joint. After a few puffs, we all relaxed. Laying my head against the back of the couch, I stared at the spackle on the ceiling. Who would try to freak out the whole school like that?

Feilding burst into the room and stared at us with her hands on her tulip-skirted hips. "So, this is what you're all up to."

Travis rolled his head in her direction and offered what was left of the blunt. The dean gave an exasperated sigh before marching up, plucking the joint out of his fingers, and inhaling like a pro. There was a long moment where I watched with equal parts amusement and respect.

"Right," she said after an exhale. "Does anyone know what happened? Did anyone see anything last night?"

"I'd like to think I'd recall seeing someone ripping animals apart and strewing them about the school."

"It's a crime scene," Feilding admitted. "I've called the authorities, so you might want to flush that joint. Whoever did this is insane and very angry at Marten Ranch."

"Who would even be mad at us?" I asked.

"Richter left angry," Felice said. "But I don't think she'd go postal on raccoons."

We started sitting up as if the thought occurred to us all at once. I was in the clique hive mind. "Sykes..."

***

The police came, followed by the FBI.

We were admittedly stoned, but it all lined up. I first started hearing the noises around the same time I ran into Sykes in the night, so he knew something was up. His disappearance followed by a hoard of raccoons and their violent deaths.

Overhearing the locations was the final nail in the coffin. The professor's desk in the library, the dean's office, on the doorstep of Dr. Nelson's office. There was one left in the kitchen, but none of the knives were missing. Altogether there were four-and-a-half animals found?

Feilding came bursting in with papers.

"I have here records of pest control. They come quarterly to check the house, and not once did anyone mention the crawlspace had been compromised."

"He opened it knowing the raccoons would come?" Travis said.

"No." Feilding frowned at him while showing the two detectives in black suits. "I think he broke it to get in and out of the school unseen."

An exterminator came into the room. "We found another...part."

"Where?" a detective asked.

"In one of the student's rooms."

My heart started pumping then. Please don't be my room. *The nightstand under my bed was still there.* That thought was like a prayer, uttered over and over again.

"Second story, left-wing, third door on the right."

Felice held her stomach. "That's my room," she said. "Which means he had to have done it after I left this morning."

That made sense. Felice was the one who had sic'd the private investigator on him earlier that year. She was the one who promised to help with all her attorneys only to advise him to surrender to the authorities.

"What time did you leave your room?"

"After six thirty," she said. "I like to drink my first cup of coffee alone."

There were other questions that followed, but the hammering in my ears made it hard to concentrate. Sykes was using the secret hallways, waiting for Felice to leave her room. What if he wasn't waiting and just missed her instead?

We weren't safe.

Estella leaned into me then. *It's too much.*

"Feilding," I said, interrupting whatever conversation was had. "We can't stay here until we know he's gone. He could've hurt Felice."

I wanted the school to remain in action as much as everyone else, but there was no way I'd let everyone stay with a psycho on the loose.

"There's no doubt about that," Feilding said. "The police need to investigate every inch of the house without students running amok. We're already arranging your flights home. Expect to be back after the New Year."

I nodded, pulling Estella in close.

"Ugh," Jacob lamented. "I think I'd rather take my chances with Sykes."

Heather patted his back. "You can come home with me if you want. I'd be all alone in Montana if you don't."

"That sounds nice, actually. Everett, are you going?"

"Yeah, my parents are on a diplomatic visit in Bosnia. They aren't scheduled to come home for another few weeks."

I detected some military vibes by the way Everett called his dad 'sir,' but I had no idea they were diplomats. There was a story there. I'd have to ask Estella later.

***

We split into two groups, boys and girls.

Room by room, we packed whatever we needed and stayed togeth-er. I only needed the important things: passport, phone, and purse. I had plenty of clothes and make-up at home. I would just do carry-on without checking any luggage on the plane and get the hell out of here.

We were coming back in January anyway.

This was just an extended break. Instead of two weeks off, we were taking two months. Though I knew we'd pay for that at the end of the school year, this was an emergency. I didn't mind staying through July, just so long as Sykes was caught.

Estella packed a suitcase, mostly with books, but Felice, Heather, and I said nothing. We just paced the room, trying to keep calm.

"You don't have a rug," Heather said randomly. I think she was in shock, but she was right. All of our rooms had a white round shag rug except Estella's. Mine was over the entrance to the secret halls, Tiffany's was under the...I gulped.

"Does your room not have access to the other hallways?"

Estella glanced up at me from her heavy black lashes. "I'm just the lucky one, I guess."

I don't know why that was weird, but it was.

What was even weirder was the police standing outside Felice's door. "It's a crime scene," the female officer said apologetically. "If there's anything you need, I can get it for you."

"I can't go in my own room?"

"Miss, I don't think you want to."

Felice hesitated at that. My stomach was aching from hunger and nausea. I hadn't eaten anything all day. Even if I wanted to, the kitchen was closed off with yellow caution tape.

"I'm not squeamish," Felice insisted.

The policewoman escorted her in. As the door opened, a flash went off, and I got a glimpse of the room. I had to clamp a hand over my mouth to keep from puking again. The whole wall was covered in blood. Someone shut the door, and a rancid, metallic scent wafted into our faces.

About ten minutes later, Felice emerged from her bedroom with roll-away luggage. Her face was impassive as she said, "All packed."

I turned to glance behind me, and the policewoman was staring at the back of Felice's head like she expected it to start spinning.

"How bad was it?" I asked Felice.

"You know how it is," she said, dragging her luggage behind her. "See one mutilated animal, you've seen them all."

I think she expected us to laugh, but no one was laughing. Her smile was gone, and she said more earnestly, "I think it was me he wanted to smear across the room."

The guys were already packed and waiting downstairs for us. It was decided among the hivemind that we would stop somewhere to eat along the way. No one wanted to linger in the house, even if most of us didn't have flights until later that night.

"Can it please not be Denny's?" Felice whined. "Isn't there something a step up from a diner around here?"

"Once we get closer to SeaTac, there is," Jacob said with a mustered cheer that reminded me of a train running out of steam.

"I'll eat anything at this rate," I said. "I missed breakfast."

Heather groaned. "That's really not healthy for you."

It's not like I had a choice in the matter. I was about to respond sarcastically but stopped short. Heather wasn't criticizing. She was putting emphasis on my health as a priority over Felice's demand for quality.

"Yeah, Felice, I'm hungry now," Everett said.

"Ugh, fine."

Our van pulled up to a diner aptly named The Diner. There were no complaints about the food. Heather and I got the pancakes. She ignored the fact that they weren't vegan, and no one said anything when she smeared a layer of butter over each one.

Estella and Jacob got the eggs benedict while Travis got the chorizo and egg burrito. Encounters of fleeing a residential psycho required eggs and butter.

I closed my eyes and inhaled. The events of that morning fell away. Everything is better with chorizo.

Everett got the biscuits and gravy with an extra side of bacon, while Tiffany got waffles. We ate in silence. Too exhausted for conversation and numb to care if the rest of the dinner stared at the curious group of teenagers scarfing down food, not saying a word.

I had just finished my second cup of coffee when my phone lit up.

"Hey," I answered.

"Are you okay?" Dad asked.

Feilding must have notified the parents. I should have thought about that. If I had just showed up at home unannounced, he would've assumed the worst. "Hey, Dad."

Everyone at the table looked up and hesitated. We didn't know how much the dean had told our parents. Did she mention raccoon guts everywhere, or did she just say Marten Ranch was closed for investigation? How much did I have to explain while my stomach was full of pancakes?

"I got the email. That doctor has been sneaking around in the crawlspaces?"

"Yeah, everyone is fine. We just didn't want to impede the investigation."

Or be murdered in our sleep.

"Okay, that's fine. We'll talk more at home. Love you, honey."

"Love you too."

Heather was making a face that suggested she was looking at a pile of adorable sleeping puppies. "Aw, I love your dad."

That was code for: I wish I had a dad like that.

I didn't blame her. From what Estella told me, her parents sounded like a piece of work. "Yeah, he's a good guy."

"So, you don't think he killed your mom," Felice said.

Her words stunned me so hard I couldn't speak. How did she know about that? Everyone else was staring at Felice too. She had been acting really weird ever since this morning.

"What?" she said, with a mouthful of fruit melody. "I thought everyone saw the documentaries."

"No, Felice," I said through gritted teeth. "My dad didn't kill my mom. She tried to commit suicide, and he called for an ambulance."

"But no one knows what happened after that," she pressed, unaware or unconcerned by the sudden tension in the room. Even the old couple near our table stopped eating.

"No one knows what happened after that."

"But the hospital forms say your dad checked her out—"

"Felice," Jacob stopped her. "We've all had a rough day. Maybe this isn't the time."

As if the thought didn't occur to her, Felice blinked and said, "Oh, right. Totally not the time. Sorry, Carlie."

Only, she wasn't sorry. It was just something Felice said when she said something off. Her apology was poison dipped in honey to make it go down easier, and I had to swallow or risk fracturing the clique. I was so close to being admitted to the sanctuary. The hivemind buzzing between my ears suggested as much. I just needed a break. We all did.

PART TWO: CHAPTER 15

I t's weird entering the place I call home.

The smells that I had never noticed before came rushing at me all at once. Sweet, smoky pipe tobacco and the lemon cleaner Francesca uses on the floors are new again. The silence is repressive. Once, I craved it after a long day of overwhelming noise. Nine-hundred students all talking at once from eight to three would still be just as draining now as it was then, but the silence is eerie.

Marten Ranch has the perfect level of occupation. I seldom hear anything from my room, but outside my door, there's always something going on. Whether it be a vacuum or the clique talking downstairs...

Pulling out my phone, I texted the group chat. *I miss you guys already.*

Heather: *Omg, you too!*

Tiffany: *Say Hi to Dad for me.*

Jacob: *HI DAD!*

The clique has decided Dad is everyone's dad after the fundraiser. I couldn't wait to tell him. Estella's flight was eight hours and a layover through customs.

Travis: *Poor Estella...*

Carlie: *I know! I was just thinking the same thing.*

The sound of a pair of slippers came sweeping down the stairs and through the hall. It would be weird if he found me just standing in the entryway like I was lost. I straightened and acted like I still belonged, threw my bag on the kitchen island as I always used to, only to stop and put it on the coat hanger like a civilized person.

No wonder my old bag got a big cut in it.

My dad was wearing his brown suit with slippers on his feet. His thin blond hair was combed over to one side. When his square face formed a smile, I smiled too and gave him a bear hug.

"Oh," he said in surprise, hugging me back. "Happy to see you too."

I had never really hugged him before. I should do that more often.

"Everyone says hi," I said.

"Everyone as in..."

"The clique," I said, like he had forgotten his seven other children. "They say hi, by the way."

"Oh, well, hello to them too."

I relayed the message that moment so I wouldn't forget. He leads me to the stools around the kitchen island before getting a cranberry-apple juice from the fridge. "So, what was the deal with that professor?"

Ugh, I really didn't want to worry him, but if I learned anything about Mom's disappearance: If I didn't tell him everything, someone else would in a far more sensationalized manner.

I started from the beginning. How the clique got weird vibes, and Felice hired a private investigator. How she found out he had a history he was hiding from everyone—even Feilding didn't know he had a misdemeanor involving an underaged girl.

"He probably got it taken off his record," Dad said. "If he was a young man when it happened, they probably gave him the option."

"Exactly! Anyway, his wife discovered he was abusing his daughters and filed for divorce and was pressing charges. He asked us for help, and we told him to go to the police."

Dad's brow raised, but he said nothing.

"He didn't want to go to the police; he wanted Felice's dad to make it go away. We were like, "No way, you need to surrender". He took off that night, and we assumed he made a run for the border."

"Only, he didn't go anywhere," Dad finished.

"And that's when he tried to intimidate everyone by leaving raccoon parts in very specific places. Like his old desk, Felice's room."

Dad's nose crinkled. "What a piece of work."

I nodded. "Yeah, it was disgusting. Everyone was puking. So, classes are canceled while they search for Sykes and clean up the mess. Feilding is going to make sure there's no way for him to get back into the school."

"What if they don't catch him?" Dad said, spinning the crystal glass. "Honey, I don't know if I want you to go back if he's still out there."

No. I shook my head. I felt everything get all hot, and my eyes instantly watered. *No. No.* I had to go back. My friends were there. My grades were good. I was good. I tried to say as much, but I pulled a Heather and started crying.

Dad's eyes went wide, and he rubbed my arm. "Okay, okay. If it means that much to you. Maybe I'll look around for personal security for you and the rest of the kids."

Yes. I nodded. That would be fine. Just as long as I got to stay where I belonged. Shaking off the upset, I took out my phone and showed him the pictures I'd taken and introduced him to the clique. Dad nodded and followed along the best he could, but I think he was tired.

"I think you work too much," I told him. "You should really be focusing on yourself. Self-care, you know?"

His expression was incredulous. "Self-care?"

"Yeah, you know. Go out for walks. Take days off. You bought that nice set of golf clubs and never once use them."

"I only got those because I had a client who was a fanatic," he explained. "I don't exactly have anyone to golf with."

That was ridiculous. "I'll go with you."

His face was a mixture of confusion. "In November?"

Oh. He was probably right. New York weather wasn't exactly prime for golf. "Okay, what about you take a day off? We can spend the day together. Get some breakfast, maybe get you some new suits..."

Dad would've been less surprised if a meteor was hurtling toward him. It was like he was waiting for a catch or condition. "Um, yeah. We can do that. Carlie, are you sure you're all right?"

"Of course," I said. Dad thought I was being weird. Like I had been strapped to a chair and brainwashed. He didn't understand because he didn't see all the work I had put in over the last few months.

I always thought myself immune to influence. Other people used all sorts of tactics for good or ill on me. There was the reverse psychology of teachers who still yearned to reach their students because the system hadn't beaten them to a pulp yet.

Then, there were classmates who wanted to see me at my worst. Goading me into acting out for their own entertainment or to get me kicked out of their class because they didn't like the way I asked questions and the discussions dragged on too long. Their interests were easy to pick up, like the scent of burning hair.

I put my hand on his and said, "I've decided it's time to set the traumas aside. To look at them as they are. I'm *not* responsible for Mom or how she hurt us, but I am responsible for my own actions."

It was time he did the same. Dad never moved on. My palm felt the smooth gold band still on his ring finger. In his heart, he was still married. We needed to put her disappearance to rest and move on with our lives.

She was a festering wound left to rot. A gangrenous limb in our family tree that infected aunts, uncles, and even grandparents. I didn't give a shit about them, but we deserved the truth. Maybe then Dad could find a way back to happiness.

The only way that was going to happen was if I irrigated the wound. Going through the box of records in the attic wouldn't feel pleasant, but it had to be done. Felice hired a personal detective, so could I if need be. Mom's case had been cold for years, but maybe in that time, new evidence surfaced.

Dad was speechless. That was okay. I'd give him time to process that.

"I'd like your consent to look through the records."

"Consent?" He repeated the word like it was some bold concept.

"Are you comfortable with that?"

He blinked. "Yeah, honey. Whatever you need. I just...can't get over how much you've changed. It's like you're a whole different person all the sudden."

"Still me," I said with a grin. "I got mad at a professor and did my thing in September."

"Oh no."

"Oh yes." I laughed. "I wrote, 'Babz is a cunt' on the side of the school. Do you know what happened?"

"Eh, well, you didn't get suspended."

"My friends had my back," I said. "They told Feilding how Richter treated me. They didn't excuse my behavior, but they helped me wash it off and do community service. Feilding listened to us. I decided to try after that."

"You..." Dad said with a mocking tone. "Community service?"

"All week! Also, I fell in love."

"A boy?"

Ew, no! Everett was...complicated. Jacob's sexuality was still up in the air. Travis, he was cool, but I didn't know if I could see him that way. He reminded me of a poet, and I've read enough to know a relationship with a poet never ended well.

"I don't have time for a boyfriend. I don't even have time for Quasimodo," I explained. "He's the residential shelter dog."

"Quasimodo, eh?" The name lulled around in Dad's mouth like he was coming to terms with it.

The highs and lows of the conversation were maxing out my poor dad's emotional capacity. His fingers were working at the sharp edges at the bottom of the glass. He was probably wishing his juice was a brandy about now.

***

Everything left of Mom was consigned to a cardboard box filled with files.

I shouldn't say everything. There was still the hovering reminder of her in the air within the house. The eyes of her portraits followed me along the photo wall, and there was always the way Dad seemed to be looking for her wherever we went. Getting him to donate her wardrobe last spring was hard on him, but he kept every single letter and update from the women's shelters across the country that benefited from the auction.

"All right, Mom," I said, shimmying the lid off the box. "Time to get rid of you for good."

Most of it I already knew from the police report about her suicide attempt and copies of the hospital records. She had taken an entire bottle of clonazepam and overdosed in the bathtub. The ambulance and firefighters arrived on the scene and got her to puke most of it out, but the hospital still had to treat her.

"Admitted to psychiatrics," I muttered as I thumbed through the details Dad acquired through other means when the hospital invoked HIPPA.

This was where things got weird.

She was in there involuntarily, and there should have been no way to release her unless it was from one psychiatric ward to another. Yet, there was an authorization to transfer, signed by Dad, to a private rehab that didn't exist.

Wouldn't the hospital check to make sure the rehab was an actual facility before waving goodbye? The FBI thought so. The hospital claimed it was a lapse in admin due to a staff shortage.

This, of course, made Dad an insta-suspect, but a handwriting analysis came back negative. I could see why. If I squinted hard enough, it almost looked like Dad's loopy penmanship. Maybe if he used his left hand and was slowly suffocated with a pillow as he signed.

All this stuff was known.

I needed more on the woman herself. Who were her friends? What did she do when she wasn't asking a six-year-old to feed her pills and pre-mixed cocktails? Her bedroom might have the answers.

Growing up, I never thought it was weird for a married couple to have separate bedrooms. Cohabitation was for poor or codependent people. And besides, Mom needed a whole closet to herself. Just how valid was that concept, given that Mom was mentally unstable? Her room was across the hall from Dad's.

Her products and perfumes were thrown away, but everything else remained unchanged. The satin sheets and a dozen pillows that matched her royal blue bedspread. The framed posters of her short career as an actress.

I only quit because I got pregnant with you...

Ouch.

My heart felt as though it were being squeezed, but sometimes it hurts to heal. Set the trauma aside. I'm responsible for how I respond to it.

Rummaging through her drawers, I found postcards from various directors and coworkers from Europe. Turning on the light to the walk-in closet, I searched for anything that I missed the first time.

If I learned anything from Marten Ranch, it was that houses had secrets.

Nothing was loose when I pulled on her custom-built storage.. No ceiling hatches. Just a closet. I hated being in her room. Even when she was long gone, I still felt unwelcome.

Don't touch my things with your dirty little hands...

I slid under the bed, working my hands around the support planks. There had to be something for me to go on. My mind sifted through all the things I could remember about her. She was beautiful and had volatile moods. One minute she would have me try on her jewelry and take photos, only to scream at me for tilting the vanity mirror the next. I remember always being afraid of her. Never knowing what would set her off.

Did she always hate me, or did she just love herself more?

It was like I died the day you were born. No more invitations. No calls from my agent. I married a rich man and had a child. My life was no longer mine.

I couldn't help but snort at that. Lots of actors had kids, and their lives didn't end. Given that her films went straight to video, she probably wasn't a very good actress to begin with. I was just a scapegoat.

Did her friends all abandon her after she had me? Doubling back to the postcards, I read the sloppy handwriting. They weren't dated, but the postmarks led right up until the time I would've been six.

That stung harder than the way she used to slap me in the face for no reason. My dad couldn't figure out why I was always covering my face with my hands and asked her about it. She lied to him just as she lied to me.

Her actor friends were still in contact; she either ignored them or found other ways to respond.

Still clutching the postcard, I stared at the date. Flipping it over, I searched for a name, but there was none. Just scratchy, barely legible handwriting with the occasional loop for some dramatic flair.

Something heavy and hard was forming in the pit of my stomach. My skin was cold, but my blood burned as I raced back up to the attic. Ripping open the cover of the box, I rifled through the papers until I found the handwriting analysis.

I smashed the postcard against the sample and screamed in a mixture of triumph and anger.

The handwriting matched.

Me: *Hey, I need to contact your PI.*

Felice: ...

CHAPTER 16

E stella: *Did you get the email?*

She wasn't using the group chat. That meant that Estella wanted to talk to just me, and it wasn't about the homework care package Feilding sent. It was annoying at first, but I needed something to keep my mind busy. What did I even do here when I wasn't in school?

It must have been so boring and lonely that it didn't take up memory space.

Lonely girl in her room with no one to talk to. Watching people on her phone live their lives, hating them for having nothing yet doing all the things she couldn't. Depressing.

Carlie: *Yeah, I'm honestly glad. It's so quiet here.*

Estella: *I'd kill for a moment of quiet. It's my cousin's Quinceañera and the entire Delgado clan is staying here.*

Carlie: *-_- How long are they staying?*

Estella: *Who knows. I think most are staying right up until Christmas.*

Poor Estella. All that beautiful weather in that house full of laughter. It was snowing in New York. I woke up just after five in the morning to one of the groundskeepers shoveling snow. Thin metal scraping against pavement over and over.

My dad didn't have creamer, so I was forced to drink the coffee black.

Francesca stopped and watched me with an alarmed scowl. "I will get your creamer right away, miss."

I looked outside, and the snow was falling so hard I couldn't see the iron fence that surrounded our property. "It's snowing really hard."

"It's no trouble, miss."

Except I knew that it was.

Dad spent most of his time in his office upstairs. None of this would have bothered me before, but I couldn't help but feel like a trespasser in the life that was once mine. Every minute of the day, the urge to return to Marten Ranch pulled in my veins. I could go back, but no one else was there other than Feilding and the cleaners.

...And possibly Sykes.

Not to mention I'd have to fly back out again for Christmas a few weeks later. No, I had to stick it out. Dad was noncommittal about taking a day off, but maybe he'd change his mind.

Carlie: *It just feels weird here. Like I'm all alone.*

Estella: **Teary face* I'm sorry, I didn't know it was like that. I wish you could be here with me. At least then my brothers wouldn't barge into my room without knocking.*

Carlie: *Ugh, boundaries!*

Estella: *Hey, what were you talking to Felice about?*

I smirked at that. Was Estella worried that Felice and I were becoming close? Not a chance. Felice was sort of mean without Jacob there to constantly remind her that she was a human being. Still, she was smart and savvy, and her fashion sense couldn't be denied.

Carlie: *I want to hire her private detective to look into my mom. She had these postcards...I just have a feeling they're related to her disappearance.*

Estella: *Okay, but you know that she is the private detective, right? She doesn't hire anyone. She does that all herself by hacking into her dad's work servers.*

The phone slid in my sweaty palm. Holy shit! That explained why she said she'd have to get back to me on that. The idea of Felice digging through my family drama made me feel gritty on the inside, as if I ate sandy mud and it wasn't going down.

Carlie: *I'll get my own investigator.*

I should have known better. We were the troublemakers, after all. Nearly everyone in the clique had history. The clique set the trauma aside but not the information they'd learned along the way. We didn't read it in an old book or take notes. The past was etched into our bones where no one else could see it. Even if the words no longer evoked the bad, icky feelings that made fires in our eyes, they remained as information.

The curiosity I discarded had never left. It was a scabby thing that refused to flake off. I wanted to know their history. Not just what they told me but the full, unadulterated version of events. And what was the deal with the sanctuary?

Feilding had police crawling all over Marten Ranch searching for Sykes. Would they find the secret place where the clique did their initiation? I was really stuck on it being a secret, hidden place, but in all reality, it might have just been the library.

But if that was the case, wouldn't they just say that?

There would be no initiation while I was stuck at home. Some things would need to wait. They wanted to show me; I could feel it the way I felt Heather's intentions on the way to the diner and the way Felice didn't ask questions when I asked for her nonexistent PI. In the same way, Tiffany and Jacob admired my dad from afar... I knew why even when they spoke little of their home lives.

Opening my laptop, I did some research of my own. The internet was an ocean of options. Saturated with Yelp reviews and websites prompting phone calls. I was paralyzed by the choices I'd need to make. How did one vet a private detective?

There had to be an easier way.

Dad hired several initially. They would be familiar with the case, but clearly, they weren't successful. So, should I even bother with them? I was chewing on my fingernails again. It was a growing occurrence ever since I took off my acrylics. I didn't have time to go to Clarkson for refills constantly, but now I was gnawing my poor cuticles raw.

This was eating at me.

I went to Dad's office only to be stopped by Thomas, the secretary. He was hunched over his laptop on the little makeshift office outside the doors. When Dad began working from home two days a week, Thomas was given the same option but chose to follow my dad home instead. Whatever.

"I need to talk to Dad," I said.

His black-rimmed glasses were as black as his hair. Thomas had mousy features and would have benefited from an orthodontist, but he wasn't terrible to look at. His British accent also wasn't the worst.

"He's in wall-to-wall meetings until six," Thomas said. His skin was as pale as the glow of the laptop screen.

Inhaling, I thought about how to not be an asshole. I wasn't jazzed about asking Dad about hiring PIs to stalk my potentially dead mom to begin with. Maybe this was a Thomas problem.

"I want to hire a detective, and I have no idea where to find a good one."

Thomas took off his glasses and closed the laptop. Without them, it was like I was looking at a different guy. Either I was getting desperate, or Thomas was getting hotter. Maybe I just never noticed him before. Why would I?

"Mr. Whittaker mentioned you wanted to look into your mother."

He rummaged around in his file desk before producing a single sheet of paper. "I went ahead and found some for you. Mr. Whittaker hired three private detectives, but only one is still an investigator. He felt she was the best of the three anyhow."

I was taken aback by this. "This was weirdly easy."

"Yes, well, it helps when you don't call me a cunt as you barge in on your father's meetings."

Oh, no. I did do that, didn't I? I cringed, and Thomas nodded. "Yeah..."

"I'm really sorry. I was so self-absorbed."

"He's right," Thomas said with a sincerity that made my feet go to jelly. "You have changed. What has that school done to you?"

I laughed. "I can call you a cunt again if it makes you feel better."

"Sort of plain on its own. Give it some flourish. Throw in some adjectives next time."

I was smiling. Why was I smiling at this? Something about his humor made my terrible behavior seem more like a sporting event that was actually fun. Not just when they run after a ball for three hours. The one with the sticks...hockey. It felt like we were playing hockey but with words.

"Like crusty?"

His dark brows raised as he said, "Yeah...just think about it. The more absurd, the better. Go crazy with it."

"I'll...I'll work on that," I stammered. Heat exploded on my face, and I turned away before he could notice. What the hell was I doing? He was in his twenties and worked for my dad.

"Nice chatting with you, Ms. Whittaker."

"Okay, bye...schnitzel cunt!" I said, not looking back.

"Read a bloody thesaurus!"

CHAPTER 17

The Christmas decorations were going up, and I couldn't help but get into the spirit. By spirit, I meant anything that isn't sitting in my room alone. Dad always works right up until Christmas Eve, and it seems like he has no intentions of changing that tradition this year, either.

I wrapped fake fur along the banisters. Hung red bows with little copper bells all over the house. Francesca and three other maids I didn't know were caught between asking me what they should do and telling me how to do it.

"We've always used the white satin ribbon like this," Francesca said as she used a hooked poll to drape it along the walls. "But if you don't like that—"

"No, I like that," I said.

It looked like the Macy's Christmas tree exploded in our house and reminded me of when I had cousins who came over to play in our scratchy, formal, red and white dresses. Once upon a time, both my mom's and dad's side of the family came every year. These days, it was mostly just the Whitakers since the Hunts all decided Dad murdered his wife. Even if they didn't believe it, they still said it for an easy buck.

Two of the new maids carried a large box from the attic.

We never had a real tree. I always wanted to go and cut one down, but Dad never had time, and I imagined it was a mess. Pine needles and resin all over the place right before a party? More work than it was worth. I was unboxing the ornaments when Thomas stepped into the room with Dad's mug.

"Lending a hand with the decorations?"

"Yeah," I said. "I'm the fluffer."

His brows arched as he stared at me. "The what?"

"The fluffer," I repeated. "The person who arranges the limbs so the tree looks full."

Thomas cleared his throat and stared into the mug. "It's a shame it's not a real tree."

"I was just thinking the same thing! I love the pine smell, but it's too much work on top of everything else."

It was a nice fake tree, though. The best money could buy. It stood nearly nine feet tall, and we needed to use hooks and ladders to reach the top. "We've had this thing since I was a kid."

"Bring back memories?" he asked.

"Sort of. There was a feeling of excitement and something else I can't really describe. But that's gone, and I don't think it's ever coming back."

Jeez. I sounded so morbid. He wasn't saying anything. *Do something, Carlie. You made it awkward.* So I did the next most awkward thing I could have managed. I laughed. Big, fake, and forced. "Sorry."

"I understand."

"Is it like that for everyone?"

"Even us plebs?" Thomas teased. "I suspect so."

"You're not flying back home?" I was eager to shift the conversation away from whatever melancholy mood I'd struck up.

"Not much to fly home to these days," he said.

There was no avoiding it. Somewhere along the line, holidays went from excitement to stress and dread. A reminder of how our families shrunk with each passing year. How we set out the plates even when the seats would remain vacant.

"You should come," I said.

Thomas smiled and shook his head. "Mr. Whittaker invited me as well. I feel it is a bit too familiar with my employer."

"You've only been working for him for like ten years," I reminded.

"Uh, five, actually. How old do you think I am?"

I was just flopping at every turn. Was I utterly incapable of having a normal conversation? Something was seriously wrong with me. I needed to get out more and talk to real people. I loved the clique, I did, but sometimes it was like speaking to an empty cardboard box. There were no definitions or virtually anything apart from the face value of their idle chit-chat.

"I don't know," I said slowly while playing with my hands. "Twenty..."

"Five," he finished. "I'm twenty-five. I graduated prep school and moved to America when I was twenty."

"Why? You could drink in pubs. All your family was there."

"Yeah, but there wasn't much else there to do. I could be a grocery clerk or a delivery driver. On the docks...or I could try something new."

A word rang from my heart then. "Brave."

He smiled at that and went back to staring at the mug. "I should get back to it. His coffee is getting cold."

For some reason, just knowing Thomas was in the same house as me made it feel a little less lonely.

The ornaments were all part of a set. Real crystal and star-shaped. Each one was slightly different, but hanging on the tree, they appeared mostly the same. The only person who knew their individuality was the person who hung them up.

Or, in our case, the three of us, because it took that many people to decorate the massive tree. Francesca was on the top of the ladder setting the tree topper. A star dazzled with hundreds of crystals that matched the rest of the ornaments.

A maid giddily plugged in the lights, and the whole thing glowed in soft yellow.

There was a sigh of awe that came from us.

"Oh, you're decorating?" Dad said.

We turned around to find him nodding in approval. "Looks good, honey."

"I only helped a little bit." Politely reminding him that there were three other women who had spent the last several days working on the decorations. I only hung up a few things. The other maid was still working on the dining room—setting the table and getting drinks ready, that sort of thing.

"Good job as usual," he said. "Did Thomas give you that paper?"

"He did. I left an email, but I don't expect an answer until after the holidays."

I was surprised he was interested. Hopefully, it was for the right reasons. We needed closure. There was a good chance they wouldn't find anything new and end up flipping through countless Jane Doe photos.

I didn't tell him about the postcard with the familiar handwriting. Or anything for that matter. He was happy I was learning and growing, but I got the feeling he expected me to revert back the moment things got hard. I wasn't some drug addict that was one glass of champagne away from a relapse. The only difference between September me and December me was that instead of lashing out in petty ways, I had people to talk to. It's not that deep.

But whatever, if he didn't trust me, that was okay. It took time, and I could appreciate that. I just hoped the family wouldn't bring out the worst in me tonight.

Dad's new partner was the first to show. He was a junior partner for years in another firm before my dad took a look at his client list and offered partnership on the spot. This must have been their first year at a Whittaker Christmas.

"Oh, wow," the wife said in awe.

His kids were young, and a smile crept along my face when their eyes flashed white and red. It was like the Christmas Jackpot was going off between their ears as they stood there before the tree.

There were presents under the tree—Thomas's work, most likely. I leaned down and said, "Do you want to see what's under the tree?"

"Presents for us?" the younger one asked.

I nodded toward the tree. "See for yourself."

Dad was a busy man, but he did make notes of names and kids. Little details he'd scrub from brief conversations over coffee or requests for time off in emails. They all probably went to Thomas, but with Dad's intention. No doubt those kids would find the hottest toy of the year or the thing highly recommended by the toy store on Park Ave.

Next were Grandma and Grandpa Whittaker. And, oh, Grandma got a new facelift. When she smiled at me, her face met the brows pinned high on her face. Grandpa was the same as always. I'm pretty sure he only wore his black tuxedo for this event and this event alone.

"Look at you!" Grandma said as she embraced me and kissed my cheek. "You've gotten taller."

"Not since I was sixteen," I reminded.

She looked me up and down before saying, "That's not what I meant. Oh, champagne..."

Grandpa was right behind her, so when she shuffled off, he was next in line. His voice rattled like a bone across a washboard. "How are ya, honey?"

"Hi, Grandpa."

"How's school? Freshman, right? That trust fund is waiting."

Of course he had to bring that up. My cousins all got theirs when they turned twenty-one, but Dad had added an addendum to mine. He wanted me to earn it. Once, I'd railed against the notion. Calling it unfair. These days it didn't feel like such a hurdle, but I might feel differently upon my return to Harvard.

He was waiting for me to answer his question with a slack jaw full of large fake teeth. I failed my first semester at Harvard before being expelled in the second, so technically still a freshman. "That's right."

"How you liking it?"

His aftershave was overwhelming but in a good way. Intoxicating, just as it was every year. "I love it," I said. "I've made so many friends—"

"There he is!" Grandpa marched toward my dad, who had emerged from his office.

I stood there alone with a sheep baying between my ears. Too old to hold a conversation they'd forget tomorrow. I shouldn't feel bad. But I always did the things I shouldn't.

Somewhere between a glass of champagne and a couple of salmon rolls later, my aunt's blonde, fluffed-up hair, followed by my aunt, waddled in wearing a fur coat. *Yuck.* What hair her husband lacked was made up for by his wife. He was already wiping his sweaty forehead with a handkerchief.

"There she is," my aunt said. Her voice was just loud in general, but when focused on me, it felt like her hot breath was going to loosen the curls I spent an hour forging with a curling iron.

"Hi, Auntie..."

"Brother said you came home early. I hope you didn't get into any trouble."

Her makeup was already caking in the creases of her face. Unlike Grandma, Auntie insisted on some skincare line advertised by a celebrity, only I think she bought it and never used it. Maybe her husband did because his face was smooth and taut like a drum. Was he number three...maybe number four.

"They had to close early for some emergency repairs," I said.

"Oh, is it underfunded?"

I shook my head. Working out the lie as I went along. "No, this was unexpected. A professor was let go and didn't take it well."

Her eyes went wide. "I think I read about that! A doctor, right? There's a manhunt. Those poor girls."

"I helped organize a fundraiser for them," I assured her with a hand on her arm. "They're going to get all the help they need."

There was a flicker in her eyes. Something racing and concerned. Like she got a whiff of gas and was worried I might light a match. "Good for you, honey."

I didn't know how to respond to that. She was commending me on doing a good thing, but the way she said it was so patronizing. Like telling a homeless person that money wouldn't solve all their problems when we all knew it would.

"Oh, Rodger, you know cream cheese gives you gas!" Auntie bellowed as she departed the conversation.

I needed another glass of champagne.

My cousins, the twins, skulked into the entryway. Both girls were wearing slip dresses, one white and the other red. At least the Whittakers appreciated a good theme. They were two years younger than me. Probably juniors or seniors in high school. Glued to their phones with their long, skinny arms. Their faces fixed with setting spray in a position that suggested they couldn't get the smell of rubber cement out from under their noses.

"Hey," I said.

Neither girl looked up. "Hey," Red Dress said.

Macy and Bailey. At some point, they went from following me around and asking to try on the things in my closet to being annoyed by my presence. I was the same way at that age, so I didn't hold it against them.

"After glass three, they won't notice if you drink the champagne," I said. "Just pour some orange juice in it."

Both girls looked up from their phones at that.

Dad had never made an issue of me drinking. Somewhere between the vacation in Greece and the one in Switzerland, it occurred to him that the rest of the world didn't care if teenagers drank. There were no hard rules, but as long as I wasn't being an ass, he just ignored it.

I was just passing along the secret knowledge of the Christmas party in the way it was passed down to me by one of our older cousins who was spending the holiday in the Swiss Alps.

That was everyone. Standing off to the side of the room, I sipped and watched as my family flocked around my dad. It was kind of fascinating. Being the most successful of the kids, it was like his rank among the family was established by net worth alone.

My aunt married well and often enough that she didn't technically work. Her husbands provided money and she, in turn, found networks for them to broaden and further entwine themselves into the

Whittaker finances. Even after the imminent divorce, there was still profit to be had.

My other aunt was CEO of running businesses into the ground. Whether genius or Dad's people, she always managed to come out wealthier for it.

Unlike his sisters, Dad accumulated his own wealth long after Grandpa's initial investment. Plain old finance investor. Nothing flashy or even illegal. He was just really good at his job, hired the right people to expand, and the Whittaker name gave him an undeniable reputation.

"Is that all of them?"

Not expecting the British accent, I turned to find Thomas. He must have been working with Dad in his office and crept out when no one was looking. I tried not to act surprised, but there was no denying the flush spreading up my chest.

"That's all of them," I said with a sigh. "You decided to come."

He gave a slight smile and said, "I have something for you."

I made it a conscious point to stop covering my chest. The dress wasn't that low-cut, but I still felt so exposed. Like I was spread-eagled and waiting for the wax with the dismissive esthetician who saw fifteen vags that day.

With Thomas beside me, I was in the picture and not staring at it from behind a red rope.

"What?"

"Don't get too worked up," he said. "I saw it when I was out shopping for the gifts, and I thought of you."

He pulled a gold threaded loop from his pocket, and out came a plastic vial with green sticks inside. "We were talking about the smell of pine. I thought you'd like to have your own little bottle of Christmas wherever you go."

I took the dangling thing and held it. Stunned into silence. My chest was doing that stupid thing where it threatened to sob, but I swallowed it back. It wasn't a big deal. Just a cute little gift. But it felt huge. Bigger than the time a boyfriend stole his grandmother's ring to propose.

"That's really sweet, Thomas."

I unscrewed the cap and inhaled. Synthetic pine and holiday spice. I closed my eyes and went back to a time when there were too many faces to count, and they were all happy to see me. When my cousins and I ran like a pack of wolves throughout the house. Snatching snacks to take into my bedroom to provide for the older cousins so they would tell us their experiences in grown-up matters. When we shredded the wrapping paper like ravenous monsters, and it piled around us so high the grown-ups had to dig us out.

My eyes found his when they opened. He had been watching me as the memories flooded back as if he was standing there beside me the entire time. There was something so intimate about it. As if he were watching me sleep while caught within a dream.

"I... If I knew, I would have gotten you a gift."

His smile was somewhat sad and twisted along his face. "You just did."

***

We abandoned the party.

If anyone noticed, no one spoke of it. I caught my dad glimpsing us as we went upstairs and sat on the top step. There was a not-so-subtle walk through the entryway, where he spotted us eating from a silver plate and laughing before he rejoined the party.

"I don't think Mr. Whittaker approves," Thomas said.

He didn't. I already knew what Dad would say, and it was hanging on the walls like portraits waiting to be acknowledged.

He's a bit old for you, isn't he, honey?

"I don't want you to get the wrong idea," I said. "I like you, but—"

"I get it," he said. "I don't exactly fit in with your kind."

What the fuck? Why would he even think that? "I was going to say you're older than me."

"Oh." His eyes were wide. "Right."

"I'll be twenty in March. Five years isn't a big deal, but I'm in college across the country. Not even drinking age. We're just not at the same point in life, you know?"

"This might be the nicest rejection I've ever had."

It was a first for me too. The only way I knew how to end relationships was to drive the torpedo headfirst into the desert. I'd walk away mostly unscathed but decimate everything around me in the process. Even deserts had ecosystems.

"I really do like you, but I'm not going to be around for the next four years. It just wouldn't work."

"No, it wouldn't, would it?"

I wanted to say more. To offer more. But promises after four glasses of champagne were pretty much null and void the next morning. Maybe after I graduated, he'd be single, and I'd be single. Anything could happen.

"Who knows what the future will bring," I said, cringing at my own cliché.

Thomas took it like a champ. Lifting his glass, we toasted to that.

"Are you coming back for spring break?" he asked. "We can't date, but I'd at least like to catch up with you."

"Deal." Normally, I'd go to Cabo or something like that, but maybe I'd make an exception. Do something healthy for a change. "You'll need to help me get Dad to take a day off. When was the last time he took a vacation?"

His face crunched as he searched for the answer. "Not in the last five years, at least. I had to send the doctor to his office for his yearly exam."

"Shit."

"I'll tell you what," Thomas said, nudging my knee with his own. "Next time you're in town, we will pick a day, and I'll reschedule all his meetings and unplug the internet. He won't know how to fix it, and he will have no choice but seek out a place for WIFI to check his emails."

I got the feeling this was a plan Thomas had been waiting to do for some time. It was nice to know I wasn't the only one who worried about Dad.

"Oh, honey," Auntie said from the entryway. "Not with the help."

"Does your pool boy know that?"

It spouted from my mouth faster than I could think. Her eyes bulged from her head as her cheeks went pink. For a moment, I thought she was going to erupt. The volume of her voice was about to increase tenfold, and she'd have one of her famous meltdowns.

Everyone would hear it. Say anything to calm her down. It wouldn't work, and the only recourse would be to end the party. No apology would serve, and there would be a snide remark for the next three consecutive holidays.

I held my breath, waiting for it, but what came out of her mouth was hot air trumpeting between her lips before she erupted into laughter. "I don't care how much Brother says you've changed; you'll always be your mother's daughter."

Touché.

There was no blow defter than evoking a comparison between my unhinged mother and me. Thomas did his best impression of a stair railing, but his knuckles were white as he gripped his pant leg.

Let her have the last word. If you don't, she's going to escalate. While she gives you shit, you're tucked away with the fact that her precious twins have gotten into the champagne and probably broken into the schnapps. One of them is puking in the toilet, while the other one is sending pictures of her boobs to a senior.

I didn't actually know if this was what they were doing. It's what I did at their age. One of the peppermint schnapps bottles was missing, and I put two and two together. I might be hanging on statistics by a thread, but I could manage the basics.

Visibly wincing, my aunt puffed with a sense of satisfaction before clucking off. The moment she was out of sight, I laughed and popped another salmon roll in my mouth.

"Are you okay?" Thomas asked.

Cream cheese was squishing between my teeth. "Hrm?"

"She's awful."

Slicking my tongue over my teeth, I made sure there was no debris in my teeth before I explained. "Only to me," I said. "People only act like that when they know they can get away with it."

"Carlie," he said slowly. "How long has she been saying things like that to you?"

That was a stupid question. "Always?"

He was frowning like I said something weird. "They're all like that when he's not looking. My mom wasn't as rich as they are; it's offensive to them. Like I'm a mutt or something."

Only mutts were incredibly cute. Not as cute as Quasi, but they were healthier. Fewer defects, and they lived longer. I had every intention of outliving my aunt.

"By the way your dad makes it sound, everyone is so kind to you."

"They are when he's looking," I offered.

"I don't mean to pry," Thomas said slowly. "But your mum, was she good with you?"

"Same deal with her."

"Right," he said with a nod. "So, when dad isn't looking, everyone treats you like *that*."

"Not everyone," I said, leaning against the wall. The champagne was rushing to my head. Bubbles, bubbles, and more bubbles. Like I was swimming in fizz.

"My grandparents are nice, and my cousins are probably cool."

At any moment, one of them would be caught puking. My aunt would blame me. Say that I was a terrible influence. My dad would be embarrassed. A lecture would follow. The usual.

Her precious girls wouldn't have even dreamed of touching alcohol if it weren't for her leading by example. Brother needs to put his foot down.

The lull of the champagne numbed and calmed the swirl of bad emotions within me. I'd say negative, but you know, negatives are not bad, just a different valuable. Not only was I fizzing. I was buzzing.

Zzzzz...Zzzz

"I think your phone is going off," Thomas said.

I frowned. Who would even be calling? It was Christmas Eve. It was probably a butt-dial or mistake. Holding out my phone, the name Estella and the image of my best friend blurred.

"Hello?"

I heard my own voice echo back to me. "Estella?"

There was a soft sob followed by a louder one. "Estella? Is that you?"

"...Carlie," she mewed.

All the bubbles popped, and the fizzy went flat.

CHAPTER 18

I stormed out of my room, armed with my bag, my thoughts only of Estella. I kept asking her what happened, only to get the same answer.

"I can't..."

I did manage to coax her location out of her. She was in the airport bathroom. It explained the echo in the call and probably why Estella couldn't tell me what was going on. Her sobs sent me into a spiral of panic. Something was terribly wrong. If I dwelled on it too long, I started crying myself.

Maybe it was the hivemind mentality within the clique, but I had a sense that I knew. She was going back to the academy for her own safety, and if home was more dangerous than Sykes lurking in the walls, that was all the confirmation I needed.

Jogging to catch up, Thomas had several prints of paper. "I got you the next flight out. There's a layover, but it will get you to Washington sooner than if you waited for a one-way."

He was so considerate.

I didn't even tell him what was happening. He just heard the tone of my voice while talking to Carlie and left. I assumed he was just trying to give me privacy, but he was booking tickets for my flight.

Thomas led me to his old Toyota and got in.

The glow of the headlights against the starless night did nothing to obscure the snowflakes warping toward the windshield like falling stars. My eyelashes were soaked with tears, and I felt perpetually damp. No amount of heat blaring from the vent could stop the shivers.

"Can I text you to make sure you get back to school all right?" Thomas asked.

I nodded.

"I'll arrange for a driver when I see you to the airport. They will be waiting for you just like last time."

His voice had that trained reassurance of a professional. Thomas wasn't on the clock, but his job slipped over his knuckles like a pair of custom gloves. "Thanks," I said. "I don't know what I'd do if you hadn't..."

Probably fly into a panic. Calling Ubers and running through the airport, screaming at people to get me on the nearest plane. Didn't they know Estella was in trouble? If my dad had a private jet, none of this would be an issue, but his wealth was a testament to not spending like a dumbass who won the lottery yesterday.

Maybe when I graduated, I'd ask him to manage my trust for me. On some level, I just assumed he would anyway. There was a difference between asking for help and forcing others to step in. It would be nice to invest all of it, but that would require a job and living within my means. I had no idea how to do that.

Did I know how to do anything?

"I'll explain everything to your dad," Thomas assured me.

I winced, and a tear escaped the waterline. It rolled down my cheek so fast that there was no hiding it. "I wanted to have a day with him. Now I go and bail on him on Christmas."

"Hey," Thomas soothed. "This is an emergency."

"You don't even know what's going on!" The whine in my voice even annoyed me.

"True, but it must be serious, right?"

I pipe down at that. "Estella doesn't cry," I said, voice cracking. It felt like my ribs were buckling under the strain. "It would be like if Wednesday Addams ugly cried in public."

His eyes were fixed on the road, but he frowned. "I'm having a hard time picturing that."

Because it wasn't a picture. It would never happen, only it was happening, and Estella was hiding out in an airport or in first class, trying to keep it together. "Something really bad happened to her."

A new fear hit me then. It was like a bomb. Stupid, fat bomb that shouldn't matter, but it did. "What if she's in economy class," I wail.

Thomas couldn't help but erupt into snickers. He caught sight of my face and straightened his professional gloves. "I'm sure she got first class. Those are always the last seats to fill."

He didn't understand. If Estella was flying coach, it meant she was stuck uncomfortably close to strangers in a vulnerable state. Imagine being wedged between a snoring person and an armrest invader when you're doing everything you can just to keep it together.

When she cried, everyone would notice, and no one would help.

If I could have one superpower, it would be teleportation. I could just appear beside Estella and hold her hand. I could buy the seat next to hers, better yet, the whole row, and fight anyone who dared speak to her. When she was safely tucked in bed, I could teleport to whoever hurt her and...

Zzzz...Zzzz

"Hey," I said.

"Honey, where are you?"

It was Dad. He knew I left him alone with his awful family on Christmas. Only, he didn't know they were awful. I could hear Auntie jabbering in the background. She was angry. Probably because she finally found the twins, and I wasn't there to blame.

Sorry, Auntie, you'll need to blame someone else. Or just hold the girls accountable for once.

"I'm so sorry, Dad. Estella is in trouble. I'm on my way to the airport."

"Serious? Like legal or that professor?"

"Something happened to Estella back home. I don't know what exactly, but I'm not leaving her alone."

It had been months since the police searched the school. If Sykes was there, they would've found him. Given the lack of news from Feilding, I assumed he was long gone. Marten Ranch was a safe haven once more. Only this time, it was sealed tighter than a dolphin's asshole.

"No, I understand, honey. This sounds serious."

"I'm so sorry," I said. "I'll call you when I know more. I'll be home for spring break."

"...I'm proud of you, honey."

A wood beam slapping me in the gut would've had less impact. I don't know why, but his words were so genuine, and the increasing pitch of my aunt's squawking wasn't nearly as amusing as it should've been.

Dad was proud of me.

"Thanks, Dad," I said with a shaky breath.

"Teenagers do these things!" someone yelled in the background.

Sounds like the family drama would carry on with or without me being in the center of it. Didn't they just know when to go home without causing a scene? I had an actual emergency on my hands. Auntie was acting like two drunk girls were the end of the day when we all knew something like this happened every year.

I ended the call. There was nothing more to say between us.

"Sounds like the Whittaker party ended right on cue," Thomas said. "But if you're not there, who will they blame?"

"Oh, they'll find a way," I said, recalling how I told the twins about the orange juice. I was just trying to befriend them. Had I known Thomas was going to be there, I would've ignored them. Next year, I'll make it a point to say nothing to anyone.

The car came to a stop. I gave Thomas one last look and said, "Thank you. I don't know what I would've done without you."

"It's my job."

No, it's not. Your job is to see to my dad's needs, not mine. You're just a good guy. Do you know that?

As I got out, I gave him one final glance. *Text me.*

He might be too old for me right now, and we're in different places in our lives, but I needed Thomas in the way a deep diver needed a lifeline. Someone to talk to that wasn't empty past the face value. A real, honest-to-God person on the other end, not a machine.

Inside the airport, people were giving me really strange looks. Like I was dressed up for Halloween. I got flagged for a pat down, only the security guy with his blue latex gloves held his hands up and said, "She's good."

It wasn't until I checked in the long panel mirror outside of a perfume store did I realize why. My long, clingy gold satin dress was too formal. Makeup streaked down my cheeks in black blur smudges, and my once-curled hair was wet and flat at the top. A total wreck.

Like I got dumped on prom night and decided to take a flight going anywhere.

I hadn't packed any clothes. Just the stuff I needed to get on the plane.

In the half-hour before my flight, I bought sweats and a T-shirt. They were clearly sports paraphernalia but way less conspicuous. The lady at the checkout line stared without shame as she checked me out. Her hands slid the overpriced sweats over the scanner without even looking.

Most people might have said something. Explained it was an emergency trip during a Christmas party, but I didn't need to justify myself to someone who'd never see me again.

After changing in the bathroom, I washed my face and found a hair tie in the bottom of my bag. I couldn't stand the idea of crocs, but there were flip flops, so good enough. My outfit said, "I don't actually belong to a gym, but this team is my whole identity."

No one stared at me as I boarded the plane.

"Excuse me, ma'am," a flight attendant said. "This is first class."

She looked me up and down like I didn't belong. Who was she to judge me? Anger flared, and I just couldn't reel it in. Emotionally empty, I needed to fill myself back up if I was going to survive the next eight hours.

"Do you see this ticket?" I asked, holding it up. "What does it say?"

"I'm sorry..."

"What does it say?" I asked again, my voice raised high enough that others were starting to watch.

"It says first class," the flight attendant said before hurrying off.

That's what I thought.

Carlie: *I'm on the plane now. I'll be there in the morning, okay?*
...Okay?

...Estella?

CHAPTER 19

I was home.

Marten Ranch Academy was cleaner— more thoroughly polished and traces of fresh paint lingered in the air. Feilding went all out on removing any trace of Dr. Sykes. Even the plaque on his door was gone. EvIf he was still lurking between the walls—I was certain he wasn't—it didn't matter.

Skipping my room, I went straight to Estella's. I didn't knock, I just barged in. Which was rude, in hindsight, but she wasn't even there.

Her bed was slept in and unmade, and her purse was on the chair. Her black polish, lipstick, and powder compress had spilled onto the floor. A passport lay closed on the ground along with some pesos.

If she wasn't here... Where did she go?

Feilding wasn't in her office, but there was a fresh stack of forms and the computer was on. No purse. She must have been out for a late breakfast. Maybe she took Estella with her.

I checked everyone else's rooms, and they were still empty. No one else was here. Which figures, since it's Christmas and all.

Carlie: *I'm home. Where are you?*

She wasn't responding.

I spent the next half hour pacing the entryway, chewing fervently on my fingernails. The sound of a car sent me lunging for the door just as Feilding stepped in. "Oh, Ms. Whittaker," she said. "I'm glad you're here."

"Estella?"

Feilding's sharp blue eyes were wide as she nodded. "She came in last night very upset. I tried to calm her, but she locked herself in her room. I...felt like calling her family was the wrong thing to do."

I was torn by that. She and her family were close. They had that kind of relationship that belonged in sitcoms and stories. The kind where a laugh came on cue and every segment ended happily — unless there was a part two — of course.

"She's not in her room."

Feilding didn't seem concerned. "I've too much work to go hunting for her. Try taking the elevator down. I trust you know what to look for."

I slowly turned to watch as the dean strutted up the stairs to her office. What in the shit was that all about? Well, that must be my one hint in finding the sanctuary.

Where does the trauma go?

Not everyone participates...I don't need to.

All the things I had overheard or been told about the sanctuary were now coming back to me all at once. Something happened to Estella. Something so bad that she no longer wanted to live within her own skin. I had to find her.

Stepping into the elevator, I pushed B, assuming it was for basement.

The metal gates closed and there I was, in what felt like a tin box rattling downward by a cord. What if it snapped and dropped? Plunging downward into what was probably the depths of hell. It continued to crank downward but in a painful lull. Each creak and metallic groan made me flinch as I was lowered into a dark chasm. Snatched away from daylight, but slowly, as if the elevator itself wanted me to know I was stepping into unknown territory.

I hit the ground with a clunk and the metal doors opened. I'd much rather they remain closed at this point, but Estella was somewhere down here, alone in the dark. Using my phone as a flashlight, the room opened to what was once a wine cellar. Brick columns supported the low ceiling and there were crates and cardboard boxes lurking in the corners.

Just a basement. I'm too old to be afraid of the dark. One foot in front of the other.

"Estella?" I called.

An exposed water pipe dripped in response. At least there were no spiders and no raccoons after Sykes got ahold of them. Cold like a tomb, I was thankful my sweatpants were thick.

It didn't take long to reach the corners of the room. That couldn't be right. Feilding said Estella was probably down here, but she said I would know where to look. What if I didn't?

Drip...Drip...

Scanning my light over the brick supports and boxes of stowed items, I didn't see anything unusual. Just some old paintings of flowers and a cardboard box that said Lost and Found. On the ground in a stack were the white shag rugs like in my room, still wrapped in plastic.

I tried pressing on protruding bricks and observed the massive cast-iron boiler that was probably decommissioned before my grandma was born. Absolutely dead. Cold to the touch but recently cleaned.

There were some bricks freshly mortared back into their places and the cement floor was vacuumed.

There was nothing here. Well, there was something, but I was too stupid to figure it out. Feilding was so confidant I'd figure it out. How disappointing of me.

In a moment of desperation, I even tried sending the elevator up. It felt clever at the time. No one would be able to see a secret entrance with the elevator sitting on top. As it moved upward, I realized why no one had thought of that.

There was no door under the elevator, and now I had no way of getting back up. Panic makes people stupid, and my anxiety levels hadn't been this high since the time I tried to buy pot in Greece using google translator only to realize he was a cop.

No, there was an answer, I just wasn't seeing it.

What would I know to look for? Feilding seemed to think I had it all figured out already. I had discovered the secret hallways on my own. Each room had one, except for Estella's, and a rug marked the entrance.... wait.

"You've got to be fucking kidding me," I said, hurrying to the stack of rugs. I pulled them to the side, two or three at a time until it revealed cuts along the brick wall. I wouldn't have noticed if I hadn't been specifically searching for it. I tried to pick at the bricks without mortar, but they didn't pop out like a door. The section wasn't wide enough for a person to even crawl through.

With all ten fingers, I pushed against it, and something clicked from the other side of the room. Yes! It was like solving a puzzle created by a dead guy who wanted to show his weird friends that he could summon demons. Only a man would risk unleashing an apocalypse for bragging rights.

A door-shaped cut out formed on the opposite wall. The little gears were working so hard as it reeled the segment away, revealing a hidden entrance. Still high on the success, I inhaled a deep breath and marched in before my nerves could register imminent danger.

***

Okay, so, this is the stuff horror films are made of.

When a secret hallway is swept and tidy, some of the scare factor is swept away with it. Sure, it's still a secret hallway built by an unhinged man from over a century ago, but it's known and maintained. No longer a forgotten secret with things lurking that have dwelled beyond what's humanly possible.

Maintenance takes the decrepit aspect away from the traditional creepy space of a cellar, and even the unorthodox like the hallways. It's hard to be totally spooked knowing that the housecleaning lady also frequents the halls with her vacuum. If she's not scared, you're probably fine.

Take these secret halls, for instance. Add a bunch of cobwebs plastered with dead spiders, skittering noises, and dust falling like ashes, and the mood changes.

"Estella?" I called.

Everything was dank and the stone walls seeped with moisture they leeched from the ground. I was in the bowels of Marten Ranch, and a fetid, sick smell was growing stronger with each step. At least it wasn't a maze of corridors. There was only one path. Without decision or recourse, it led onward.

I couldn't imagine the clique traveling through here willingly. Estella? Yeah, this was her scene, but Jacob would probably have an asthma attack. Heather would start crying. And Tiffany? She would be so annoyed by the endeavor.

The confinement of the walls gave way all at once, and I found myself standing in a circular room. In the center was a massive black statue that depicted a monster of some kind. Not the one with fangs and hair or scales like the dog-eared page in Estella's book. This was about as tall as my Christmas tree, still standing proudly and covered in crystals. It was light absorbing black. It had a dark wisdom in its goat face. Standing tall, its clawed hand was held outward, as if asking me to take it.

Something about it was beautiful. Words rippled through me that promised little things.

Self-worth... Generosity... Freedom. You'll never fear the dark again, and at the end of every day you'll find that you have everything you need.

Was I promising myself those things or were they spoken from the statue? It was hard to tell because it was my internal thoughts but not things I'd ever barter my soul for.

No soul required.

Either Estella set off one of her peyote smoke bombs, or I was having a moment with a demon statue in the secret basement of my school.

"Estella?" My voice echoed alarm. I couldn't take my eyes off the statue. Oh shit, why couldn't I look away?

"I'm here," she said gently. "Don't be afraid. It only shows you your true desires."

"So, it won't make me sign a contract in blood or anything sketchy, right?"

"Black opal is rare, near impossible to find in this quantity," Estella said, approaching the statue. She patted it gently on the buckled flank. "it's said that black opal has a power unlike any other. But at the end of the day, it's just a gemstone."

At this, the whispers shrank back to the recesses of my mind, and I was able to look away. Whatever power the statue had; it was me who had given it. I felt a little sheepish, but it's not every day one encounters a giant demon statue under their junior college.

"So, this is the sanctuary." I gazed around the room. There were four paths not including the one I took to get here.

"We wanted to show you sooner," she said. "But Sykes got in the way."

I looked at her then. Estella wasn't wearing her goth makeup. Her face was bland and plain, like her goth makeup was her real face and someone was covering it up. A soft, pink sheen was on her lips...was she wearing lip gloss?

And her outfit. It was black because all her clothes were black, but she wasn't wearing fingerless gloves. No fishnet stockings, no buckle boots. Just a stylish yet simple black knee-high dress. Her hair was in a high ponytail, and she was wearing gold hoop earrings.

"Who are you, and what have you done with Estella?"

She giggled warmly. Not something Estella would do either. "It's me, Carlie. I just want to be less angsty-looking. I can't pull off the angry goth girl image forever."

I was shaking my head. Estella was lying. This wasn't her. "What happened?"

At this, she frowned and said, "Do you want to hear a sad story that will keep you up at night, or would you rather have a tour? You've been dying to see this place, and now you're here—"

I didn't give a shit about the sanctuary. "No, I want to know what happened to you."

She sighed. "I guess I owe you that much."

I was shaking my head. Estella didn't owe me anything. Why would she even think that? She was acting like whatever made her cry was some overblown incident. A spider in a bathtub or a bee flying into her room.

"Come on," she said, taking my hand. "Let's go to my room."

***

Sitting on her bed with her across from me, I noticed her fingernails. She had removed her black polish, but a purplish stain remained. That's what happens when you don't use a clear coat first. Estella would just paint layer over layer. Each chip was touched up until was just a glob of cracking polish. Only then, she'd file over it and apply a new coat.

She realized I was staring and tucked her hands under her legs. "You probably have questions."

Uh, duh.

She frowned as if recalling the event was a nuisance. I took her hand. "Just take your time."

Shaking her head, Estella laughed. "I just don't want to upset you. Promise me that you'll keep in mind that I don't feel it anymore."

My stomach turned inside out and back again. What did that even mean?

"My whole extended family was at Casa Delgado. Tons of people, half of them I barely know. One of my second or third cousins, Jesus, raped me."

It was my worst and largest suspicion but hearing her say it was like being waterboarded. Just when I thought I could catch a breath, the words echoed again and again. I was drowning in anger; in a feeling I could only describe as icky. Estella was violated in her own home by a member of her own family.

I tried to stammer out words, but they were malformed and wrong.

She was still holding my hand. As if I were the one who needed the support.

"Did you tell anyone?"

She shook her head. "I saw what happened to one of my nieces when she mentioned he groped her. I'm not going to put myself in that situation."

Of course. Forcing a family to face a truth so ugly they lash out and blame the victim. It was easier that way. Rather than face the fact that you love a monster, it's better to sweep it under the rug. That was a truth all too common in most rape cases. Funny enough, it was always the ones who protected the rapist that always asked the same question. *Why didn't you tell anyone when it happened?*

"Did you go to a hospital?" I asked.

Estella shook her head. "I can't even step outside without my family insisting they need to *protect* me."

There was a bite of irony in her voice. Bitter and frail, but it was there. She was angry about what happened. Maybe it was denial that made her appear like all was fine on the outside, but I doubted it.

"It's not too late," I said. "We can call the police. Get a rape kit done. At least then, if you decide to press charges, you'll have proof."

"The average rape kit is backlogged for years," she said. "Besides, my family lives in a different country, remember?"

But we had to do something. I wanted to say it, but this was her body we were talking about. My unsatiated desire for justice wasn't a factor in this. "Whatever you want to do," I said. "You have my support."

"Thank you," she said. "I needed to hear that more than anything."

And I meant it. If she wanted to hire a hitman or cut off his penis. Whatever she wanted, I was going to help her make it happen. I'd book tickets to Mexico and graffiti every billboard that surrounded the Delgado residence.

Jesus Delgado is a rapist.

"What's the plan?" I asked.

She blinked and stared at me as if I asked what shade of pastel she planned on wearing. "The plan?" Estella said. "It's the same as it's always been. I'm going to Oxford after I graduate from Marten Ranch. I'm going to study archaeology and specialize in occult."

No, not that, about Jesus.

"This was just a bad moment in time. It doesn't matter."

"Estella, this guy hurt you and you're telling me it doesn't matter?"

"It gave me an opportunity," she corrected. "Before this happened, I didn't have a traumatic event to sacrifice on the altar. I got to interact with a literal demon because of this. It's a dream come true, really."

Oh, the room suddenly got all hazy. My vision went in and out as I processed what she said. "Demon?"

"Like the one in my book," she said. "He feeds on our trauma, and we get to live our lives without it."

"Are you shitting me?"

"I know it's a lot. But just know that I made a massive breakthrough in my research because of this."

Where does the trauma go?

It wasn't going on a shelf in a dusty library or in a burning jar of peyote...a fucking demon was eating it like canapes. I didn't know if I could really believe this. It was more likely that Estella was having a psychotic break and had invented the story.

The statue in the sanctuary could've easily inspired a traumatized girl who loved demons into thinking one had saved her from the pain of reality.

"You're chewing on your cuticles," she said. "I have a balm for that. It tastes like ass, and you'll think twice next time."

With my cuticles oiled in something that had no scent, I left Estella's room. She assured me that there was no further need to return to the sanctuary and that she'd go to bed. I knew for a fact she didn't have a secret path through the walls, but I was reluctant to leave.

"Are you sure you don't want me to stay?"

"I'm fine," Estella said. "More than fine. I've experienced something life changing. Imagine the thesis I'll be able to create with this. It will change how people see pagan religions and even the world itself!"

My stomach sloshed around as I mulled that over. I couldn't let her carry on like this. She needed a doctor. At least some Plan B. Tomorrow morning I'd go to town and get some from a pharmacy. Would it even work? My brain was tired and between the time zones, I had no idea how many days it had been since she'd been raped.

I just hoped she'd take it.

Back in my room, I took out my phone and saw that Thomas had texted and a soft warmth staved off the chill of the room.

Thomas: *Did you arrive safely? Is your friend okay?"*
Carlie: *She's not, but I'm here with her. Thx.*

Estella was definitely not herself. I fully expected the next few days to be rough. All at once, reality would hit her. I feared what would happen then.

Maybe it would've been better if some demon had sucked out the pain of what happened. The knowledge would still be there, but she'd be free of the aftermath. No soul-breaking panic at the most inconvenient times. Nightmares would resume in the form of realizing she was naked in class or that her teeth were falling out.

What would a person be if they didn't have to carry those burdens?

Imagine it. Instead of the temporary burning clean alcohol numb or the self-destruction of drugs, there was a place where trauma could be consumed and processed without the consequences. I think I'd sleep well at night knowing that the worst emotions of my life were being digested by demon bile, never to return.

But that was Estella's fantasy, not mine.

I created a group chat with the clique, save Estella and wrote: *SOS...*

CHAPTER 20

"**H**oney, I'm home!" Jacob called from the entryway.

He and Felice were the first to come back to school on New Year's Day. Tiffany arrived later that day. Travis couldn't get away from his family until the third. Heather was meeting Everett's parents but would be arriving the next day.

All the while, Estella's delusions continued. She was Ophelia, wandering around the empty academy in a sheer black nightgown with a short satin slip underneath.

"I don't know why I never wore this before," she said with a sigh. "I think I was too hung up on my family's false sense of modesty."

Her socks had little cartoon witches riding brooms. "Cute socks," I said.

"Diego got them for me. I didn't like them because I felt like they trivialized my academic pursuit, but they are kind of cute, aren't they?"

The clique found us in the dean's private library, where Estella was lounging on a chaise, doing her best impression of a storybook damsel.

Right away, the others locked eyes on Estella. I hadn't told them what happened—it wasn't for me to say—but I did say that she was going through something major.

"Cute socks," Jacob said.

"I know, right?" Estella said with a giggle.

The corners of Felice's eyes were threatening to twitch. She was keeping it together, but it was like she knew something was really off. Tiffany sat beside Estella and said, "Did you need to use the sanctuary?"

"Finally, right?" Estella said. "It was incredible."

Tiffany nodded. "Do you feel comfortable sharing what happened?"

Estella held in her laughter at the question. "Does it matter?"

"It does," Felice said. Her arms were crossed like an angry mother. "If someone hurt you, it means they could hurt someone else. You don't want that, do you?"

At this, Estella came back to the real world for a moment. "I didn't even consider that. My cousin... He raped me over Christmas break."

Jacob was slick white, and his face was buried in his hands.

"Thanks for sharing that with us," Tiffany said.

Felice nodded and said, "Okay." Then she walked off without another word. Jacob got to his feet and headed after her. I followed them out and interrupted whatever they were muttering about.

"I want in."

Felice narrowed her eyes. *Will she flinch at what comes next? I don't think she will.*

We're in dangerous territory, Felice.

She's cool. I got this.

"What's his name?" she asked.

"Jesus Delgado," I said. "What's the plan?"

I wanted to hurt him. Consequences and all that be damned. If I never slept another unmedicated night, I was willing to pay the price. Felice had ways. Even I was aware of that much. She could make him disappear, and our hands would be clean.

Estella would come back to me when she was ready. When she was safe.

"Give me a few hours," Felice said as she stalked away. "I need to make some calls. After that, we'll go over our options."

I nodded. Jacob was rubbing his hand through his hair, disrupting his perfect coif. "Carlie, I don't know if you understand. Felice means to—"

"Kill him," I finished. "He deserves it."

Jacob got new frames for his glasses over break. They were Gucci. Black with gold hardware. Nice. But his eyes were watery and full of worry. Was he worried about me or Estella? Maybe he was concerned for everyone involved.

"I saw the sanctuary," I said. "Estella thinks a demon ate her pain."

"That's how I'd describe the process. She will be a little weird for a few days. She shouldn't have been alone, though."

For some reason, I thought if I saw the sanctuary, I'd have all the answers, but that wasn't it. Now that I knew where it was, I didn't care so much about what the clique did beneath the cellar. Estella was all that mattered.

"And after that?" I asked.

"Hopefully, she'll be back to her old gothy self."

"Can you show me how it works?" I asked.

Jacob stopped rubbing his head. "I would, but I don't know how it works. Only Estella and Felice can make it work."

"Then how does it work?" I pressed.

"It's a lot like the smoke show Estella did up in her room," he said. "You don't take anything, but you see things. It's different for everyone."

So, it was a ketamine shroom fest that Estella concocted from one of her books. She said there were no drugs involved but based on experience with her, Estella didn't consider hallucinogens or other natural substances as drugs.

I didn't either, but after eating a magic mushroom-topped pizza at a party, I decided hallucinations weren't for me. It was probably different in Estella's mind because it wasn't intoxicating, but more dissociative.

But anything that sent me running through the woods naked and thinking I was being chased by gnomes was not a good time in my book.

"Okay," I said. "Let me know when Felice does her thing. I'm going to stay with Estella. Keep an eye on her and make sure she doesn't climb any willow trees."

"Fortunately, we don't have any at Marten Ranch."

No, but there was a nearby brook.

CHAPTER 21

I t was officially the second semester. I hadn't been expelled despite the graffiti incident. Two teachers were down, but they weren't missed. Dr. Nelson was more than happy to teach history. He saw it as his rightful place in the academy.

"Instead of bouncing from one country to another," he said, "we're going to study Europe's history through periods. Starting with the dark ages all the way to the industrial era. As interesting as inbred royalty is, I'm not going to expect the class to remember them."

Oh, thank God.

European history was fascinating, don't get me wrong, but the ever-shifting territories and endless Georges were impossible for me to keep track of. Give me a block of time where cool shit happened, and I'm golden. Ask me which George was alive during the inquisition, and you'll get your car keyed.

Estella listened politely and nodded when Nelson made eye contact, but no one was home. The fire that once blazed in her eyes was gone. Replaced by a glazed-over, vacant expression.

Jacob said she'd be weird for a few days. That she shouldn't have done their little ritual alone. What if she gave too much of herself and couldn't come back? No, she had to come back. Maybe she was just hiding because Jesus was lurking in her shadows. Too afraid to be herself, Estella armored her heart and the things that mattered most.

"This is going to be the most boring semester ever," she muttered as class ended.

"...It's history," I said. "With your favorite professor."

"Yeah, but we learned European history last semester. Is it too much to ask that we learn something outside the white colonist gaze?"

For someone who could actually keep up with everything Europe did in five hundred years condensed into a semester, this was not surprising. It wasn't weird. Totally something Estella would say. *Who are you, and what have you done to my friend?*

"I agree," Tiffany said. "Chinese history is fantastic; Egyptian has just as much inbreeding if that's what the curriculum needs."

"I think logistics are an issue with Chinese history," Jacob said. "There's no way we could get through all that history in one semester. We'd need a year or more."

"Why is Europe so important anyway?" Everett asked. "Plenty of cultures around the world were just as innovative, and they didn't have to steal it along the way."

Honestly, I didn't give a shit what Nelson taught, just so long as I could get a good grade out of it. I just had one priority: graduate Marten Ranch. That was the extent of my academic goals.

"I'm sure Oxford will have different history class options," I said.

This was a small school. Yeah, we covered Europe last semester, but Marten Ranch was a junior college. We were still the fish in the bag, separated from the rest of the tank. Once we acclimated to the water, they'd dump us in with the rest.

The one-sided debate ended when Ms. T came in.

As if calculus tamed her hair and her personality, the professor went over the curriculum and the textbook with a subdued demeanor. Sad for her, but good for me. Towards the end of the semester, the formulas programmed in my calculator were starting to pop up errors as Ms. T's lessons extended past their abilities.

Lunch was once again Cobb salad. Heather was back in her vegan leather saddle, and she was more focused on Everett than ever.

"I just loved his family," she said. "They're so interesting and worldly."

There was a glimmer of something like pride in Everett. "I think you're the first girlfriend they've ever liked."

Peach color blossomed on her cheeks. "I may not be a princess or a Duchess, but they were welcoming all the same."

"Hey," he stopped her short. "They don't care about all that. Besides, I burned those bridges a long time ago."

The confusion on my face must have been apparent. Felice grinned at Everett. "Believe it or not, Everett has quite the story."

"We don't do that, Felice," he reminded her sternly. "What happened before we came to Marten Ranch doesn't matter."

Felice sighed and leaned against her chair. "I know, but it was impressive. Knowing you now, no one would ever think you were the type to hustle diplomats. I just think it's cool. Eat the rich, you know?"

Everett was staring at his plate. Was he ashamed? "That's not who I am," he said. "I just ran with the wrong crowd and got caught up in something too big for a kid."

"California is going to be great for you guys," Travis said out of nowhere. He was probably trying to change the conversation. Felice loved to poke and prod, but she was easy to derail.

"If I get accepted," Everett said.

"I know you will," Heather said, smiling across the table at him.

"Have you finally come to terms with him being a vet?" I asked.

"If he wants to be a vet, that's fine," she said. "We can make it work. Who knows, we might start a non-profit for helping animals. The next ASPCA."

"Just don't forget the Sarah McLachlan song," Felice quipped.

A split second of silence followed the chuckles before Jacob began singing the saddest song ever to grace the small screen. I snickered as Everett shook his head, trying to contain the grin. Heather's sweet soprano joined in.

Oh no, were we singing?

Estella joined in softly, and before I knew it, I was mouthing the words as well. The entire class was singing with various levels of irony before the crescendo into earnestness. Knowing I couldn't sing to save my life, I lip-synced, and as I did, I noticed something.

The saddest, most profound song that evoked pity in millions of people...felt like nothing.

They were hitting the right notes. Keeping the correct tempo. Everything was accurate, yet the words were hollow. Instead of a song, it felt like a monotonous droning. Automatic in execution yet absolute in its soullessness.

The saddest song other than the Titanic song, and hearing the clique sing it, nothing stirred within me. Not even the nudge of pity. It was a mockery of grief, and the worst part was that *they didn't even know it.*

***

Lindt resumed class as if we never left.

Humanities, the great poets, and all that, but this semester would have an emphasis on Greek philosophy. It would tie into the newly re-vamped writing class afterward. Which made way more sense. Having people write after being inspired by the greats made more sense.

As long as they didn't expect me to write like one.

It wasn't until I checked my phone after class that I saw multiple texts.

Felice: *My bedroom, tonight.*

She must have gotten something done or was about to. It would have been nice if she conferred with us first, but Felice didn't need ap proval from anyone. I thought about my own private detective digging up dirt. She told me there would be no updates until her investigation was complete. I just had to be patient.

Then there was one from Thomas. A thousand butterflies launched all at once in my chest as I read his message.

Hope all is well. Your father closed a substantial deal and is rather excited.

Being "just friends" sucked when there was no alternative.

It was one thing to decide I wasn't interested and insist friendship was the only option, but I really liked Thomas. I wasn't expecting him. Why couldn't I have noticed him a few years from now? I smacked my head with my fist a few times, but it didn't help.

"What's with you?"

I didn't realize it, but Estella was standing in the entryway with me. Everyone else just disappeared when I read his text. "I feel so stupid, Estella..."

I told her about Christmas and Thomas. Her eyes went all wide and giddy like a middle school girl. Not that I was much better. I was so utterly ridiculous with how much I liked him. I don't think I had ever had a crush on someone before. Mostly, I'd accept the attention to see what would happen. Nothing ever happened.

No walking on clouds or intrusive daydreaming. For a long time, I felt like I was just incapable of love, but maybe I didn't believe I deserved it until now.

And when I finally took an interest in someone, he was across the country. Working for my dad.

"I think it's cute," Estella said. "I get why nothing can happen, but that's just going to make you want him more, you know?"

Maybe she was right. Right now, he is forbidden fruit, even if it didn't feel that way.

"I can't explain it," I said. "He's special to me. Like how my mother's perfumes were special to her. I don't want to wear it so often I can't smell it anymore, but I never want to wash it off."

"You should write that down."

I laughed. We just finished reading love poems. Maybe those old horny bastards influenced me more than I realized. "He's my friend. I'm scared I'm going to fuck it up like everything else."

It was hard to fuck anything over three thousand miles away...

"Have you talked to Dad about it?"

Even she was referring to him as her dad now. I liked it when Estella said it, though. Deep down, it felt like I had siblings. Weird, politically correct siblings that wore gloves while reading books and knitted beanies for fun. But they were *my* siblings.

"Oh, ew," I said. "I don't want to get him fired."

Estella gave me her *Are you serious?* face. "Dad wouldn't fire him. You don't even need to tell him who you're interested in. Just get his perspective.

It was no mystery. Dad had seen us talking on the stairway. If by some chance he didn't read the room, Auntie certainly did. Who knows what version of events she told. Maybe that was why I should talk to him. Just so he knew I wasn't trying to sabotage anything or sleep with his assistant just to get his attention or something.

"You're right," I said with a heavy sigh. "I need to explain to Dad that I'm not boning his assistant."

Only that I want to and can't cause life is unfair. It didn't help that both he and I shared the common thread of making sure my dad took care of himself. Whatever I learned about Mom, I would talk it over with Thomas before telling Dad. Whenever that happened.

What if Dad already knew what happened to Mom?

That sent prickles up my spine. If he knew what happened to her, why would he hire all those detectives? Just to cover his ass? Doubtful. If Dad was remotely capable of disappearing someone, he would've moved on by now.

Carlie: *Hey, has Dad mentioned anything about you and me? Should I make sure he knows we're just friends?*

Thomas: *Um, I don't think he's upset that we talk. He asked me to tell you about the deal.*

Woah. How did I feel about that? Good and yet not. If this was anything like the awkward attempt to introduce me to his former partner's son, I'd need to snuff it out right away. I was in college, and Thomas was twenty-five. That was two years away from Heather's baby-making era.

"According to Thomas," I told Estella. "Dad isn't mad about it."

"See," she said as though that solved everything.

What would the person formally known as Estella think? It was hard to tell. We never talked about boys—or girls—I didn't even know what she was into. In a way, we might have bonded over that. I know her family desperately wanted her to date. The only reason they approved of her going to college was to meet a boy.

As if a woman can't go to college just to learn.

I imagined she'd remind me to stick to my own goals first. Graduate Marten Ranch, then Harvard, and get my trust fund. But that meant picking a major, and I had been avoiding that, like the discount mall on Black Friday.

Felice: *Are you coming or what?*

I thought she said tonight. Class had ended less than an hour ago. Whatever, I guess we're rolling on Felice time.

"I got to go," I said, hoping Estella wouldn't pry for a reason. "I'll see you at dinner?"

"Okay!"

She was skipping away. Real, honest-to-God skipping. I shuddered in revulsion. What have you done to yourself, Estella?

CHAPTER 22

F elice's room was pristine once more.

Fresh paint and new blue floral bedding, complete with a white shag rug in her closet. Hardly anything personal. Her bed was made military fashion with the corners tucked in. Loose ends were not her style. No photos of family or keepsakes from home. Her makeup was put away in a professional kit that folded into a black alligator skin case. It was like no one lived here.

The only thing personable in Felice's room was Jacob, who sat on the edge of the bed. He was slouching as if the weight of the deed was too heavy.

"Finally," she said when she answered the door and let me in.

I sat on the reading chair that was similar to my own, only I'm pretty sure this was new or reupholstered because the fabric was stiff like no one ever sat in it.

"I tracked down Jesus," she said without ceremony. "He's a bad mofo. Not only did he rape Estella, but he has links to the cartel and is on the FBI terrorist list."

Jacob's brows raised over his glasses. "Terrorist list?"

"Our friend Jesus has been selling drugs and weapons all over South America. He hasn't tried the U.S., but he's linked to the collapse in Venezuela."

Ah, yes, conservatives favorite argument against socialism. Not that I gave a shit about economies or socialism. I just got so annoyed with the discussions that I researched the Venezuelan economic collapse for myself. America wanted to use it as an example of the pitfalls of socialism, except they liked to omit the cartel's hand in everything.

Could it have worked if the cartel didn't plow through the country with their American-bought Hummers? Probably not. I don't know. There's a reason I don't study economics.

"Jeez Louise," Jacob said.

It was the most Jacob-thing he could have said.

"So, all around terrible guy. We knew that the moment we learned he raped Estella," I said. "What are we going to do about it?"

In my mind, he didn't need more crimes to warrant whatever we did next. It would help Jacob sleep at night, but I couldn't sleep until he was gone.

Felice was looking at me, then Jacob, and me again. It was like she was deciding something. There was one unspoken rule in all this. None of us would use words that implicated us in a crime. We treated it as if one of us was wearing a wire.

"I'd like to treat him the way we treated Sykes," Felice said. Only, she wasn't talking to me.

Jacob was rubbing his face. "That resulted in some consequences. The sanctuary has been different ever since."

Her eyes flickered at me, and Felice was smiling. Something Estella said instantly came to mind. *You've excited her.*

No one had directly explained the sanctuary, but I knew where it was and what it did. The how was still a little iffy. I had a sour feeling in my gut that I was about to find out. "What do you mean it's been different?" I asked.

"Estella used it after we put Sykes in there," he said. "She should be more like herself by now, only she's not. I think Sykes contaminated it somehow."

Wait—What?

As if understanding, Felice explained. "We thought that if he went through the sanctuary, Sykes might come out a better person. Someone who'd atone for his crimes."

"Only, that didn't happen," Jacob said. "Turns out that taking away trauma doesn't make someone a good person."

I nodded. If they had just trusted me, I could have told them that. Instead, Estella was broken. If Jesus was gone, she'd return to normal. I don't know why I was so convinced of that, but it had to be true. Estella couldn't achieve her goals in her current state.

She was probably still dreaming of demons or whatever Estella dreamed about, but she was convinced they were real. That objective, scholarly mentality was gone, and no one would take her seriously at Oxford.

"So, you want to get him into the sanctuary and see if it will remove enough trauma so that he is...less evil?" I could feel the heat rising in my face. "You want to put him under the same roof as Estella."

"She'd never know," Felice assured me. "That's where you come in. I want you to take her to your house for spring break. I'll handle the rest."

This was reasonable enough that the steam was evaporating. Estella would come to my house and not be around her family. She would meet Dad and Thomas. I'd make sure she got plenty of shade and the world's best pizza.

"Okay," I nodded. "This could work."

"Yeah, but what if it messes up the sanctuary so bad it's no longer a safe space for us?" Jacob argued. "Carlie hasn't even been given the chance to try it."

"I don't care," I said. "If it means keeping Estella safe, I'm willing to spend the rest of my life shackled to my baggage."

He relented with a heavy nod. "It's your choice. It's just not fair."

Life isn't fair, Care Bear.

The truth was finally out, though. The reason the clique didn't bring me to their sanctuary was because Sykes had ruined their safe space. He tarnished it with his rottenness. He probably had a bad trip and freaked out. They didn't want me in the sanctuary because it was no longer sacred to them.

It was the weirdest *it's not you, it's me* reason I'd ever heard.

Unlocking my arms from around my chest, I said, "Okay, so how are we going to get him here?"

"Easy," Felice said from her vanity. "I'm going to tell him Estella is pregnant and going to get an abortion if he doesn't come and stop her."

I'm sorry...what? Why would a rapist want the proof of his deeds there for everyone in the family to see?

"Estella's family is devoutly Catholic," Jacob explained.

"I went to Catholic school. Incest and rape aren't great, but an abortion is a terrible thing in every case."

"He will come," Felice said. "I'll make sure of it. We just need to make sure Estella is far from here when he is."

"And if it doesn't work on him?" Jacob asked.

"It doesn't matter," she said. "All he needs to do is cross the border. The FBI would love to get their hands on him either way. It would just be nice if he confessed to everything instead of hiring a lawyer."

This was a plan that all of us could support. Not a word would be spoken to anyone else outside this room. In the meantime, we would continue as if nothing was going to happen. I'd slowly introduce the idea of Estella coming home with me in the next few months. Hopefully, I wouldn't need to talk her into it.

I seriously doubted she would want to go home after what happened, so I had that on my side. Dad would be thrilled if I brought a friend home. It would be a first in Carlie Whittaker history. She would be the only other member of the clique to meet Dad and Thomas too.

There were so many angles I could come at it, and I had months to make it happen.

CHAPTER 23

Lindt eyed the essay I dropped on his stack of papers. "Hipparchia. Interesting choice. What made you decide to write about her?"

"I wanted to write an essay based on a female philosopher."

"The Cynic who threw away everything to live like a beggar."

"She loved her husband and his way of life."

Lindt eyed my Versace bag before saying, "Indeed."

It was romantic, which is probably why her story survived, even when only one of her writings did. That, and my only other option was Hypatia, but I couldn't stomach how she died. Imagine being flayed alive with seashells by an angry mob. All because she dared to teach at a university. Not a visual I wanted right after lunch.

Estella was smiling at me from the door. She was wearing a dark gray shirt with a jean jacket. More and more, packages were arriving at the school for her. Clothes that were lighter in color and theme. She was slowly phasing out her old clothes with various excuses.

"Some of these are so old," or "I'm tired of constantly sweating in all black."

"Maybe it's because you have a Crates of your own," she teased.

I'd slap her along the head if I wasn't afraid I'd do more damage to her brain. Instead, I rolled my eyes.

"Thomas only sends me updates about Dad. Come on, let's walk around outside. I'm getting cabin fever."

Operation: Dad Takes a Day Off was in full swing.

"I could use the vitamin D," Estella agreed.

It was nice to be outside. Spring was in full bloom. The Pacific Northwest had more shades of green than I thought possible. Nothing beat upstate New York in the fall, but there was almost an Asian quality about the native plants. The cherry blossoms had fallen, and everything was covered in tiny pink petals. There was also yellow pollen stuff everywhere too.

We spotted Travis inside the greenhouse. He smiled and waved as he transferred little pods into planters.

"You think he's growing pot?" I asked.

"No!" Estella gasped. "Feilding would freak out."

Every word that emerged from Estella's mouth was more embarrassing than the last. Feilding was not the sort of woman who freaked out. And needing vitamin D? It was grating my nerves. Why couldn't she just snap out of it already?

We took the trail to the hilltop when we went on these walks, averaging twice a week. Sometimes the rest of the clique joined; sometimes they didn't. Everett was volunteering at the humane society on most days. I asked him to give Quasi my love. I wanted to go too, but if I did, I might return to school with a dog.

Feilding wouldn't freak out. She would calmly and quietly go to the bathroom and shit a brick.

"Hey, so I got an idea," I started. "It's cool if you don't want to, but spring break is coming up. How would you feel about going to New York?"

Estella nearly fell off the tree that had fallen along the trail.

"That would be amazing! I've never been to New York."

"Cool! So, it's settled. You'll get to meet Dad."

"And Thomas." The way she said it. Elementary school kids had more maturity than her in this state.

A noise escaped my lips then. An annoyed huff that I tried to restrain, but it was too late. Oh no. The worst thing I could do was pick a fight with Estella before getting her to New York. She couldn't stay here over spring break.

"Sorry," she muttered in a defensive tone.

"Stop it!" I said, losing all control. "Just stop being like this!"

My heart was pounding in my chest. I didn't want to screw this up, but there was no way I'd survive an entire week of her like this without breaks.

Estella folded her arms. "Like what?"

"I just want you to be yourself again."

She wasn't quite angry. I'd take angry. Estella could slap the shit out of me, and I'd be glad for it. Instead, she doubled down.

"I am myself."

"Ever since you went to the sanctuary. You've been different."

"Happy. I am happy, and you don't like that. Carlie, sometimes it feels like we were only friends because I was the only one as miserable as you."

Okay, that stung. The earrings were coming out. The gloves were off. It was time to show her how much of a bitch I could be. "I'm miserable? I didn't surrender my pain because it was too much for me. I own it!"

"And we all feel sorry for you because of it!" she yelled. "Poor Carlie. She will never know what it's like to be free from her mommy issues. You'll never be one of us."

One of us? Like she thought that would bother me? She had no idea that she was the one on the outside. Felice, Jacob, and I had a plan. We were going to fix her, and when this was all over, Estella would know just how wrong she was.

"You're not happy. You're just hiding from the fact that you were raped."

Something in her face warped then. Like she was suddenly reminded of the truth. Her face broke, and Estella started to sob. No, I didn't mean that. Shit.

"I'm sorry," I said. I tried to approach her, but Estella backed away. "What happened to you was awful. It wasn't your fault. But you need to face it."

Smearing her tears away with the palm of her hand. Estella looked upward and shook her head. "You're such a hypocrite. I need to face my trauma, but you get to cover yours with sarcasm and graffiti."

Taking in a deep breath, I nodded. "You're right. I am a hypocrite. But you're not. Estella, you're the coolest person I've ever met. I don't want you to change because some shitbag hurt you."

She was full on crying. Her eyes were locked on mine, and I was melting under her gaze. "I want you to go to Oxford. Break the mold with your combat boots and be the leading occult expert in the world. I want you to go down in history without compromising who you are." Okay, now I was crying. "Don't let him take that away from you."

For a split moment, I saw a spark in her. Estella was still in there.

"What do you even want from me?"

"I just...I want you to talk about it. When you're ready. I want you to be okay."

"Like the demon in the sanctuary," she said. "You want to eat my pain?"

I was fairly certain this wasn't an insult. Most people would be offended if someone compared them to a demon, but Estella wasn't most people.

"Yes," I said. "I want to eat your pain so you feel less of it."

"Well," she said with some indignation. "Why didn't you just say that?"

And just like that, all the tension wafting in the woods was gone.

She told me about that night. I listened and asked her how it made her feel. Estella sort of skipped around and peddled back as she tried to explain and fill in the back story, but I didn't really care how she told me just so long as she kept talking.

It was like she was trying to remember how it went down herself.

What I found most poignant was that the trauma hadn't left at all. She might have been acting strange, but it was more like she was impersonating the clique. Estella hadn't set the trauma aside; she buried it and hoped it would stay dead.

After she told me her story, I was more certain than ever that the sanctuary didn't do a damn thing for her.

"Estella," I asked. "What was it like? Performing the ritual in the sanctuary?"

She shrugged. Her eyes were red from crying. "We blindfold the person first and set them before the statue. We light the incense I make myself and chant to summon the devouring demon and offer our pain. He sort of sucks it out and goes back to the shadows."

Okay, really creepy, but okay.

"What happened when you tried it?"

"I felt it," she said. "It pulled something out, but maybe it took the wrong thing. I don't know. I just know that nightmares still happen, and I still get panic attacks for no reason. I had to start taking my Xanax again."

I thought about what Jacob had said about the sanctuary not feeling safe after Sykes. Of course, there was no grounding Estella in reality, so I tried to explain it a different way. "Jacob said that the demon was different after Sykes."

She nodded. "He's no longer content with bits and pieces."

...Right.

"What if we go to therapy?" I asked. "I'll go if you do."

She smiled at me with her waterlogged face. "They do online therapy now."

We spent the rest of the afternoon researching for therapists. I didn't think I needed one, but if it got her to go, I'd do it. She found one that specialized in her damage, and I found one that specialized in mine.

"Do you still want to come home with me on spring break?" I asked, embarrassed that I even needed the validation. There were reasons, after all.

She grinned and nodded. "I don't want to sit around here with Feilding."

No one wanted to sit around with the dean. Brainwashed by demons or otherwise.

CHAPTER 24

No one ever told me that therapy would be tough.

Leading up to each session, I was so nervous that it was a struggle to eat my Cobb salad. Twice a week, I'd find myself staring at the perfectly arranged chunks of ham and neat pile of shredded cheddar cheese. The sulfuric scent of the halved hard-boiled egg became more prominent and dared me to try it.

My therapist was a woman covered in tattoos and piercings. Cool and approachable on the surface, but she found ways to cut into the ulcer I didn't even know was there.

"How do you feel about the private investigator finding answers?" she asked.

"Well, if I had them, maybe I'd be able to move on. Maybe Dad would move on."

She nodded but was gauging my response with those laser-focused eyes. "Do you feel like if your dad moves on, you can too?"

Maybe. If there's hope for him, there's hope for me, too, right?

"Okay, let's walk this through," she said. "You learn the worst about your mom. She's passed away. What's the plan after that?"

I slapped my hands on my lap. "I don't know. I tell him. He gets a girlfriend, I go back to Harvard and graduate."

She was frowning. "That's going to be your homework. On Thursday, we'll revisit this. I want you to focus on how you plan to deal with it emotionally."

How do you plan to deal with emotions? Was that even a thing? I didn't just set time in my busy day for meltdowns. *Oh, yes, I can fit the death of a parent into my schedule somewhere between calculus and a Cobb salad. I will mourn for approximately five minutes and fifteen seconds before doing yoga with Estella.*

That was also a thing now.

Estella's therapist suggested she take the time to focus and meditate by doing yoga. Only, Estella didn't exactly do athletic activities. I did hot yoga to keep my Hot Girl Summer body year-round but fell out of that once I started going to college.

I love Estella, and I think I love her more when she tries to do yoga. While she still isn't herself, it's like yoga reminds her that death is imminent. Life is pointless pain. And all the other goth mentalities she once believed.

"You need to eat," Heather said.

The image of Estella in the crow pose is swatted away like a plume of cigarette smoke.

"I know."

"I think what you two are doing is so cool," Travis said.

"Big brass balls," Everett agreed.

It felt good to have their vote of confidence. Estella smiled as she stuffed a cherry tomato into her mouth. "My anxiety has been the main focus," she said. "Carlie has been teaching me yoga, and it really does help."

"I didn't know you did yoga!" Heather said.

"My ass didn't get this way with Cobb salad."

Seriously, when were they going to change the menu? Was there some unspoken rule that Cobb salad was the one true salad? Would a shrimp Louie kill anyone?

Felice nodded intently like she was making mental notes about the benefits of yoga. I could foresee some nightly sessions in her future.

"It's just," Jacob said. "This is what we mean when we talk about setting the trauma aside. You two are taking accountability for yourselves. Making changes for who you want to be as people. I love it."

No—there was a huge difference between what we were doing and what the clique had done. Estella and I were going to therapy. Facing our bullshit and unpacking it. We opened the luggage, took out the tangled mass of who we were, neatly folded it, and sorted it out in a new storage solution.

The clique blindfolded themselves, inhaled some mystery incense, and sat in front of a creepy statue in hopes that all their icky feelings would slither away. Heather couldn't help but be drawn to such a concept. Her parents were new age and did everything their Guru told them to, but Jacob? The fact that he couldn't see the irony in his own words was astounding.

I couldn't imagine most of the clique fully understanding what they had done until after the fact, which meant that someone in the clique was the instigator. Lying and promising it was easy and cruelty-free. No harm in trying since it wasn't tested on animals, vegan, non-GMO, and sustainably sourced.

My bet was on Felice. She didn't flinch at extremes. As far as I could tell, Jacob was her Jiminy Cricket. Without him, her plan of world domination would be complete.

"It's work," I said. "But it's changing the way I think about things."

"Spring break is coming up," Felice said. "Are you still going to Carlie's, Estella?"

Estella brightened with the mention. That, and I think she still wasn't ready to focus on *the other thing*. "Carlie is going to take me to Broadway."

I nodded. "Nevermore is back on the stage."

There was a collective *Oooo* from the clique. Name a person who doesn't love Poe. I'll wait.

"That's perfect," Felice said, but she was looking at me.

It was her way of confirming that the plan was in motion. Estella was going to New York, and Felice had Jesus on the hook. Her phone had the FBI on speed dial. All there was left to do the thing. I didn't imagine their little ritual would work on a cartel rapist, but they were going to try anyways. I just hoped the FBI had enough on him that they didn't need a confession.

Felice seemed to have it in her head that everything would happen safely. Like Jesus wouldn't bring a gun. Or that he'd even go down into the creepy bowels of Marten Ranch. A lot could go wrong between here and there, but nothing shook Felice when she had her mind set.

What part Jacob played in all this was still a mystery to me. He wasn't exactly the tough, backup kind of guy. More like the emotional support of the operation. The tiny voice of sanity. The reminder to not just lock Jesus in the cellar and leave him to rot. They could leave Jesus down there in the dark for all I cared, except that I didn't want to risk him escaping or Estella finding out.

No one ever found Sykes...

And no one really knew how Edgar Allen Poe died either. Some thought it was part of a voting scam; others just thought he went on a bender and died. Still, he died all the same, but his work managed to endure and influence literature. No one would miss the HPV sores of the world like Sykes or Jesus.

"And I'm going to meet...Thomas." Estella said with a flare of dramatics.

"Carlie's poor boy," Felice sighed. "The love that can never be..."

I was about to stand and yank the tablecloth out from their basic asses. Cobb salad everywhere. I bit my tongue instead. The more I reacted, the more they'd keep at it.

"I think it's very mature," Heather interjected. "Just because we like someone doesn't mean we need to date them."

"Exactly," I said.

"Sometimes we're just afraid of love," Tiffany said.

"He's old," Felice said, wrinkling her nose.

"He's five years older," Heather argued. "That doesn't matter in the long run."

Folding my arms, I sat and chewed my tongue raw. No, not going to say anything. They were going to talk about it whether I wanted them to or not. Feeding the gossip by getting defensive would only make it worse.

"Are we done?" I asked.

The room went quiet then. A bunch of mischievous students who were caught in the act. Sometimes, I felt like I was the oldest in the clique. I couldn't help but giggle at their stupid, buttoned-up facial expressions. It was so corny, but the clique started laughing too.

We laughed and laughed...

CHAPTER 25

We spotted Thomas in the loading zone.

He wasn't wearing his glasses, and my heart inflated like a balloon taking to helium. It was annoying, really. There I was, mid-vigilante operation, knocked breathless by the way he stopped to stare at me.

"Hi, welcome home," he greeted. "I'm Thomas."

"Estella," she said with a whisp of a voice.

Being on the clock, Thomas opened the passenger doors for us before putting our luggage in the trunk. Estella was making a silent wow face at me.

"Stop it," I whispered.

"He's cute!"

Duh? What did she expect? The image of Quasimodo flashed in my mind. My first love was named after the hunchback of Notre Dame, after all.

Everett had been taking pictures and sending them to me during his volunteer work. Every time I saw those stupid, googly eyes and that tongue that was the length of his body, I let out a little squeal and told him he was a good boy.

Okay, so maybe I didn't care about appearances, but that just meant I wasn't shallow.

"He's hilarious, too," I said.

And charming. The British accent probably helped a lot with that. Thomas was pathologically polite, even after being called a cunt for the last five years. And to be fair, they only started working from home a few days out of the week last year. The doctor said that Dad's blood pressure was high and he needed to take it easy. This was as close to relaxing as my dad would permit.

So, I didn't really see Thomas until he was parked outside my dad's office in a makeshift work area.

The driver's side door opened, and he slipped in. We were in my dad's black town car, and I found myself longing for the rattle of the Toyota. The smell of Thomas—not a new car scent.

"Is our operation still a go?" I asked.

"Thursday," he said, glancing at me in the rearview mirror. "He thinks he will be spending the morning in a meeting with a new client. Those can take all day. But they will mysteriously cancel same day, leaving him with nothing on the schedule."

Excellent.

"Good work."

"Mhm."

Was he acting shy? I grinned at the thought. He didn't know what Estella knew and didn't want to accidentally out himself as the guy in my text messages. Nothing inappropriate, of course. It was more like we were co-parenting Dad than anything.

"Are we taking Dad on a spa day?" Estella asked.

A massage wouldn't kill him, but I couldn't imagine Dad going along with it. The moment they stuck the cucumbers on his eyes, he'd probably eat them and check his phone for any change in the stock market the moment no one was looking.

"I don't know what we're going to do with him," I said. The truth was, I didn't know Dad. All I knew was how he reacted to me and his work. Not his likes, not his dislikes. I'd have to lean heavily on Thomas, the more engaged parent.

"What do you think, Thomas?" I asked.

"He would get a massage," Thomas suggested. "He's been complaining about his shoulder. He also is in dire need of new suits."

"Do we need to set up an appointment?" I asked.

"I've already taken the liberty."

Estella was squirming in her seat like the seatbelt was the only thing that kept her from jumping up to squeal. "I can't wait to meet Dad! This is so exciting. Oh my god, is that the naked guitar player?"

"No," I said. "That guy performs in Times Square—that's just a homeless man with a guitar."

She gasped. "New York is so crazy. I love it."

We had barely left the airport.

Thomas kept glancing at her in the mirror, but he said nothing. It wasn't until we got home and I gave Estella the tour of the house that he worked his way beside me while she was having an in-depth Spanish conversation with Francesca that he said something.

"Is this the one?"

I nodded. "She's working through some things."

"Right. Is there anything I can do to help her feel safe?"

In his mind, she was behaving strangely because she didn't feel comfortable in her surroundings. The truth was much sadder. Estella was pretending to be someone else because she didn't feel safe in her own skin. Her therapist said as much.

Even after she admitted it didn't work, Estella still clung to the idea that the sanctuary cured her somehow. She just wasn't ready to face it yet.

"I don't think so," I said. "She's doing intensive therapy, but it's just going to take time."

Thomas's jaw clenched, but he kept his feelings to himself.

"We're going to make sure justice is served," I promised myself more than anything.

He only nodded. Not asking questions. There wasn't so much as a flicker of concern with the concept of taking matters into our own hands. Thomas clearly approved...but how far would he go in that belief? Was it safe to tell him everything?

I wanted to. More than anything, I wanted to tell him everything. To confess to someone with feet in the real world in hopes that he'd pull me back.

"One of my mates back home had a kid sister who ran into some trouble," he said. "The police didn't take it seriously. So, we beat him bloody and left him at a bus station."

I couldn't help but smile at him. He revealed a new side of himself. His face darkened. In an instant, he went from a frumpily polite Brit to a Bond villain. It was sexy. Maybe I shouldn't think so, but I found his violent side utterly endearing.

"This guy is bad, bad," I explained. "He's killed people. On the FBI terrorist watch and everything."

"Do what you need to do," he said with a deep breath. "Just don't get caught."

"This is the extent of my part," I said. "Bringing Estella here, keeping her safe."

"Good."

Dad wandered out in a burgundy suit that was probably bought in the nineties and brown suede slippers. Dear God, Thomas was right. Too tight around the middle and sagged about the shoulders, his belly was pushed over, making him look more overweight than he was.

"Dad!" Estella said, breaking from Francesca to wrap him in a hug.

I snorted in laughter as she hugged a complete stranger. Dad was alarmed but embraced her and said, "Hi, Honey."

"I may have alerted him to the situation. He had a lot of questions after Christmas."

"Fair and valid," I agreed.

"I might have also told him about the ribbings your aunt gives when he's not looking. He was surprised at first, but after a while, he decided it made a lot of sense."

Okay, but that wasn't Thomas's place. I tensed, not wanting to be annoyed with him, but I couldn't help it. "You didn't need to do that."

"Someone needs to be on your side."

He was trying to defend me. And yeah, it was sweet, but I didn't want that. My behavior over the years was my fault. I keyed her car the time she made a comment about my mom's side of the family being right to abandon me. I was the one who handed the keys to the liquor cabinet to her second or third husband after they spent a ton of money on his rehab.

Yeah, her words were not okay, but my actions were worse. They shouldn't be justified or excused in the way my dad always did. It made me incapable of handling the real world when consequences came, whether they were deserved or not.

"I know you're just trying to help," I said. "And I love that you have my back, but I need to own my shit."

He eyed me with a wry little smile. "Therapy is working out then, is it?"

I sighed. "It sucks, and I feel like a puppy getting my nose rubbed in my own shit...but yeah. It's working."

"Honey," my dad's voice edged with desperation. Estella was still wrapped around his middle while he froze as he attempted to navigate the fragile terrain.

"Oh, shit. Dad, this is Estella, my best friend."

"It's so good to finally meet you!" she said.

"Oh, Estella," Thomas said. "Let me show you to your room. It's next door to Carlie's."

At his prompt, Estella released Dad from the hug and followed Thomas away from my befuddled dad. "She's friendly," he said, straightening his tie.

"She's having a hard time. After what happened, she's sort of checked out."

He looked so sad by that. Dad watched her bounce up the stairs, all smiles and giggles. "You didn't want her to go home and be reminded."

"It's just not a good idea."

Dad nodded. "She's welcome here anytime."

He always did have a soft spot for a woman in trouble. I think that was the reason he donated so much to the Sykes family. Why he loved Mom the way he did. I still hadn't heard back from the investigator, but I did ask her to dig into the entire clique as well as Mom.

***

"You could just ask for an update," Estella said.

She was probably tired of watching me refresh my email. We were trying to play Scrabble, but I wasn't great at it to begin with, and Estella knew twice the number of words as me. I should have stipulated no Spanish, but that felt a little racist.

"I should!" I said, refreshing again just in case. "I'm paying her, after all. I should at least get an update."

Estella nodded as I punched out an email to the private investigator. "Aren't they supposed to let you know when they find anything?"

What if that was the problem? What if my mother's case remained just as cold today as it was ten years ago when the police closed it? I had been so certain that the postcards had meant something that I hadn't considered that they led to a dead end.

That might be worse than learning Mom was dead. She was already dead in my mind, but to learn nothing might be worse. It meant her grave wasn't a shallow one. That whatever events led to her disappearance were so elusive that it might have been random.

A case of hospital negligence was shredded and scrubbed from all records. Or maybe she wanted to get away from me so badly that Dad signed her release under the condition that she never show her face again. I didn't think he'd lie about that, and the signature on the release paperwork was definitely not his, but that didn't mean it wasn't someone working for him.

There were a slew of temp workers before Thomas got the job as Dad's assistant. Then again, maybe it was the same person, and I just didn't notice because I never saw the person at the desk. Suspicion raged in my mind as self-doubt came creeping in.

Estella placed a hand on my phone and pushed it to the bed, forcing me to look into her deep brown eyes. "It's going to be okay."

My jaw got all tight as I swallowed back the urge to cry.

Then, my phone buzzed.

That was fast...

It wasn't an email, but it was a text from Felice.

No words, but there was a little purple devil emoji with a vicious smile.

CHAPTER 26

For all his obstinance, Dad wasn't all that upset with the ruse.

Of course, there was a tense moment where he looked at the three of us and said, "You had this all planned out, didn't you?"

"You need a day off," I said. Unlike Thomas, I didn't have a job on the line, so I was willing to take the brunt of his anger.

Only, Dad wasn't angry. Not with us at least. He shook his head and said, "All this just to get me to take a day off."

We started the day by going to his favorite Bodega. He got the same bagel he always got before we went to a men's clothing store that smelled like new fabric. Which is a lot like the new car smell but without synthetic fibers.

Estella and I sat on a white sofa and drank Earl Grey while Dad was standing on a round platform, getting measured by a thin man wearing a suit without the jacket. His crisp, white linen shirt was ironed so precisely that it was impervious to the constant motion of his arms as he stretched the tape measurer in every which direction.

"You know, Carlie," Dad said, "I just can't get over the changes you've been making this year. I'm proud of you."

"She's been going to therapy too," Estella boasted.

My face got a little hot. It might have just been the steam from the tea, but praise is new for me. Dad assessed his new jacket and was nodding at himself in the mirror in approval. "Therapy? I tried to get you to do that after the bathroom fire situation, but you refused."

I cringed at the memory. Estella's lips quirked into a curious smile.

"I found out one of the girls in middle school was writing shitty things about my family in her diary. So, I stole it and burned it in the bathroom."

Dad turned to look at me then. "You never explained why you did it."

I never explained myself to anyone.

Did it really matter why I did something if it was illegal, against school policy, or outright awful? Whenever I crossed that line, I was beyond reason, and the why didn't matter anymore. My therapist thinks it stems from not wanting pity.

If my actions are really just reactions to someone being a dick, it means they hurt me more than I'd like to admit. By allowing others to know they've caused me pain, it means I'm vulnerable. And eliciting pity from a man whose done nothing but pity me my whole life was just gross.

"I'm trying to be more transparent," I said, scratching my arm. "And communicate when I'm pissed instead of destroying things."

This was a lie, of course.

Even as I spouted my therapist's buzz words and talked about honesty, I was waiting on an update from a private detective to give me the backgrounds on our friends without their or even Estella's knowledge.

While we were at it, I was also lying to my best friend and plotting the arrest of her cousin. So transparent and honest. I was on track to receive a Nobel prize.

But let's be clear: I don't feel guilty about it.

Jesus Delgado needs to be behind bars. Estella will never feel safe again if he isn't. She's already delved so deep into her façade that I'm not sure she can get out even if she wanted to. Her therapist still can't touch the topic. Sometimes, Estella feels like she can't breathe and thinks she's dying. I can't change these things, but I can make the world a little bit safer.

As for the background checks on the clique...Yeah, I was probably in the wrong here. I could just ask them, but when the investigator asked if there was anything else I needed, there was.

What were they were before the clique came to Martin Ranch Academy? It might be the missing puzzle piece in the mystery of the sanctuary. The reason they were suddenly good might be because the clique was never that bad to begin with.

I knew that to be true for Jacob, so it might have been the same for everyone else. Rather than seek therapy, they turned to some ritual they found in an occultist basement and subscribed to the same mentality highlighted in a self-help book in yellow. They probably used gloves while reading the self-help book before carefully putting it back on the bookshelf because all of them understood the Dewy Decimal System.

The only thing that threatened to punch a hole in my theory was Felice. She was faking it. I knew that now. When the clique laughed, there was a five-second delay before Felice laughed too. She reserved her judgment after the clique gave their consensus. And when she wanted to border on illegal, it was like the clique couldn't hear it.

So, what was the deal?

Might have been hypnosis.

Someone hired a hypnotist for Dad's fiftieth birthday. I learned that not everyone could be hypnotized, but some were super suggestible. It had nothing to do with temperament either. Just one of those brain things where some people can quit smoking or be awake during surgery and feel no pain, while others are unaffected.

"What do you think of this color?" Dad asked.

Glancing up from my tea, I realized he found a nearly identical brown suit to replace the one I hated. "Dad, no brown suits."

"It's nice!" It might be for some people, but Dad had a reddish tone to his skin. His hair and suit were dangerously close to becoming homogonous in color. Even Estella was shaking her head.

"I hate black suits," he grumbled. "Make me look like I'm going to a funeral."

"What about a gray suit?" Estella asked.

"Oh, that would be nice," I agreed. "You can get shirts in colors other than white, Dad."

The brown suit was rejected, and Dad was sent back to try on something else. He was still muttering about black suits, and I had to fight back the laughter. Estella was shaking her head. "He's ridiculous. I love him."

"Me too."

***

Dad and I watched Estella's face as she took a bite of her first New York slice.

Her eyes lit as the cheese stretched, and she tried to sever it. Enveloped in the bliss that only a folded slice of pepperoni pizza could provide, I got the sense that everything would be okay. I usually avoided pizza, or anything with carbs, really, but this was a special occasion.

Estella stood in Times Square and got her typical tourist selfie. She sent it to the group chat.

Jacob: *Aww!*

Heather: *... You got sauce on your face.*

Travis: *Laughing Emoji*

I checked, and shit, she did! I licked my thumb and rubbed it off so she could retake the photo. Old Estella might have melted into the void at such a gesture, but new Estella only closed her eyes and waited. Dad was watching in mild fascination but winced a little when I went for the sauce. What else could I do? It was really stuck on there.

We stood on the docks while Estella snapped pictures of the Statue of Liberty.

"Are you sure you don't want the tour?" Dad asked.

"No, I don't really do boats. I'll be right back."

He waited until she was a good distance away before speaking. "So, I've noticed you and Thomas are getting acquainted."

I had been waiting for this to crop up. "We're just friends," I said.

Dad made a noise that suggested he didn't believe me.

"I really like him, but long distant relationships don't work. That and he's working for you. It makes things weird."

"So, should I fire him?" I jerked my head in his direction just as he cracked a smile. "Kidding."

My phone was buzzing with notifications, but I just assumed they were responses in the group chat. Estella's saucy face would be everyone's favorite photo for the next few months.

"Thomas is my connection to the real world," I explained. "Like, the world outside of college, you know?"

More than anything, that was the basis of our friendship. Not his looks or wit. It was the fact that we both cared about my dad and that Thomas kept me grounded when I wanted to slip into the whirlwind of ethical and organic possibilities with the clique.

"I wouldn't be mad if you were..."

He thought I was lying. Why would I even lie about that? My nostrils flared as I pressed my tongue to my teeth. "And I wouldn't deny it if we were."

"He's a good guy. I didn't expect much when I hired him, but I'm glad I gave him a shot."

I scowled at Dad then. Was he trying to play matchmaker (again), or was he trying to coax a different version of events out of me? Even when Thomas told him about how obnoxious Auntie really was, he still believed her instead of me.

"I'm not banging your assistant!"

Pigeons scattered and flew away, and people were looking at us. The prickle of self-awareness felt like needles along my neck.

He chuckled at my outburst. "You still don't like your old dad butting into your love life. I get it."

Did *anyone* appreciate their parents nosing in their private lives? Though, in retrospect, I was weirdly shy about my feelings for Thomas. Even the mere mention of him was enough to set me off. I didn't care if Heather and Everett were sickly sweet in love. Why did I hold myself to different standards?

Might be something I brought up with the therapist.

"He's almost six years older. It might not seem like a big deal, but we're at different places in our lives right now."

Dad was staring at me. I could feel his eyes assessing me. *Who is this person? What has she done with my daughter? Maybe she locked her up and threw away the key. I should check the cellar of that school. There might be a weird demon statue in there...hmm.*

"You're careful with your heart," he said. "If I had been more like you at your age, I wouldn't be where I am now."

"Loaded with a fabulous daughter?"

"Alone."

Ugh, that hurt in the marrow of my bones. He never spoke about it until now. "You can date too, you know. One way or another, she's not coming back."

Estella waved at us from the edge of the pier. I waved back, and she returned to taking photos. Now she was volunteering to take photos for strangers. This could be a while. Goth Estella would've been able to read my expression and the energy around us. She'd come charging in complaining of the wind and salt air and save me from this terrible conversation.

"She was afraid I'd leave her," he said. "Thought that if she went to get help, she'd come home to find another woman had taken her place. I promised she'd always have a home with me."

She'd always have a home with me...

"Would you break your promise for my sake?" I asked. "Because I don't want her to ever come back."

He didn't answer, but I didn't need him to. Dad was going to stew on that for a while, and I was okay with that.

My phone was itching in my pocket, begging for a glance. Willing to do anything to indicate the conversation was over, so I checked it. As predicted, the clique was carrying on about Estella's selfie, but there was also an email. My eyes zeroed in on the name of the sender. It was the private investigator.

CHAPTER 27

The email itself only contained a sentence. "Call me when you're alone."

I shivered against the damp salt air. It couldn't be good news. That much was obvious. Might as well have said *we need to talk*, or *I've been looking at the numbers and...*

A hand eclipsed my vision.

"Yoo hoo," Estella said. "Are you home?"

"Sorry," I said. "I'm just distracted."

Goth Estella would have known. I wouldn't have needed to say it out loud. There was no update on Felice other than her little devil emoji, but Jacob was in the group chat, so I guessed all was well. Estella may never be the same again, but at least her family home would be safe enough to return to. I hoped that when her family relayed the sad news, the shell she created would crack under the resonance of her laughter.

The horn sounded, and I flinched. "Right of way," Dad yelled out the window. "Learn it, asshole."

I laughed, ignoring the tingling all over. For whatever reason, Estella was entirely unbothered by the traffic. "Can you believe this shit?" Dad yelled to no one and everyone at the same time.

She must have found something important, but the thought of it kind of freaked me out. I asked and paid for this service, but now I wasn't sure if I wanted it. I really didn't want it in the form of a phone call, either. What was it with old people and calling? If I had a mental breakdown, the private investigator would hear it.

One thing was for certain, I wasn't going into this alone. Estella couldn't be in the conversation, but I could drag Thomas in. He'd be the moral support for the consequences of my not-so moral investigation.

Estella was staring at me.

Her brain might have been a little scrambled, but not to the point of oblivion. "The PI emailed me. She wants to talk alone."

Estella took my hand, and I leaned my head on her shoulder. The funny thing about her was that while sitting, we were pretty much the same height. It was only when she stood that it became apparent that I was six inches taller. It was like a fun party trick that she couldn't turn off. Where did the rest of that girl go?

"It will be okay," she said.

How do you know? ...I wish you could still hear me.

***

Thomas got my text.

I overheard their conversation from the second-floor stairwell. He muttered some excuse about needing something at his desk before the weekend, but Dad wasn't having it. "Came to say goodbye to Carlie?"

"Uh, yes, I should do that."

"I'm going to bed early," Dad announced rather loudly. "I took one of Carlie's sleeping pills. Trying out my new headphones..."

He had absolutely no shame. Not at all. One day, I'd get him back. Dad was bound to flirt with someone, and when he did, I was going to scream those words before literally putting headphones on because gross.

Thomas came up the stairs; he glanced back before saying, "He's up to something."

I grabbed his hand and dragged him into my room. Waiting was the worst, and I had no patience for polite British fumbling about being in a girl's room. "Dad secretly hopes we'll fall in love," I said. "Wishful thinking."

"Oh."

It wasn't until I registered the tone of his voice that I winced. "No—sorry. I didn't mean it like that. I'm just freaking out."

He wrapped his arms around me then, and all the tension went soft like warm putty. "We'll get through this," Thomas whispered in my ear.

I rested my head on his chest for a moment. It felt good. Safe. Whatever the PI had to say, it couldn't affect me here.

With a deep breath, I dialed her number. Thomas only let me go when she answered but stayed within reach in case I needed him.

"Ms. Whittaker?"

"Yes," I swallowed the egg-sized knot in my throat.

"I didn't email you until I was certain of my findings."

"Well?"

There was a sigh from over the phone. "You were right about the writing samples. We don't have a lot to go on, but the signature on the hospital forms matches the writing on the postcard."

My pounding heart was making it hard to think. "The director."

"Fernando Simmons lives in Europe these days. Mostly associates with nepo babies in the art scene. I found a woman in Brussels who matches your mother's description. She changed her name, but I'm sending you a picture now."

The phone rattled as I held it up to see the text image. Different hair, but the face was the same as the woman in the portraits. She was alive the entire time, probably watching the Lifetime documentaries about her disappearance and laughing at our pain. She was finally famous; that's all she ever cared about.

I couldn't respond. It was all I could do just to breathe.

"I'm really sorry," she said. "I'll send you all the information I found."

Mom abandoned me. She really did just decide to run away from her whole life and start a different one. It was like getting stabbed in the chest with glass. Shards splintered and pierced through my flesh and bones. Impossible to remove, the fragments worked their way toward my heart.

All she had to do was say she didn't want to be a parent. Dad would've gotten a full-time nanny, and she wouldn't have to be my mother, just so long as she stayed. Fucking coward. Too afraid to be honest, she left us waiting and wondering all these years. Not once did she think to reach out or apologize.

"Okay," I said. "Thank you."

I just needed to hang up the phone. Thomas was still holding me, but he had to lean against the wall to support both of us. Tears were rolling down his face, but he remained silent like he didn't want me to know he was crying on my account.

"Also, I'll send those background checks of your friends. Ms. Whittaker, you need to be careful. Those kids are dangerous."

I couldn't take any more. I hung up and let the phone slip through my fingers before sobbing into Thomas's chest. "She faked her own death to get away from me."

Why did she hate me so much? I was just a kid. I was six. How bad could I be? Maybe if I didn't touch her perfumes or stayed out of her room, she would have stayed. If I didn't seek out her approval or tell her I wanted to be like her when I grew up. Did my dad know all along and just let her go, or was he just another casualty?

My face was a hot, wet mess that chafed against Thomas's black button-up shirt. He kissed my forehead and said, "She didn't deserve you, and she knew it."

She wasn't happy, I knew that much, but to leave us in such a chaotic way was fucking spiteful. She wanted us to suffer for no other reason than the fact that we didn't live up to her expectations.

"If she wanted to leave, she could've just left. She ripped my entire life apart."

My mother wasn't dead. She wasn't a Jane Doe waiting to be claimed. The terrible things we imagined befalling her every night never happened. Felicity Whittaker wasn't happy, and she wanted to make sure we wouldn't be either.

Thomas's lips brushed the top of my head. There was warmth where he grazed my eyelids. I didn't want to feel this way anymore. Lifting my head, my lips met his. Soft and sad but full of promise.

Slapping at the light switch, I made the room dark before leading Thomas to my bed.

PART 3: CHAPTER 28

Bled dry of tears, it felt as though I'd withered. My body was still the same, but I was so much smaller on the inside. Getting up to go to the bathroom was a struggle. Fine motor mechanics were best left to the pros. The toilet paper roll was empty.

"You have to tell him."

At some point in the night, Thomas put one of my nightshirts on me. The very idea of putting on clothes was exhausting. Chanel was printed on the front, so I'm guessing that's where it came from. He slid it over my head and helped guide my arms through the sleeves like he was dressing a child. I'm so pathetic.

I shook my head before sitting on the bed facing the window. Just barely dawn. The sky was an eerie blue.

"He should know, but I can't..." Even finding the fucking words was hard. "He doesn't deserve to feel this way."

"It's different for you," Thomas said, rubbing my back. "She might have been his wife for a few years, but she was your mother. You have every right to feel like this, but I don't know if he will feel the same."

Probably, I don't know. It felt like a train wreck in my head, and I just wanted to go back to bed. All this time, she was alive. Probably watching her own documentaries and family interviews and laughing the way God laughs at us. Did it make her feel powerful to be featured on that late-night rotation between Unsolved Mysteries and infomercials?

The most polarizing and elusive case of the decade... What happened to Felicity Whittaker?

Now that I knew, I wished I didn't. If my mom was that messed up, what did that say about me? The girl who looked for her face in every crowded place, and her dad, who still checked the Jane Does if they matched the description.

His doctor made house calls because Dad was too busy at work but never too busy to check the morgue. I couldn't tell him. Just imagining the words in my mouth was enough to make my eyes well up. It would be worse for him to see what it was doing to me. I couldn't pretend anymore.

"Is it a dick move to ask you to talk to him?"

"I was rather hoping you'd let me," he said. "I think you both need time to process things before talking about it."

I nodded and laid back down to sleep.

Thomas had left. Presumably to tell Dad the awful truth, but when I woke, there was a glass of ice water, an iced coffee, and a chocolate chip muffin on the nightstand. He must have gone out for food. Not wanting to appear as though he stayed the night even when Dad already knew.

Dad said I guarded my heart. More like I yanked it out and slammed it in a locker door several times before sleeping with the guy I really liked and didn't want to screw things up with.

But I didn't regret last night. It just meant we needed to talk.

Bitter coffee and semi-sweet chocolate worked their magic. Still felt like I was hit by a train of runway models wearing stilettos, but now with more energy. The detective left attached documents in my email that I'd ignore. No more bad news for now, thank you very much.

Estella wandered in around ten. Climbing into bed with me, she held me. I didn't hate it. "I overheard Thomas talking to Dad. I'm so sorry, Carlie."

Ugh, how bad was it out there? *Please don't cry, Dad. We're not worth it.* I've only seen him cry a few times, but when I'm responsible—and I usually am—I'm the worst person in the world. Guess he knows now where I got it from.

"I always felt like she hated me. Now I know it's true. I just wish I knew why."

"It sounds to me like she didn't hate you. She hated herself."

Her words didn't slow the dull ache or stop the nausea. It was more like someone turned on a light. If I hated myself, what would I do? I'd start new. Change my name and be a whole different person in a new place.

Maybe she hated how she treated me and felt guilty—like she didn't deserve my adulation. Rather than continue to screw up something too bad, she left before making it worse. The pieces fit better in my mind because I could see myself doing exactly the same thing.

I wondered what she'd say if I called her. I was willing to bet I had her phone number somewhere in the slew of attachments in my email.

There was a knock at the door. Estella got up and opened it. She looked at me and said, "I'm going to get packed for the flight, okay?"

Dad stepped into my room. He had been crying. Fuck. His face was redder than usual. "Hi, honey."

"Hi," I said weakly.

He frowned and sat at the edge of my bed. "We knew it wasn't going to be good news. At least she's alive, and you know I didn't do any of those things the documentaries suggested."

There was never any doubt of that in my mind. I knew he was still in love with her. In some idiotic way, we both were. The only people who thought otherwise were her side of the family, and they just wanted someone to blame.

"Did you have any idea?"

"Maybe I should have. I knew she was having an affair. Jim advised I not mention it to the police. They'd see it as a motive."

"Why not just get a divorce like a normal person?"

Dad laughed at that. "She always did have a flair for the dramatics." Only the B-rated kind.

"Did she leave because she hated me?"

"No," he said with a certainty that almost made me believe it. "Your mom was so happy when she found out she was pregnant. About six months after you were born, she started to have these fits. Post-partum wasn't talked about a lot back then."

Logically, this all lined up neatly in a row. It wasn't my fault. I had a sick mom who only got sicker after having me. But that didn't lift the shroud of guilt and shame that clung to me. I thought I was past that abandoned little girl mentality, but in so many ways, she was still here.

I didn't need her. I had a dad who loved me. I had friends. Possibly a boyfriend? The jury was still out on that. I didn't need her. I could repeat that to myself a thousand times over, but it would never stick.

"I think I'd rather her be dead."

Dad sighed. "I don't blame you. Parents have this unhinged urge to protect their children. I want to do that for you, but some things are just out of our hands. We leave it up to our kids and hope for the best. And if I know you, I know you'll become successful despite her."

There was no doubt about that in my mind.

I would graduate from Marten Ranch and move on to real college. The second my trust fund was open, I'd use some of it to travel to Brussels and slap the ever-loving shit out of her. Maybe I'd fuck her boyfriend. Smash her car. As much as I could get away with before my passport got taken. Then, I'd invest wisely. At least she didn't have any more kids. One was enough, apparently.

"I should pack."

Dad took that as a sign to leave. "If you need to talk about it more," he said. "I'm just a phone call away. I love you, honey."

You and my therapist both.

"I love you too."

***

Thomas kept eyeing me during the drive to the airport. He looked anxious. Like he would burst at the seams if he couldn't say whatever needed to be said. With Estella beside me, it was hard to have *that* conversation, but we wouldn't get another chance to say it in person.

"Thank you for everything," I told him.

"If you need anything, call me."

I nodded. God, I hated how desperate he sounded. "Summer break is going to be delayed because of the school closure, but I'll be back home in July."

"I wouldn't want you to..." he struggled to find the right words. "Avoid certain college experiences."

"The class has eight students. It's not like I'm missing anything."

"Still. Should you find opportunities to... you should try them. I will remain at Mr. Whittaker's side regardless."

I'll remain at your side regardless.

"Likewise."

"Oh, for crying out loud," Estella burst our awkward bubble. "I was in the next room. I know what went down."

Thomas nearly swerved off the road. "Fucking Christ!"

Laughter came out of me then. It was foreign and not my own, but it came out. "So, friends and then some."

He recovered enough and nodded but kept his eyes on the road. "No promises, no expectations."

Estella bit her bottom lip and smiled at me. I wanted to smile back, but it felt so empty and forced, I gave up. She took my hand. "You'll feel better back at school."

"What if I don't?"

"You know we can help."

She meant the sanctuary. My stomach squelched like my organs were rearranging themselves. Instead of taking Estella's pain, it took the best parts from her. Subjecting myself to the same process didn't sound promising. But then again, what would I have to lose when there was nothing left but pain?

CHAPTER 29

Water spilled over the rim of the clawfoot bathtub and puddled at my six-year-old feet. Her glassy eyes never once looked at me. Not even when I handed her the pills. Swallowing gulps of bathwater to wash them down. The only communication between us was when she extended her hand for another.

Do you want to help Mommy? Of course you do. You love your mommy, don't you? You'd do anything for her.

I counted as I waited for her to signal that she needed another. In my mind, they were vitamins like the kind I took each morning. Only mine had cartoon characters on the bottle and were chewy. Hers came in a boring plastic orange bottle.

No cartoon characters or adverts, just yellow pills. Doctor prescribed vitamins. And you should always take what the doctor gives you. Like the time I got an ear infection from the swimming pool. Dad said I had to finish the antibiotics even if they tasted like pink chalk and my ears stopped hurting.

She closed her eyes for a few minutes before sinking nose-deep into the water. Bubbles guggled where her nose was. Mommy could hold her breath for a long time. She learned it from one of the big movies she was in, where her character slept face down in a pool. But Dad said I should never try that.

Coughing and cursing, Mommy opened her eyes and slapped at the water. It was like she was mad at it for waking her up from a nice dream.

Outstretching her hand, I gave her another pill and watched as it began to melt in her wet hand. Another mouthful of bathwater washed it down. Bubbles and all! She would probably get diarrhea or, at the very least, a tummy ache.

It must have tasted awful, but Mommy always took her pills no matter how yucky they were.

"Having you was a mistake," she told me with a waterlogged voice. "I'm not a parent. I'm a star."

It never felt good when she told me those things, but she only said them when she had too many bottles on her nightstand or when the doctor didn't give her enough medicine. So, I didn't say anything. I just sat with her words and let them twist inside my tummy.

Her head lulled on the rim of the tub. "How many pills did I take?"

"Fifty-two," I said, holding the empty prescription bottle. Or was it twenty-two? I could count to one hundred, but sometimes I skipped around on accident.

Spoilers: There weren't fifty-two pills in the bottle. If there were, she wouldn't be in Brussels pretending I didn't exist. She'd be rotting in a coffin and a sad segment on the local news.

"Count the bubbles, okay, sweetie?"

"Okay, Mommy."

That was my second mistake. I didn't do as I was told. The moment I saw bubbles, I ran from the bathroom and found Francesca. She was the one who pulled my mom out of the tub and called the ambulance.

Sometimes, in my head, it was Dad that came to our rescue. Sometimes he also wore a cape like Thor. But in truth, he worked too much and had little idea what his wife was up to.

Strange men asked me questions, and Mommy puked in the bathroom. Still clutching the bottle, I gave it to a large, outstretched palm. Their faces were creased and sad when they looked at me. I hated it.

Francesca was crying. She was speaking rapidly in Spanish and motioning at me like I was the problem. If I wasn't there, Mommy wouldn't take pills until she fell asleep.

Dad later explained to me that Francesca wasn't angry with me at all. She was furious with my mom and was threatening to quit if he didn't hire a nanny. The housekeeper was advocating on my behalf. But the moment is still ingrained in my mind, and I can't link the truth with the memory.

***

I go back to Marten Ranch Academy.

Laying in my bed, these were the things that went through my mind every night. I missed the Ambien prescription like a child missed their favorite stuffed animal. I left the bottle back in New York. Maybe my therapist would write me another prescription.

I rehearsed the right words. The ones that would make the therapist think it was her idea to give me the sleeping pills and not my own.

Circumventing the sob story was a non-issue now. I no longer cared if people looked sad when I talk. Estella had updated the clique on what the private investigator found, and no one brought it up. Even Ms. T — who was oblivious to the world — gave me an extension on my homework. I didn't ask for it, but the blank page was apparent to everyone.

What no one ever tells you about depression is that it's exhausting. The brain power it takes to breathe and pump blood eats away at the reserves. I thought depression consisted of, "boo hoo, I'm sad."

But I was so wrong.

Numb and tired. In a way, it made some things easier. Final exams were discussed, and I didn't get that nervous squelch. It helped that passing those finals wouldn't make or break me. If I bombed the exams, I'd still pass the classes.

I watched the clique pull out their black latex gloves and pay homage to the old rare books Dr. Nelson brought to class, and mine remained unopened. He didn't say anything, and Estella shared her book with me. She showed me pretty depictions of human sacrifice and bizarre medical cures, like putting birdseed on a sick person's feet or drinking urine.

I didn't even wrinkle my nose at the thought.

It took all I have just to get out of bed and get dressed in the morning. Estella reminded me to shower, and thank God for the housekeepers and dry-cleaning service Jacob sent to my room.

I didn't want to be this way. I hated myself for allowing Mom so much power, but self-loathing only made this worse. Why couldn't I just say, "Fuck her!" and be done with it? I did say it, multiple times a day, but my body didn't get the memo.

We ate our Cobb salads and attended classes, only no one asked me to share anything in writing. Which was a shame, really. I'd taken to writing. My little stories were so bleak and depressing, they'd make Cormac McCarthy stories sound like a pleasant stroll on a yellow brick road.

Lindt found my depression "transformative." My homework was always the first he collected, and he read it while picking up the rest of the clique's assignments.

"You'd make one hell of a writer, Whittaker," he said one day after class.

Who knew all it took to be a brilliant writer was self-hatred and a downward mental spiral? I thought of Hemmingway and decided writing wasn't for me. Sure, he was charismatic and interesting, but he also killed himself.

"Reminiscent of Hunter S. Thompson, but with a feminist gaze," Lindt says.

"Didn't he kill himself?" I ask.

Lindt eyed me from the top of his reading glasses but didn't answer. Judging and assessing.

"Don't worry," I say. "I'm too spiteful for that."

Estella was back to wearing black again. Pulling the reserves from the far recesses of her closet, she wore a black pleated skirt with a black polo shirt. Her hair was down and flat around her face, and it was almost like seeing someone just as sad as myself.

Only, her fingernails were still clear coated. The purple stain from years of black polish was gone and her makeup was less elaborate. A smoky eye and some lip gloss. I knew she was doing it for my benefit. A shade more familiar. Like she was in mourning on my behalf.

"It's okay to explore your darkness," she said. "Just don't let it consume you."

I wasn't on some adventure of self-exploration. This wasn't the dark hour in the heroine's tale. It was clinical depression. Anti-depressants take four to six weeks to kick in; I'd talk to my therapist about that too.

Just for shits and giggles, to remind myself that I was there, I asked Estella if she wanted to read my stories.

"Those are just for you."

She didn't want to know. It was too much for the thin shell she'd developed for her own survival. But the real Estella was still inside somewhere. I was the opposite. The protective layer was all that was left of me. A husk was all that was left of Carlie Whittaker.

CHAPTER 30

Somewhere between wallowing in sadness and my therapist wanting to bump up our sessions to three times a week, something in me snapped like the filaments in a glowstick. It was angry. It started with the glaring, still-ignored email that I couldn't delete from my otherwise empty inbox.

I called Thomas to talk—since everyone assured me they are there to talk—only he didn't answer. It was midnight here, which meant it was three am back in New York, but that didn't stop the rage from rushing up my throat like bile.

The sheets smelled like fabric softener. Overwhelming and so chemical that I couldn't lay with my face smashed against the pillow because the fresh scent ran up my sinuses like a snake in the drain.

Gathering all my notebooks I had been writing in over the last month, I marched up to the dean's private library and dropped them beside Feilding's fireplace. I was tired of being sad. I annoyed myself with my own misery.

I watched the presto log catch fire and burn good and hot before feeding each sad journal to the flames one by one. They sizzled and cracked, and it was like I was in middle school all over again. Lighting diaries on fire in the girl's bathroom.

Once they were layers of paper-thin ash, I head to the library. It was late, well after midnight, so no one saw me printing out the background checks and information the private investigator sent me. A black and white photo of my mom wearing couture sunglasses, smiling at a greasy man wearing a fedora like he thought it was still the early two-thousands.

The private investigator found her fake name and all the means to contact her. If I had to feel like this, so did she. It was the least she could do. More than anything, I wanted her to know how much she'd hurt my dad when he didn't deserve it. How he picked up the pieces and made us feel like a family. If something ever happened to him, it would be her fault.

While the rest of the background checks printed, I dialed the number.

"Hello?" a confused woman answer. It was probably midday where she was.

"Count the bubbles, sweetie," I say. My anger was red lining. It was hot in my throat, and my words were covered in acid.

She didn't respond.

"I should have never had you. I'm a star!" I mimic.

"Oh..." She started sobbing. "Carlie..."

She would have none of me. Not my name, and not a single word of who I was. I only delivered her own words back to her so she could relive them and rot on the inside from their poison. The way she poisoned me.

"Don't touch that with your grubby little hands."

A man answered next. "Who is this? What do you want from my wife?"

"Your wife?" I echoed back. "Your wife! I'm going to tell the world about her. Everyone will know she faked her death to become famous because it's the only way she could get on TV."

"I can pay you," he said. "Whatever you want—"

"I want her ashes so I can dump them in the toilet before taking a massive shit on them!" I screamed like a wounded animal caught in the grips of a rusty trap. The only way to escape was by gnawing off my own limb, and I would do that if only to remind her that she nearly destroyed us.

Before he could say anything else, I hung up and threw my phone into the dark because I hated that too. The screen shattered across the library, and I cackled like a villain. High on pain and vengeance, I used the school laptop to forward all the information on Felicity Whittaker to Lifetime and several news outlets that were particularly cruel to my family.

The responses begin rippling in my inbox, but I didn't answer them. They could eat their own words after researching for themselves.

A picture of Felice Lakewood rolls out of the printer. She's standing against a wall holding a letterboard. A mug shot!

"Oh, now this is precious," I said to myself.

Felice Lakewood, several DUIs, but the charges for manslaughter were dropped. There was also a string of brutal murders surrounding her high school, but she always had an alibi. If I knew anything about Felice, I knew she was careful.

Everett Milonakis was nearly charged with embezzlement at the tender age of twelve. I nodded in appreciation. Didn't think he had it in him. Before he came to Marten Ranch, he was found unresponsive at a party. Dead for five minutes. Impressive.

Jacob Mounts, clean rap sheet. That was just boring. His parents really were just assholes, I guess.

Heather James...cut the breaks on her ex's car.

Tiffany Nguyen was charged with multiple charges of minor shoplifting. That was certainly brow raising. Who knew she was a kleptomaniac?

I got to Travis Gates, and there was no rap sheet, but there was a long-term hospitalization. No specific reasons, but no one stayed in a hospital for three months without good reason. And if it wasn't announced on social media, it was probably mental health related. He told me he tried to commit suicide when we ate chips with the homeless guy. That must have been it.

Something about reading Travis's background brought me back to reality. I slowed, and the room around me became more prevalent again. I was sobering. No longer drunk on revenge, and shame was setting in.

No, I had no reason to feel ashamed. I wasn't in the wrong. It wasn't my fault my mother was a cruel, drug addled bitch who took it out on me. Why should I have to carry that weight when she was drinking mimosas and appreciating the beautiful, European landscape?

There wasn't a doubt in my mind that she didn't give a flying fuck about what she had done to my family, so why couldn't I let it go too?

There was one way...

CHAPTER 31

"Are you sure you want to go through with this?" Felice eyed me skeptically with her crusty eyes. It was five in the morning, after all.

There was no other option in my mind. "Everyone else did it," I said.

"Yeah, but you were pissed when Estella changed."

"Don't you see?" I asked, fully aware of how unhinged I sounded. "If I do it, Estella being different won't bother me anymore because I'll have changed too."

"Okay, but this time, we're all going to be there with you. No solo trip to the sanctuary."

I shook my head. "No solo trip."

'Cause let's be honest, I had no idea how it was done in the first place. I was at the mercy of the clique. I couldn't stand another moment of this. Icky on the inside and empty on the outside. I wanted to smile, to use gloves when reading old books. I wanted to enjoy volunteer work and be a good student.

I used to watch the girls on the school ground double Dutch with jump ropes. How I seethed with envy as the ropes spun so fast, I couldn't follow them. Too proud to ask for help, all I could do was watch and writhe in my own incompetence because it took two people holding ropes to even try.

It was easier to pretend I didn't care, only now I did care. This wasn't double Dutch; this was my future. I couldn't live the rest of my life like this.

If the sanctuary can save killers and kleptos, it can save me too.

"All right," she said. "I'll get everyone together. We will plan a time after Feilding goes to bed. On the weekend, so the staff is gone."

"Thank you," I whispered. "Thank you."

I didn't sleep that night. It felt pointless to sleep for four hours only to drag myself out of bed. Instead, I caught up on homework. Running on manic fumes, I raced through the work and double checked my calculus. Ms. T wouldn't need to give me any more extensions.

I'd be able to see the world untainted by trauma. No more self-sabotage.

Thomas called me during class. I had my phone on silent but called him back during break. Tucked between a podium with a vase and the curtains in the corner of the room, my eyes no longer scanned for anyone happening by.

"Hey," he said. "Is everything okay?"

I had every intention of lying, but when I opened my mouth, the truth came out. "No..."

"I'm so sorry," he said. "Do you want to come home?"

"No. I will be better soon."

"What does that mean?" His voice was thin. One wrong word, and he'd get on a plane and crash my plans. I had to say something optimistic—and quick.

"I'm seeing my therapist three times a week, and she gave me anti-depressants. The professors are super understanding, and Mr. Lindt says I'm doing amazing work."

"Oh." He didn't sound like he believed me for some reason, but it was all true. "That's good, then. When I saw you had called so late, I was worried..."

"I'm sorry," I said. "I just miss you. My friends are going to throw me a party this weekend, and I just couldn't stop thinking about you."

I hadn't thought about him at all because I was a shitty person doing what shitty people do. Redirecting a man from the glaringly obvious is all too easy. But maybe after the ritual, I'd be someone Thomas deserved.

"I admit, I think about you far more than what's good for me."

Thinking about me at all wasn't good for anyone.

"I have to go back to class," I said. "I just didn't want you to worry."

"Right. Well, keep in touch, okay? Day or night. I don't care."

***

The clique was already gathered in Felice's room when I came in. All of them wore sullen expressions like they were about to discuss how to proceed with my last wishes. It's not like I was dying, I was being reborn.

For the first time since I came back from New York, I was hopeful. I was sleeping and I even brushed my teeth.

"Hey, Carlie," Jacob said.

"There are a few things you need to know," Estella said, not waiting for the formalities. "The experience is different for everyone. Like the peyote thing we did on Halloween."

I'd managed to put that much together myself. The reason why Estella described it as a demon eating her pain, yet Jacob experienced a formal process…clearly some hallucinations were involved. The little bundle of incense Estella left untouched in her nightstand probably had something to do with it.

"For me, it was standing on a cliff while watching the first dawn," Heather said.

Everett smiled like he was recalling the best moment of his life. "I was being snuggled by puppies and kittens."

"We'll be with you every step of the way," Travis said. "You won't be alone. But I've been where you are now. I wouldn't wish it on anyone."

His was the opinion I really wanted the most. "It really worked for you?"

Travis nodded. "This place changed my entire outlook on life. I've never felt so comfortable in my own skin as I do now."

"But it doesn't always work the same," Estella reminded him.

It only took a massive fight between us for her to admit it. Was she pissed at me for going to Felice instead of her first? I should have, but Felice was the queen bee in the clique. Everything had to go through her.

"That's because you went in alone," Tiffany said. "If you had just waited, we could have guided you."

Estella shook her head and stepped into the shadow of the dresser. "That's not why."

Before she could say more, Felice redirected. "The point is, we don't know what you'll see, but we will be there to help."

Anxiety was clawing its way up my back. I had to do this. There wasn't any other option. Not unless I wanted to fight with medication or be in therapy for years. Those things might help, but I wanted to be free of it all.

I wanted to watch the news blow up with reports about the mother who abandoned me and feel little more than sympathy. *Poor woman, she probably has mental issues. Imagine that man living under scrutiny for fifteen years. Oh, their poor daughter.*

Then, I'd dismiss the empathy with a simple scroll of my phone.

Compassion without investment. A clinical type of caring that I could leave at work when I came home for the evening. To set the trauma aside. Empathetic towards victims, but not to the extent that I wanted revenge on their behalf. That was what I wanted.

Maybe then I could fill the husk with enough *Live, Laugh, Love* mottos that I too could believe it.

"Whatever I have to do," I said. "I'll do it."

Felice looked around the room at the others. There were no objections. "Okay. We'll get started."

CHAPTER 32

They blindfolded me before leading me to the sanctuary. I shivered as someone took my hand. Almost twenty and I never shook the fear of the dark. Anything could be waiting for me there; the worst thing would be nothing. Just a big, vacant nothingness without limits, and that's where I was at this moment.

"It's not necessary," Estella says. "She's already seen it."

"We're going by the book this time, Estella." There's a hint of agitation in Jacob's voice. I know he didn't approve of her going in alone, but it was the first time I caught any animosity from him about anything other than black belts paired with brown shoes.

With my eyes covered, I heard everything.

The slight edges of their words and the unscripted conflict bubbling underneath. The drips and drops of the leaking water pipe. The groan of the elevator. Without seeing where I was, my hearing painted the picture for me.

There was a smell I didn't notice before. Sulfur or porous rocks...brimstone? The word felt right even when I didn't know if it was true.

"It is necessary," Felice said. "No one is to venture into the other chambers."

"We need to stick together," Jacob added.

I was pushed to a kneeling position as the hands that guided slipped away. Floating in endless darkness, the only source of grounding I had was the concrete against my knees. *Just breathe. It won't be like the time you ate shroom pizza. You won't be running around in the woods naked being chased by Gnomes.*

A lighter clicked, and I smelled something sooty and sweet. The air grew heavy around me as Estella led a chant. The others joined in, depriving me of not only smell but my hearing as well. Touch was the last sense of self I have left.

Panic came in waves then. Like I was trapped in a cave quickly filling with water. I inhaled big breaths and held them before releasing and gasping for more.

"Don't fight it," Heather said somewhere nearby.

Easy for her to say. I wanted to listen, but I couldn't help but fight back. Something engrained within me wanted to resist. Claw the blindfold off and face the creepy statue that I knew was in front of me. I could feel the coolness radiating from it. Icy breath that increased with each incense-laden gulp of air.

That was when I lose my sense of touch.

My knees were numb from the concrete. I could have been floating for all I knew. I gripped at my sweats and even the texture was all wrong. It was not cotton, and the countless knits and rows were no longer there. It was smooth and hard.

Was I grabbing the statue? I couldn't tell.

I was holding on to something, and it was alive but not. Moving but not breathing. Existing yet not. My feeling hands worked along the grooves and etchings, and it shifted into a different position. The statue was moving.

"Give it your pain," Travis urged.

How do you give pain? It was easy to inflict it—I'd done that to so many—but to give meant the statue must be willing to accept it. "Is that what you want?" I asked. "Do you want my pain?"

My hands found a large tusk, worn from use, and my fingers bounced along a series of teeth like a stick along the xylophone keys. This couldn't be real. I wanted to take off my blindfold, but I hesitated. What would I see if I did?

On Halloween, everyone saw something different. The clique saw fish, sunsets, flowers. What would I see? Felice saw nothing. What would it mean if I took off the blindfold and just saw an empty room? What would I do then?

I was holding something in my arms. It was too big for me to wrap around, so I petted it like I would Quasimodo. It nudged my chest as if beckoning for more. A giant beast asking for kindness, not pain.

The chanting came back in clips, like a detuned radio. Estella's voice was rising above them all. She wasn't saying what the others were. Her words were urgent and pleading.

"What are you doing?" Felice shouted.

Something was wrong.

The nudging at my chest became a sudden push, and there was a lightning strike of pain. Stunned by the pain, I couldn't make my arms work. Shrieks from the clique echoed in my broken head. I felt for the fabric around my eyes. Felice's Gucci scarf.

I yanked it down just in time to see a hulking glass-work beast charging at Travis. The statue was alive. I couldn't breathe. Rattled to my core with fear that had me spasming against the wall.

The beast statue was glimmering in the low light. Black shards splintered off like fur or scales—it was too hard to make out which. Claws and teeth and tusks. It bellowed so loud I had to cover my ears. It swiped for Travis and enclosed him in its birdlike talons before shoving him into his mouth.

I was screaming. Begging. Heaving. Powerless as the beast ripped Travis in half and devoured the upper half. Blood was raining from its jaw as it finished him off in two more bites.

This was real. This was fucking real, and Travis was eaten right in front of me.

He didn't even scream. Why didn't Travis scream?

The monster twisted its neck like a bird as it eyed me as it approached. It sniffed, inhaling so hard my clothes were pulled upward. It was so stupid, but all I could think about was how broken my dad would be if I died. I didn't care about being ripped apart; I just didn't want Dad to know I was dead. I didn't want him to lose everything he had only to die alone at his desk.

Then, whether by divine intervention or something else, the monster jerked upward suddenly and took off running on all fours into the darkness.

And for once, I had a reason to be afraid of the dark.

***

Something wet and hot in my hair roused me.

A few candles were still lit, and it was enough for me to see blood on my hands. Red and wet. I wiped it on my sweats and sat up. No one was in the room, and the statue that was once the crown jewel was also gone. Was I petting the statue? There was no way the clique carried off that statue, so maybe I wasn't in the room I thought I was in. My mind probably pieced together what I knew of the sanctuary and filled in the gaps.

"Estella?" I called, wincing as a ringing sounded between my ears.

Where the hell did everyone go?

I got to my feet and picked up the candle. It was one of Estella's. Long and deep yellow, it smelled like beeswax.

"Estella..." a voice trailed from one of the many dark corridors. I went in the direction I thought it came from.

It was a long corridor that split off like some crazed labyrinth. The voice could have come from any direction, but I kept to the left. Wherever it led to, it would ultimately take me back.

The way that voice called for Estella... I was certain it was Felice, and she was up to no good.

The clique must have seen the monster too. They knew it killed Travis. Why the hell would they summon that thing? Maybe it wasn't real. Like the peyote. In my depressed state, I hallucinated a monster killing Travis, and none of this was really happening.

Only, if that were true, where was everyone else?

Left, dead end. So, I took the next left, and then another, and the light flickered. There was air circulating the room. Something glinted from the corner. It was a candle holder with a few surviving stubs. I lit it and kept moving, bringing light to the new chamber.

It wasn't as big as the main one, but it must lead to somewhere.

"She's a liability..." someone said. It sounded like Heather.

Everett's voice was a frantic whisper. "We never signed up for this. This is not what we do."

I opened my mouth to call out, but something stopped me. Who was the liability, and what was it they didn't want to do? I shook the notion from my head, and the lights went hazy. I probably had a concussion. I was confused and needed to get help.

But first, I had to find Estella.

"Guys?"

"Carlie?" Heather called.

"I'm here," I said, so relieved to hear a familiar voice. "I'm here."

Heather emerged from a hallway. Her long hair was coming undone from the braids. Everett came up behind her; his red polo was smeared with dust and cobwebs. "What happened?" I asked.

"It was Estella," Heather said, wrapping me in a hug. "I don't know what she did, but nothing like that has ever happened before."

That couldn't be right. "She wouldn't..."

"We need to get out of here," Everett said.

I agreed, but I wasn't going to leave her. "You should go," I said. "I need to find Estella."

"We can't do that," Everett said sharply.

The clique made a vow to stick together. It seemed they intended on keeping it. "Okay. Let's find the others first."

Head injury or no, the silent exchange between the couple was sketchy. They weren't here to find the others. They were acting weird. I needed to get Estella and get out. Whatever they had in mind, it wasn't good.

"You're hurt," Heather said, pushing back my blood-plastered hair. "Let's get you back, and we'll find the others."

"And then what?" I asked, stepping back.

Heather smiled like a saint, but Everett was staring at her like he wanted to do anything but be involved.

"It's for everyone's safety," she insisted. "Estella almost killed us. Travis is dead. We can't let that little psycho hurt anyone ever again."

I stepped back two steps. Dread and nausea were having a co-ed party in my stomach. "What do you plan on doing?"

"The right thing," Heather said. "You said it yourself—she's never been right since she came here on her own. What if it possessed her and lured us down here for a feast?"

Everett's jaw was locked so hard I could see his tendons straining underneath his skin. "We don't know what Estella was trying to do," he managed. "We don't know why she did that."

A dizzy wave threatened to knock me off my feet.

"She tried to kill you." Heathers words were like a shotgun hitting point blank. If I had the capacity for disbelief anymore, I would have said it wasn't true. "It was gunning for you. If Travis hadn't stepped in..."

Heather was weeping now. Sad, mournful sobs that echoed within the husk. I didn't even stir. Had the monster taken my pain before scampering off? Or was there just nothing left?

I felt pity for her, and I was sad for Travis. His family would be devastated, and there was nothing left to bury. But it was only sympathy I felt.

What the fuck was wrong with me? I watched him die. Horribly, for that matter. But there was no anger or raging grief. My sadness for him was a disgusting neutral. Like the dust and cobwebs, it was nothing a good shower couldn't wash away.

"We need to find the others," I said.

Everett nodded. Taking Heather by the hand, we each grabbed a candle and waded into the darkness.

The clinking of claws and scratching at stone dogged our steps, making our throats dry and silent. A single wrong turn could bring us face to face with the beast. Maybe it was what we deserved. Playing with forces we didn't understand, trying to bend a demon to our will like Robert Lacourt once did. That's what the clique had been doing, only they were in various stages of denial about it.

While others saw happy things on Halloween, I saw the monster in Estella's book. The very thing that was trying to kill us all now. What if all of this was my fault? We manifested whatever visions into reality, but mine was a literal fucking monster.

"Let's try this way," Everett urged.

The next room was circular, smaller than the central chamber, but the smell was overwhelming. A mixture of sewage and something like despair. The monster wasn't the only horror that awaited us within the sanctuary.

CHAPTER 33

The room had a black void in the center. At first, I thought it was a trick of the candlelight, but the sole of Heather's shoe skidded as Everett yanked her back from a dark pit. A shrill wail came from her lips as Everett pulled her into his chest. "Shh."

Standing at the cusp of the pit, I held a candle over the void. Two figures lay at the bottom. They moved when the light hit them. Like frightened baby possums, they winced and flinched. It wasn't anyone from the clique.

"Kill me," Sykes said with the casualness of ordering coffee. "Kill me."

The disgraced professor was mostly intact. In the place of his arm was a bloody stump. The second was a Hispanic man that had both legs stripped clean of flesh, leaving nothing but the bones. He trembled violently as Jesus Delgado stared at the wall.

"Kill...Me..."

"Don't look, Heather," Everett warned, but he was looking at me.

Felice had done this. She insisted that she was going to call the FBI for Jesus. That Sykes simply ran away. All along, he was here, being feasted on by a literal fucking demon.

"Estella didn't do this," I said. "She was in New York with me when Felice lured Jesus here."

"You knew?" Everett's pitch was raised.

I shook my head. "No, I had no idea this was what she had in mind. Only that she was going to try and make him confess to his crimes to the FBI."

"She said the same about Sykes. He was here the whole time."

That meant he couldn't have been responsible for the raccoon slaughter. "Why do that?" I asked. "The raccoons."

"Because I wanted to attend the winter fashion show," a voice came from behind us.

I spun around to find Felice in front of the only exit. She was holding the iron-rod poker from Feilding's library. "That, and Sykes kept escaping. I'd find him crawling around in the secret passageways with the vermin. He must have followed what was left of my ex. Naughty professor."

"You put Mike in here?" Everett asked.

I didn't know who that was. Felice smiled bitterly. "I saw the way he looked at Heather. I did you a favor."

"What the fuck, Felice," Everett was yelling. "What the fuck is wrong with you?"

"Carlie, don't act so surprised. You met him, but you were so drugged on sleeping pills you might not remember. I'll give you a clue," Felice said before making a horrid panting noise.

Yup, going to puke.

I heaved, and bile came spewing from my mouth. It burned in my sinuses. Felice laughed.

The noises between the walls. It was Felice's partially eaten boyfriend, desperate to escape. She killed and mutilated the raccoons for no other reason than to see a fashion show. The expression on the cop's face when she left her room. It was suspicion.

"But you did the ritual," Everett said. "After Jacob. You were changed."

Felice rolled her eyes. Her response was a sudden rush. She swung the iron rod at Everett, knocking him back. I lunged at her, trying to stop her. Soften the blow, anything. There was a horrid gush of air as Heather went rigid.

The spiked end of the poker was embedded in Heather's side. She had moved at the last moment, blocking Everett to take the blow herself before they both fell back into the pit with a liquid thud and a splintering crack. He was screaming then. Not in horror, in pain.

I couldn't do anything for them with Felice charging my way.

It was all I could do to duck her swings and take off running towards the exit. I'd come back for them, but I needed to be alive to do that. Their screams filled the narrow passageways, disorienting my sense of direction. Felice must have lit some candles on her way to the pit because they were neatly set in each corner.

My mind whirled with the casualness of it. Felice was strolling through a dark maze with a demon on the hunt, lighting candles as she went.

That evil bitch. I couldn't help but feel envious. It must have been nice to fear nothing. To feel nothing. This wasn't the time to be pouting over emotional baggage. It also was not the time to be afraid of the dark.

The only way I could throw Felice off my trail was by putting out the lights. I ran over, grabbed one, and stomped out the other two candles clustered together in the corner. Hopefully, that would confuse her. Blinded by the sudden change in light, I had to feel with my other hand while my eyes adjusted.

Passageway after passageway, I put out the lights save my own. I could hear Felice laughing in the distance.

"Only one of us fears the dark, Carlie. It was the first thing I learned about you. The way you jump into bed like something is going to grab your ankle. The nightstand under the bed was a solid move. That's when I knew you'd be a real contender."

I was running. My candle barely hanging on to the little whisp of fire. There were no specific thoughts going through my mind. The words *crazy bitch, crazy bitch* flashed neon red. I had to find Estella and get somewhere safe.

A flesh-eating demon was the secondary problem compared to Felice.

"Carlie," a male voice said from the darkness. It was Jacob. The candlelight glinted in his glasses. "She's..." I couldn't make out the words. My throat burned, and my lungs were spasming for air.

He took my hand and led me through the dark, but I yanked my hand away. "You helped her."

"I know."

That wasn't good enough. For all I knew, he was leading me straight for her. "Why?"

"She said she needed me," he said in the dark. "That I could save her from herself."

My mind went back to Jacob's baggage. His mother was a pill fiend, not unlike my own. He wanted to help her get better in ways he couldn't help his mom. Even if the demon gobbled up his pain, there was still a predictive reaction.

Jacob would always seek out the damaged woman and try to be her guiding light, only he picked the worst possible kind. "You can't help that."

"I get that now," he said, annoyed that I'd even suggest it. "We really did try to help Sykes, but she knew what would happen to Jesus and did it anyway."

"Didn't the devouring demon cue you in that you were in trouble, Jacob?"

"It wasn't alive then," he said, urging me forward. "It never moved until tonight. They just screamed as they were being ripped apart by something unseen."

Then what changed? Estella might have actually brought it to life. Did she want to kill us? My first and best friend wanted me dead. Not all that surprising, but still, fucking ouch. Couldn't she just break up with me via text message?

"And Mike was just a happy accident?" I accused.

He stopped. His Nikes skidded across the stone floor. "You know Mike?"

"He was the reason for all the creepy noises in the walls. She fed him to the demon first."

Jacob let out a soft moan and let go of my hand. "She said he transferred after they broke up."

Well, clearly, Felice wasn't the type to take rejection with any sort of grace. I needed to get away from him. Jacob was a liability to my safety. At any point, he might decide to help Felice if she told him the lies he wanted to hear. At the same time, he knew the sanctuary better than me.

"We need to get out," I said. "How do we find the central room?"

Jacob wasn't moving. "What have I done?"

Grabbing his hand, I pulled, but he wouldn't budge. "Jacob, we need to move."

A light from a cell phone illuminated the area enough for me to see that we were at a dead end. Felice had caught up to us. She wasn't doing her creepy smile, but her eyes were fixed on Jacob. "You're turning on me now?" Felice said. "When I need you the most. You're just like everyone else."

He was shaking his head. "You lied about Mike. About Sykes. You knew what would happen because you did it before."

"They were terrible people," she said. "If we turned them in, they would be unleashed into society without rehabilitation, and they'd hurt more people. You know our justice system is a sham."

"Mike wasn't," he said. "He was our friend, Felice."

"Your friend. My ex," she said. "When Estella showed the statue to me and told me what it was, she couldn't see the potential I saw. Robert Lacourt made this place to house the demon trapped in that statue. She said it was safe if we offered sacrifices willingly."

"So, you sacrificed your pain," I said.

She snorted like I said something stupid. "It didn't want me. I didn't have anything it liked. It feasted on the pain of everyone else, but not me. When Mike ended things and told me he was transferring, I saw an opportunity to feed it something more."

"You killed him just to see what would happen?" Jacob was yelling and crying, slumped against the wall.

"Once the demon realizes I will feed it more than just scraps, it will do my bidding. With that kind of power, just imagine what I'd be capable of."

"Okay, no one in the world wants that for you," I said.

Felice's lips scrunched as she gripped the poker. Holding it like a bat, she came swinging. I had no way out. I couldn't avoid the hit, so I threw the only thing I had, the candle. Hot wax that had collected around the stem splattered on her face. She screamed and swung wildly with her eyes closed.

Jacob shoved me out of the way just as the rod came at me, and she struck the wall. Sparks arced across the walls, and in a moment of genius, I plucked the phone out of her back pocket. It was still in flashlight mode. We took off running, abandoning Felice in the dead end with the only source of light.

Her enraged screams echoed in the distance, and it was only then I could breathe. We were safe for now, but I couldn't say the same for Estella.

CHAPTER 34

Jacob managed to lead us in the right direction. We were back where this awful night started. For the first time, I notice the patterns of brickwork along the floor. It was like thousands of arrows pointing to the center circle where the statue stood dormant. I still wasn't clear on the events that brought it to life, but if Felice was to be believed, it had consumed enough people to become animate.

It wasn't me who brought it to life, and it probably wasn't Estella either.

"Estella!" I screamed. "Estella! Central Room!"

"Shh," Jacob said, covering my mouth with his dirty, sweaty hand. "Felice is still out there."

I slapped his hand away. "What do we do, stand here and be quiet? Hope everyone finds an emergency exit?"

My sarcasm wasn't lost on Jacob. "Ringing the dinner bell isn't a great idea either."

I tried to laugh, but it came out more like a cough. Frantic Jacob was way more fun than regular Jacob. I'd always wanted to sneak into his room and unmake his bed and mismatch his socks just to see him frazzled. I think we both would have preferred mismatched socks over demon and psycho killer.

"Okay, think," I said. "Was there a stop gap? A magic word to stop the process?"

"Like a safe word?" Jacob said without a shred of irony.

"Anything like that?"

"No."

There had to be a way to put it back. The only person who might know is Estella, but there was no sign of her. *Come on, Estella, where the hell are you?*

She tried to warn me about Felice several times before. So, I was confident she booked it in the opposite direction, but what if Estella got caught by the demon? Worse, what if she tried to find it and dispel it but couldn't.

"Do you know where anyone else is?" Jacob asked as he paced the floor.

"Heather and Everett are in the pit with Sykes and Jesus," I said. "I think Everett is hurt, but they're all still alive."

"We should get them and send them up the elevator," he said. "At least give them a chance of surviving."

But if we both went, there was a chance we'd miss Estella. "You should go," I said. "I'll wait here. If Felice comes..."

I honestly didn't know what I'd do if Felice came. Nor did I think it would matter if we were together or separated. Her intent to kill wasn't some accidental disaster. It was raw and overwhelming. She wouldn't stop even after the breath left my body.

It was nothing like the romanticized serial killers portrayed in podcasts or tv. She wanted nothing more than for me to cease existing. Felice came at us with pure adrenaline and wild strength. There was no talking her down, and fighting back was a fat chance in hell, but it was all I had.

"Okay," he said. "Stay here. I'll get the others out. It's the least I can do."

"How long are you two going to keep talking like I'm not in the room?"

My heart plummeted as Felice came swaggering toward us. "You know I've been here the entire time...just waiting for you to notice and get a head start."

Something was coming up the steps behind her. Prowling on all fours with sharp, crystalline spikes for fur. Opalescent scales shimmered on its underbelly. Felice found the demon, and she intended to unleash it on us.

"I've memorized every corner of the sanctuary in the event that someone got spunky. There's no escaping me."

"Felice," Jacob whispered. "Step to the left."

I looked at Jacob. Even after all this, he thought he needed to protect her.

She frowned and went silent. The demon snorted from behind her. Felice mouthed the word *fuck* before dodging out of the way. As terrifying as it was, I was relieved that she hadn't somehow teamed up with the demon. In her arrogance, she didn't even consider that it was right behind her.

Affronted by her sudden movement, the demon pounced, but its nails had no traction on the smooth floor. "No!" she screamed. "I will continue to feed you. Don't you want that?"

The demon whipped around the room, herding Felice as it went. I crept into the shadows and waited for the inevitable. It was way easier to outrun the demon than it was to escape a psychopath. "Jacob," I whispered.

He wasn't listening. Instead, he broke into a run toward Felice.

"I taste bad, remember," she said, extending her hand. "You don't like my meat, but I can give you good food. As much as you want."

Everything inside me twisted in knots as the demon sniffed her hand as if it were debating on her words. It had to be sentient on some level; otherwise, how would it know to feed on the clique's trauma and not the rest of them?

It opened its mouth sharp like glass and spoke then. It was a language I didn't understand, but it was posing a question. If we didn't stop her, Felice really was going to have a demon doing her bidding.

Anyone who posed a threat, disliked, or straight up bored her would be fed to the demon in the way Mike, Sykes, and Jesus were. Slowly and deliberately as it savored their agony. The panic to do something to try and stop it was overwhelming, but what could I do?

"Yes, I can feed you all the delicious morsels," she said, taking a step closer to the demon.

"Felice," Jacob said softly. He was approaching her from the side like he intended to stand between them. "You don't need to do this. We can just walk away and forget this ever happened."

She hissed at him and moved in a way that suggested she was trying to block him. *Jacob, no. Get away! Felice isn't going to listen…*

I couldn't say it, or I'd alert them to my presence, but the tears were rolling down my face because I knew he'd be the first person she'd feed it. *She doesn't care about you. Trust me. She isn't capable of it. And that's not your fault. You didn't do anything wrong. She's the husk. Not you.*

As if getting a whiff of Jacob's was like smelling fresh tartar, the demon lurched back on its haunches. It craned its neck as its black opal eyes fixed on him. Frozen in terror, Jacob stared back at it. He was as good as dead.

"I don't need you anymore, Jacob. You served your purpose."

"No!" I screamed.

In an inexplicable moment, Felice popped Jacob along the back of his skull with the handle of the poker. He sagged to the ground in a rumple of Calvin Klein, and the demon lost all interest. Its sights were once again on Felice.

In hindsight, Felice had saved Jacob from being devoured. Maybe there was a tiny shred of goodness in her. A chink in her titanium hide. There had to be. Why else would she spare Jacob?

"Not that one," Felice said. "I have something much better for you."

Felice was striding toward me the way a panther glides toward its prey. The demon followed at her heels. Everything went slow motion then. The shadows that once concealed me were evaporating, and there was nowhere left to hide. Even if I ran, I wouldn't make it to the closest corridor.

I was trapped and about to be fed to Felice's demon.

So, I did the only thing I could do. I charged at her. My hands gripped anything they could. Hair, iron, whatever. I scratched at her with my broken, chewed-up fingernails and kicked at her with all my might.

This stunned her somewhat, like she didn't expect anyone would fight back. Felice let go of the poker and punched me in the head. My ear screamed in pain as the tender, vulnerable flesh was struck, but that only spurred me on. I stabbed her eyes with my fingers and wrenched the poker just a little bit more from her grasp.

Her face was rage personified. There was a rapid succession of slaps to my face. Each one a shock to my system. I let go of the poker, but she lost balance without me holding it. Hooking my leg around one of hers, I fell like dead weight. The poker smashed into her chest, and

Felice wheezed and gasped for air. Wherever the demon was, whatever it was doing, I didn't care. My only goal was to take Felice out.

No commander, no army. At least, that's what Mr. Lindt said.

I straddled Felice, pinned her arms with the poker, and proceeded to punch her head as hard as I could. No one ever tells you how much punching someone's head hurts. Even with white-hot adrenaline coursing through my veins, I felt my knuckles fracturing.

The tiny bones in my hand screamed in pain, and there was blood. It was probably my blood. Felice kept jerking her head at the right moment, and my blows slid off her cheeks. She wriggled an arm out from the poker and grabbed a thick handful of my hair, yanking me to the side.

She was on me then. So quick, I couldn't see how she did it, but I felt the poker whack against my back as the wind was knocked from my lungs. I gasped for air, but nothing came. It was like drowning without water. I flailed and grabbed her wrist, but it was locked tight on my scalp as my jeans scraped against the stone.

"This is what you want to eat," she said. "Nice and ripe. She's no virgin, but I'll get you one of those next."

There I was, face to face with a flesh-eating, soul-destroying demon. And I realized she's referring to Estella. Even a deranged psychopath knew that rape didn't qualify as losing one's virginity. It was so politically correct that I couldn't help but laugh.

Felice looked down at me. "Really?"

"You really think you can contend with Estella?" I said. "You don't stand a chance."

"You're totally gay for her, aren't you?"

It just didn't feel like the time to consider that possibility. The demon also seemed curious about this as it paused and waited for my reply. Maybe it just didn't want to eat me. It had the chance when we started the ritual, and yet it didn't. Instead, it nuzzled me. It gave me a stupid, stupid idea, but it was all I had.

"It's her you want to eat," I say. "Full of malice and evil. You'll never taste anything so awful in your existence."

The demon wasn't moved. So much for that idea.

My fingernails dug so hard into Felice's wrist, she grunted in pain as I drew blood. It fell in splatters on the floor and rolled down my hands. It was slick, and I lost my grip. But not before all the spikes on the demon flared and, it drooled white foamy sap.

Seeing my plan working, I clawed more and more at Felice's arm. I left gashes and hit a vein. Blood began to spurt, and the demon made a shrill noise and took a swipe at us. Felice was forced to let go of my hair, and I fell face-first on the floor before scrambling away. My nose wasn't broken, but it was a close call.

"No!" Felice screamed. "Not me. You don't want me."

Her wrist was a bloodied, mangled mess, and the demon's blood lust was too intense, even if every fiber of her being tasted like rotten garbage. Felice turned to run, but she smacked into something and fell to the ground.

CHAPTER 35

Still eating stone tile, I saw Felice slide to the ground. Her eyes met mine before they flickered into oblivion. I watched her slide out of my vision as her long acrylic nails feebly dug for traction. There were sounds then. Horrible, ripping, snapping sounds and grunts of pain. Wet and splooshing. I didn't want to know.

I rolled over and smiled. Estella was kneeling over me like some gothic saint. Her lips weren't black, and she was wearing dark blues, but she would always be a goth in my heart.

"You're okay."

"I'm sorry," she said. "I saw it breaking free from the statue. I tried to stop it but—"

"Shh," I said. "I know, but we need to send it back."

Estella helped me to my feet. Felice's body was gone. Only a spill of bright, fresh blood remained, but something was wrong with the demon. It was on all fours, and its spikes were standing on end. It shuddered and made a soft growl.

"Is it hurt?" I asked. "Was Felice so nasty that she poisoned the demon?"

"He's not a demon," Estella said. "He's a god. Just a very old and forgotten one. Every culture has something that describes him, and he has countless names. Robert Lacourt thought he was a demon and was wrong."

She was watching it like it was a deer in the forest. Mystical and magical. Never mind the dead bodies. She was Estella, after all.

"What's the difference?" I asked.

"Mortals can control demons. Same can't be said for gods. We offer; they accept or reject. But he's been here too long. Too alone and hungry to remember what he is. When Felice fed him Sykes and Jesus, it must have warped him somehow."

So, she knew about them. I had hoped she'd never find them. I didn't want her to know what I was complicit in. I lowered my head. "You should know that I helped get Jesus here," I confessed.

Estella didn't say anything, but her throat bobbed. "I know. Seeing him half dead in the pit helped me forgive him."

"Heather and Everett?" I asked.

"They're heading upstairs. We need to deal with him before we can retrieve Jacob, though."

"Did you see Tiffany?" I asked.

Estella shook her head. For all we knew, Tiffany might have gotten eaten too. She was standing next to Travis when he died. "Okay, so, how do we get rid of him?"

The demon was licking the blood and making a weird coughing noise that reminded me of a cat coughing up a hairball. Felice had made him sick. He was bloated on evil and the pain of nearly a dozen adolescents. No longer thinking or feeling, just drowning in pain that wasn't his own.

"Do you trust me?" Estella asked.

She was going to make me do something I wouldn't like. "Unfortunately."

"You have a connection to him," she said. "You saw him on Halloween, and when we started the ritual, he didn't try to eat you. I think...you can help."

"Me?"

Estella nodded.

Yes, let's send the depressed, maladjusted shoe addict to cure a god's tummy ache with the touch of her hand. And yet, something within me pulled. I wanted to help him. He didn't deserve to be trapped down here for a century in a statue. Fed nothing but despair and poison.

I inhaled a deep breath. Okay, here goes nothing.

Approaching slowly and directly, the demon—god, whatever—flinched, and his spikes flickered. "It's okay," I said. "I'm not going to hurt you. I don't want anything from you."

He made a cooing noise and lowered his head as I came closer.

"You're sick," I said. "Their pain made you this way."

I placed a hand on his snout, and his nostrils flared at the touch. "It's all right."

There was something so sweet and broken about him. It reminded me of Quasimodo. Terrifying on the outside, but there was a gentle wisdom somewhere within. I embraced him, guiding his giant head to my chest. I didn't know what I was doing, but it felt right.

"Give that pain to me."

All at once, memories came rushing into my head. A car ride with a pretty blonde girl accompanied by the biting slaps of a belt. Sorrow and joy intermingled in a setting sunset. Eating peanut butter out of a jar on a kitchen floor and crying all alone. More memories came, but faster, crashing into my psyche all at once.

My head fell back as I screamed.

These were the memories of the clique. The pain the forgotten god had collected. I took them all and felt the stone crumble between my hands.

Collapsing to the ground, I sobbed in a pile of black opal. Never again would I be able to forget their pain, the things that shaped their lives. But more than that, I'd never be able to shake the fear of nothingness that once belonged to Felice.

Estella was holding me. She said nothing, and just let me lean into her for a while.

"Is it over?" Tiffany said.

"Have you been lurking over there this entire time?" Estella asked.

Too dazed to respond, I looked at her and understood why she'd surrendered her pain. Her mother had abandoned her like mine did to me. She didn't change her name and fake her death. Her mother slowly strangled their relationship for the sake of a new husband.

At least I wasn't alone in this.

"What else could I do?" she asked. "You guys are cool, but I'm not about to die for you."

"Coward," Estella snapped.

Tiffany shrank back at that. She was ashamed. "Yeah, maybe. But no one else is going to take care of my grandparents and little brother."

"Can you wake Jacob up?" I asked.

Estella had to help me to the elevator while Tiffany roused Jacob. "Wake up, you fat shit," she grunted as she pulled him by his arm.

Jacob moaned before waking up with a start. "What happened? Where's Felice?"

"She saved you," I told him. "Rather than let him eat you, she knocked you out."

Clamping a hand over his mouth, he regarded the puddle of blood on the floor. "Then she's..."

"Yeah," I said.

There were no more questions after that. Jacob didn't want to know how she died. We'd all had enough of blood and gods for one day. Leaning against the elevator cage, I paused. "Hey, grab some of that opal."

Why?

It's a surprise.

Estella shoved the biggest and best chunks of the opal into her pockets before pushing the button. I sighed in relief as it went up. Returning to the first story of the house was like stepping back into reality. It was dawn, and the hellscape that was the sanctuary was far removed, like a nightmare I couldn't quite recall.

Everyone was standing on the stairway outside the house as an ambulance loaded up Everett and Heather. They held hands until their respective gurneys were carted into separate vehicles. Feilding was arguing with a police officer about something.

The teachers weren't at the school because it was a weekend. Marten Ranch Academy was empty.

"I have no idea where Sykes is," Feilding said as I stood in the doorway. "We need to make sure all the students are out of the house! Why are you not listening to me?"

"Ma'am, you're under arrest for aiding and abetting a criminal."

They were going to arrest Feilding? I didn't think so.

Turning around to head inside, I went into the kitchen and grabbed a bottle of shitty cooking wine and a lighter. Going back into the elevator, I said a prayer as it lowered. The glacial speed of the elevator gave me time to uncork the bottle and take a long, hard drink before stuffing a rag inside and allowing it to soak.

I lit the rag and threw it at the boxes and pallets. Glass shattered as flames erupted on the dry boxes beside the sanctuary entrance. Pushing the button to go back up, I watched as the flames spread. Smoke was already working its way upward to the floorboards.

Harboring the trauma of nearly a dozen people, I was still me. My actions were still my own. And I was choosing to make it hard to find evidence.

Back outside, I sat beside Estella and the others. We were being treated for minor injuries, and the police were grilling us about what happened.

"Was Sykes in there?" one asked.

I nodded. "He took Felice," I said. The tears came easily. "None of us knew he was there until it was too late."

"We tried to find her, but..." Estella broke off.

Oh, so tragic. Good girl.

"She wanted to be a hero," Jacob said. "She was convinced he was hiding somewhere, but none of us believed her.

The police officer broke at the sight of Jacob crying. "Hey, bud, it's going to be okay."

A window shattered in the distance. Everyone jumped at the sound. "Shit," the cop said. Turning around, he yelled at the firefighters. Smoke was enveloping the whole downstairs and fuming from cracks in broken glass.

Estella raised one brow, and I shrugged.

This is always how gothics end. She of all people should know that.

CHAPTER 36

"Here we are," Thomas said, navigating the dorm with luggage in each hand. "Room twelve is yours. And no, there is no room thirteen. I inquired."

I followed Estella and Thomas into a room so small our two suitcases each would barely fit. There was no private bathroom, and no closet. It smelled like musty sheets and moths. There was no air conditioning, just a radiator beside a window.

I wiped a cringe from my face when Estella turned to smile at me.

"It's great, right?" She was wearing dark grey again, slowly fading into black socks and Mary Janes.

"It has potential," I managed.

"Things are a little different across the pond," Thomas warned. "You'll have a lot of adjusting to do."

The dorm was only designed for one person, but Estella (and Dad) talked them into allowing two. Oxford was happy to accept us based on Feilding's glowing recommendation and our essays about surviving a harrowing first year. It also didn't hurt that a certain cold case shook America and Europe when the mystery of Felicity Whittaker was proven a hoax.

These days, Dad wasn't all that interested in what the news had to say. After stepping down as partner in his firm, he became a consultant for a select few clients but spent his days with a divorcee with three children my age.

I was happy for him.

"Are you sure this is what you want?" Estella asked.

"To major in history and archeology? Yes. I mean, I healed a freaking god and sent him home. If that's not a sign, I don't know what is."

Besides, if I didn't have Estella's back, who would?

"Oh, that reminds me," I said, searching my pockets. "This is for you."

Estella's eyes flickered from the box and back to me again.

You're not getting down on one knee, are you?

Oh, my God, no. Just open it.

She gasped at the yellow gold ring with a beautiful black opal crowning the center. I'd added a little skull on each side of the mount just to make it extra Estella. I showed her mine, too. White gold because yellow gold wasn't for every skin type.

"What kind of stone is that?" Thomas asked.

"Black opal," I said. "One of the rarest gems in the world."

"Beautiful." He wasn't looking at the stone.

Estella stayed in the dorm while Thomas and I went on a walk. He pointed out different things and telling me about British life. It was an overload, and I forgot most of what he said. But I learned that anything enjoyable to be found was either at a historical site or a pub.

"You're going to get burnt out with all the flying," I warned.

He shook his head. "No. My mum, on the other hand... She might burn me out."

With Dad working less, he didn't need a full-time assistant. After Marten Ranch Academy burned down, he did feel that he needed someone to keep an eye on his girls, however. With an ailing mother a few villages away, it only made sense that Thomas made use of his dual citizenship.

"I just hope the Delgado's don't cause you any trouble," he said.

They'd tried their best to keep Estella from going to Oxford. When she refused to come home for the summer, they cut her off financially in hopes that she'd return, but she was an adult with scholarships, and whatever else was left, Dad gladly funded.

"I don't know what they can do," I said. "She's an adult."

"Powerful families have a way of making things happen."

He underestimated Estella's power.

While we didn't make it a point to raise demons or gods, we'd tried a few seances with minor success. Estella said we needed to find older energies. Places with history. Europe would provide ample materials for our research.

"Why archeology?" Thomas asked while we sat together on a park bench. "I didn't know you even liked history."

"I like certain types," I said. My fingers traced over the stone. "I think it chose me if I'm honest."

He made a considerate *humph* sound and focused his gaze on the pigeons.

We sat in silence for a time. The birds randomly scattered from a nearby building where a shadow grew despite the overcast day. It flexed before shrinking back into the recesses, only people were too busy to notice. That, and they never saw the things they don't wish to see.

Oxford would be very interesting.

www.ingramcontent.com/pod-product-compliance
Lightning Source LLC
Chambersburg PA
CBHW051103030726
47504CB00006B/1765